THE THINKING MACHINE

Being a True and Complete Statement
of Several Intricate Mysteries which
came under the Observation of
Professor Augustus S. F. X. Van Dusen,
PH.D., LL.D., F.R.S., M.D., etc.

JACQUES FUTRELLE

Edited, with an introduction and notes,
by Leslie S. Klinger

Introduction and notes © 2023 by Leslie S. Klinger
Cover and internal design © 2023 by Sourcebooks and Library of Congress
Cover design by Sourcebooks
Cover image: *Frankenstein, 9–11 and 15–17 September 1977, Presented by
Worms Theatre Center, 2000 hrs, Taukkunen Barracks.* Jim Thorpe, 1977. Prints
& Photographs Division, Library of Congress, LC-DIG-ppmsca-43487.

Published by Poisoned Pen Press, an imprint of Sourcebooks,
in association with the Library of Congress
P.O. Box 4410, Naperville, Illinois 60567-4410
(630) 961-3900
sourcebooks.com

This edition of *The Thinking Machine* is based on the first edition in the Library of Congress's
collection, originally published and copyrighted in 1907 by Dodd, Mead & Company. The
stories in this book were originally published in 1905 by the *American-Journal Examiner*.
Illustrations by Troy Kinney and Margaret West Kinney accompanied the original publications
of the stories, and some were included in the book. They are reproduced in this edition.

Library of Congress Cataloging-in-Publication Data

Names: Futrelle, Jacques, author. | Klinger, Leslie S., editor.
Title: The thinking machine : being a true and complete statement of
    several intricate mysteries which came under the observation of
    Professor Augustus S.F.X. Van Dusen, Ph.D., LL.D., F.R.S., M.D., etc. /
    Jacques Futrelle ; edited, with an introduction and notes, by Leslie S.
    Klinger
Description: Naperville, Illinois : Library of Congress/Poisoned Pen Press,
    [2023] | Series: Library of Congress crime classics | Includes
    bibliographical references.
Identifiers: LCCN 2022061911 (print) | LCCN 2022061912 (ebook) | (trade paperback) | (epub)
Subjects: LCSH: Van Dusen, Augustus S. F. X. (Fictitious
    character)--Fiction. | Detective and mystery stories, American. |
    College teachers--Fiction. | Boston (Mass.)--Fiction. | LCGFT: Detective
    and mystery fiction. | Short stories.
Classification: LCC PS3511.U97 T48 2023 (print) | LCC PS3511.U97 (ebook)
    | DDC 813/.52--dc23/eng/20221230
LC record available at https://lccn.loc.gov/2022061911
LC ebook record available at https://lccn.loc.gov/2022061912

Printed and bound in the United States of America.
SB 10 9 8 7 6 5 4 3 2 1

To those two persons who made The Thinking Machine possible

*J. L. E., who opened the way, and L. M. F., who
guided, advised and encouraged the hand that
labored, these tales are gratefully dedicated.*

"Look out for a shot," warned The Thinking Machine sharply.

CONTENTS

FOREWORD

Crime writing as we know it first appeared in 1841, with the publication of "The Murders in the Rue Morgue." Written by American author Edgar Allan Poe, the short story introduced C. Auguste Dupin, the world's first wholly fictional detective. Other American and British authors had begun working in the genre by the 1860s, and by the 1920s we had officially entered the golden age of detective fiction.

Throughout this short history, many authors who paved the way have been lost or forgotten. Library of Congress Crime Classics bring back into print some of the finest American crime writing from the 1860s to the 1960s, showcasing rare and lesser-known titles that represent a range of genres, from cozies to police procedurals. With cover designs inspired by images from the Library's collections, each book in this series includes the original text, reproduced faithfully from an early edition in the Library's collections and complete with strange spellings and unorthodox punctuation. Also included are a contextual introduction, a brief biography of the author, notes, recommendations for further reading, and suggested discussion questions. Our hope is for these books to start conversations, inspire further research, and bring obscure works to a new generation of readers.

Early American crime fiction is not only entertaining to read, but it also sheds light on the culture of its time. While many of the titles in this series include outmoded language and stereotypes now considered offensive, these books give readers the opportunity to reflect on how our society's perceptions of race, gender, ethnicity, and social standing have evolved over more than a century.

More dark secrets and bloody deeds lurk in the massive collections of the Library of Congress. I encourage you to explore these works for yourself, here in Washington, DC, or online at www.loc.gov.

—Carla D. Hayden, Librarian of Congress

INTRODUCTION

On October 30, 1905, journalist Jacques Futrelle claimed his place in the pantheon of crime fiction with the first appearance in the *Boston American* of his classic tale, "The Mystery of Cell 13" (later retitled "The Problem of Cell 13"). The story—about a man who bets that he can escape from prison—was published in six parts as part of a contest: the best solution submitted by a reader before publication of the final installment would win a prize of fifty dollars.* "The Problem of Cell 13" and its protagonist, Augustus S. F. X. Van Dusen—known as the Thinking Machine—were so popular that Futrelle eventually published more than forty stories about his sleuth. Futrelle's work was unsurprisingly compared immediately (and favorably) to the extremely popular stories of Sherlock Holmes that continued to appear in the press. For example, Rafford Pyke, in the *Bookman*, exclaimed that "in sheer inventiveness and ingenuity, [the

---

* The contest for "The Mystery of Cell 13" ended on November 5, 1905. According to E. F. Bleiler, in his introduction to *The Best "Thinking Machine" Detective Stories* (New York: Dover, 1973), the contest was won by Mr. P. C. Hosmer, who was never heard from again as a writer (vi). The newspaper ran additional contests relating to further stories by Futrelle; nothing is known of their outcome, but the circulation of the newspaper rose dramatically.

stories in *The Thinking Machine*] at times surpass the now classical problems which interested the mind of Sherlock Holmes."*

As well as Holmes, Van Dusen had an even earlier predecessor: Edgar Allan Poe's Monsieur Dupin, whom critic Harold Orel characterized as "an ironic and occasionally saturnine sleuth, bookishly appreciative of the arts, given to epigrams, unastonished by human depravity, and convinced of the value of studying truth 'in detail.'" Orel suggested that early American detectives all essentially copied Poe's creation. He assessed the Thinking Machine as "a wonderfully imposing structure... He was not lovable. His brisk, contemptuous tone toward those who doubted his faith in human reason marked him as the logical—and ultimate—extension of Dupin, the thinking detective... This kind of detective-hero is, to be sure, a special creation: nothing more can be done to characterize him."†

Van Dusen is indeed far from an attractive character. He is described as "slight, almost childlike in body; and his thin shoulders seemed to drop beneath the weight of his enormous head... His brow rose straight and dome-like and a heavy shock of long, yellow hair gave him almost a grotesque appearance."‡ He is disdainful of those who do not follow his methods. "You ought to know that two and two make four, not sometimes

---

* *Bookman* (New York), 25 (June 1907): 433. "Rafford Pyke" was a pseudonym of the *Bookman*'s polymath editor, Harry Thurston Peck, who helmed the magazine from its birth in 1895 until 1907. Peck and his friends, the prolific writer Caroline Wells and Arthur Bartlett Maurice, the junior editor of the *Bookman*, were true devotees of the Holmes stories and coined the term "Sherlockians." One may therefore take these remarks as high praise indeed!

† Harold Orel, "The American Detective-Hero," *Journal of Popular Culture* 2, no. 3 (Winter 1968): 395–403.

‡ "The Thinking Machine," originally published in *Associated Sunday Magazines*, January 20, 1907, and used as the introductory story in *The Thinking Machine on the Case* (New York: D. Appleton, 1908), 5.

but all the time,"* he admonishes a client. Yet this is a pose, as Benedict Freedman points out:

[This] is essentially homage to the perennial ideal of perfect logical thinking, perfect, flawless, ineluctable, all-encompassing... Homage but double-edged. For what makes Futrelle's [stories] permanently readable is that he has introduced elements of doubt, even mockery, into his portrait of the perfect deductive thinker... It is not some theorem of Boolean logic that solves the problem of Cell 13 but such homely bits of folk wisdom as newspapermen will do anything for a story or small boys for a ten-dollar bill. Van Dusen's deductive prestidigitation is magnificent. It rivals Dupin at his best and throws Holmes completely into the shade.†

Van Dusen is not a true scientific detective, in that he uses little or no science, just intellect. In this respect, stories of the Professor are quite different from the early work of L. T. Meade's *Stories from the Diary of a Doctor* (1894–96) or the Holmes tales containing tidbits of science. Van Dusen's cases are precursors of the science-oriented stories of R. Austin Freeman's Dr. Thorndyke series (beginning with *John Thorndyke's Cases*, 1909), the tales of Edwin Balmer and William MacHarg (*The Achievements of Luther Trant*, 1910), and dozens of stories about Craig Kennedy by Arthur B. Reeve (beginning with *The Silent Bullet*, 1912).‡

While other writers of the day were focused on the strange and the outré (what E. F. Bleiler, the anthologist who almost

---

* "My First Experience with the Great Logician," *Associated Sunday Magazines*, January 20, 1907.

† Benedict Freedman, "The Thinking Machine," in *The Mystery & Detection Annual*, ed. Donald K. Adams (Beverly Hills, CA: Donald K. Adams, 1972), 79–85.

‡ Craig Kennedy was also hailed as "the American Sherlock Holmes." See Arthur B. Reeve, *The Silent Bullet* (Naperville, IL: Poisoned Pen Press in association with the Library of Congress, 2021), part of the Library of Congress Crime Classics series.

single-handedly brought Futrelle to the attention of modern readers, called "stories of incident or situation"*), Futrelle's tales were grounded in the everyday. Futrelle included a Watson-like companion in the form of Hutchinson Hatch, a realistically drawn newspaperman possibly modeled on Futrelle himself (or at least his self-image as an eager and tenacious reporter). Futrelle's representatives of officialdom—most notably Detective Mallory, who is the only police official actually named in the tales—were not dim, just limited, as the police of the day were. In crafting mysterious but ordinary problems, Futrelle successfully used what one reviewer called "perverse ingenuity" to "build a mystery backward from an obvious solution into a something that is so fair an imitation of a blind maze that it may be mistaken at a casual glance for the real thing."† This is naturally enough what mystery writers—at least those who write "puzzle" mysteries—do: devise the solution, then work backward to conceal the clues.

A later judgment of Futrelle's work by anthologist, critic, and scholar Howard Haycraft found that, "except for occasional 'dating' incidents inherent in the mise-en-scène, there is little in [Futrelle's] writing to indicate their prewar vintage. The concept of the problems is essentially fresh and modern, and the style is straightforward and agreeably free of the pomposity which characterized too much of the detective fiction of the time."‡ Yet Harold Orel, in 1968, had a contrary view: "[Futrelle's] confidence in intellectual processes now seems to be arrogant, but in the innocent years before World War I it cheered us on." This was, as Ellery Queen and others were to label it, the first golden

---

* Bleiler, *The Best "Thinking Machine" Detective Stories*, vii.

† Review, "The Thinking Machine," *New York Times*, April 6, 1907, 202.

‡ Howard Haycraft, "America: 1890–1914 (The Romantic Era)," in *Murder for Pleasure: The Life and Times of the Detective Story* (New York: D. Appleton-Century, 1941), 83–102.

era of crime fiction, when readers were eager to believe that the power of the mind alone could right the wrongs of the world.

There is no question that "The Problem of Cell 13" is one of the most admired creations in the history of crime fiction. It has been anthologized dozens of times. Harlan Ellison called it "a once-in-a-career jackpot of a story."[*] Was Futrelle a one-hit wonder? As the following stories illustrate, Futrelle had a gift for originality, for clear, unambiguous writing, excitement leavened with wit, and a "strange, buoyant enthusiasm," in the words of Bleiler.[†] Ellery Queen, writing in 1948, called Professor Van Dusen "as fresh and fascinating today as when he first appeared in covers."[‡] Futrelle's legacy was cemented after his tragic death on the *Titanic* in 1912. "Had Jacques Futrelle lived beyond his thirty-seventh year, he might well have become one of the two or three leading names in the development of the American detective story," summed up Howard Haycraft. "As it was, he brought to the genre a lightness of touch in advance of his time, and even by present-day standards his plots are still artful and his narratives readable."[§]

There have long been rumors of more Thinking Machine stories in the Futrelles' abandoned luggage on the *Titanic*, but these are undoubtedly lost forever. We must be content with those that have been published, where two and two is *always* four and logical thinking is enough to solve the worst human problems.

—Leslie S. Klinger

---

[*] Harlan Ellison, "Introduction," *Jacques Futrelle's "The Thinking Machine": The Enigmatic Problems, of Prof. Augustus S. F. X. Van Dusen, Ph.D., LL.D., F.R.S., M.D., M.D.S.* (New York: Modern Library, 2003), xxix.

[†] Bleiler, *The Best "Thinking Machine" Detective Stories*, viii.

[‡] Ellery Queen, *Queen's Quorum: A History of the Detective-Crime Short Story as Revealed by the 106 Most Important Books Published in this Field since 1845* (Boston: Little, Brown, 1948), 53. Of course, Queen included *The Thinking Machine* on his list of "most important books."

[§] Haycraft, 87.

THE PROBLEM OF CELL 13*

I

Practically all those letters remaining in the alphabet after Augustus S. F. X. Van Dusen was named were afterward acquired by that gentleman in the course of a brilliant scientific career, and, being honorably acquired, were tacked on to the other end. His name, therefore, taken with all that belonged to it, was a wonderfully imposing structure. He was a Ph.D., an LL.D.,† an F.R.S.,‡ an M.D., and an M.D.S.§ He was also some other things—just what he himself couldn't say—through recognition of his ability by various foreign educational and scientific institutions.

In appearance he was no less striking than in nomenclature.

---

* First published as "The Mystery of Cell 13" in *Boston American*, October 30, 1905.

† A doctor of law. This is an advanced degree, not to be confused with the juris doctor (JD) degree attained by all lawyers who do not enter the profession through practical training (also known as an LLB or baccalaureate degree of law).

‡ Fellow of the Royal Society, the preeminent English scientific body. Founded in 1662, it was formally named "the Royal Society of London for Improving Natural Knowledge" by King Charles II in 1663. There are many royal societies in England— e.g., the Royal Society of Chemistry, which recently named Sherlock Holmes as a Fellow—but only one "Royal Society."

§ Presumably a master of dental science (or dental surgery). Confusingly, this is a more advanced degree than the common DDS (doctor of dental science) and is usually only attained in connection with a dental specialty.

He was slender with the droop of the student in his thin shoulders and the pallor of a close, sedentary life on his clean-shaven face. His eyes wore a perpetual, forbidding squint—the squint of a man who studies little things—and when they could be seen at all through his thick spectacles, were mere slits of watery blue. But above his eyes was his most striking feature. This was a tall, broad brow, almost abnormal in height and width, crowned by a heavy shock of bushy, yellow hair. All these things conspired to give him a peculiar, almost grotesque, personality.

Professor Van Dusen was remotely German. For generations his ancestors had been noted in the sciences; he was the logical result, the master mind. First and above all he was a logician. At least thirty-five years of the half-century or so of his existence had been devoted exclusively to proving that two and two always equal four, except in unusual cases, where they equal three or five, as the case may be. He stood broadly on the general proposition that all things that start must go somewhere, and was able to bring the concentrated mental force of his forefathers to bear on a given problem. Incidentally it may be remarked that Professor Van Dusen wore a No. 8 hat.*

---

* As a practical matter, hats rarely are larger than eight and one-eighth (twenty-five inches) in the crown. This fact is intended to convey that Van Dusen is highly intelligent. It is well established that a large head generally indicates a larger than average brain size. What is not established is that the size of the brain has any relation to intelligence. That notion was an essential premise of the pseudoscience of phrenology, propounding the idea that measurements of the skull could reveal intelligence and even personality. The "big head = big brain = intelligence" equation was first espoused by the Viennese physician Franz Joseph Gall, who laid out his theory in an October 1, 1798, letter to Joseph von Retzer, explaining—his tongue, we might assume, at least partly in cheek—"A man like you possesses more than double the quantity of brain in a stupid bigot; and at least one-sixth more than the wisest or the most sagacious elephant." Even Sherlock Holmes, though perhaps only pretending to believe it, suggested that the possessor of a large hat, one Mr. Henry Baker, was highly intelligent: "It is a question of cubic capacity," Holmes told Dr. Watson. "A man with so large a brain must have something in it." Arthur Conan Doyle, "The Adventure of the Blue Carbuncle," in *The Adventures of Sherlock Holmes* (London: George Newnes, 1893), 160.

The world at large had heard vaguely of Professor Van Dusen as The Thinking Machine. It was a newspaper catch-phrase applied to him at the time of a remarkable exhibition at chess; he had demonstrated then that a stranger to the game might, by the force of inevitable logic, defeat a champion who had devoted a lifetime to its study.* The Thinking Machine! Perhaps that more nearly described him than all his honorary initials, for he spent week after week, month after month, in the seclusion of his small laboratory from which had gone forth thoughts that staggered scientific associates and deeply stirred the world at large.

It was only occasionally that The Thinking Machine had visitors, and these were usually men who, themselves high in the sciences, dropped in to argue a point and perhaps convince themselves. Two of these men, Dr. Charles Ransome and Alfred Fielding, called one evening to discuss some theory which is not of consequence here.

"Such a thing is impossible," declared Dr. Ransome emphatically, in the course of the conversation.

"Nothing is impossible," declared The Thinking Machine with equal emphasis. He always spoke petulantly. "The mind is master of all things. When science fully recognizes that fact a great advance will have been made."

"How about the airship?" asked Dr. Ransome.†

"That's not impossible at all," asserted The Thinking Machine. "It will be invented some time. I'd do it myself, but I'm busy."

---

* The incident is recounted in more detail in the chapter titled "The Thinking Machine," in *The Thinking Machine on the Case* (New York: D. Appleton, 1908), 1.

† The first sustained and controlled heavier-than-air flight was achieved by Orville and Wilbur Wright only a few years earlier in 1903. It was therefore no great feat of prognostication to foresee an "airship," by which Ransome presumably means a vessel that can carry passengers and cargo through the air.

Dr. Ransome laughed tolerantly.

"I've heard you say such things before," he said. "But they mean nothing. Mind may be master of matter, but it hasn't yet found a way to apply itself. There are some things that can't be *thought* out of existence, or rather which would not yield to any amount of thinking."

"What, for instance?" demanded The Thinking Machine.

Dr. Ransome was thoughtful for a moment as he smoked.

"Well, say prison walls," he replied. "No man can *think* himself out of a cell. If he could, there would be no prisoners."

"A man can so apply his brain and ingenuity that he can leave a cell, which is the same thing," snapped The Thinking Machine.

Dr. Ransome was slightly amused.

"Let's suppose a case," he said, after a moment. "Take a cell where prisoners under sentence of death are confined—men who are desperate and, maddened by fear, would take any chance to escape—suppose you were locked in such a cell. Could you escape?"

"Certainly," declared The Thinking Machine.

"Of course," said Mr. Fielding, who entered the conversation for the first time, "you might wreck the cell with an explosive— but inside, a prisoner, you couldn't have that."

"There would be nothing of that kind," said The Thinking Machine. "You might treat me precisely as you treated prisoners under sentence of death, and I would leave the cell."

"Not unless you entered it with tools prepared to get out," said Dr. Ransome.

The Thinking Machine was visibly annoyed and his blue eyes snapped.

"Lock me in any cell in any prison anywhere at any time, wearing only what is necessary, and I'll escape in a week," he declared, sharply.

Dr. Ransome sat up straight in the chair, interested. Mr. Fielding lighted a new cigar.

"You mean you could actually *think* yourself out?" asked Dr. Ransome.

"I would get out," was the response.

"Are you serious?"

"Certainly I am serious."

Dr. Ransome and Mr. Fielding were silent for a long time.

"Would you be willing to try it?" asked Mr. Fielding, finally.

"Certainly," said Professor Van Dusen, and there was a trace of irony in his voice. "I have done more asinine things than that to convince other men of less important truths."

The tone was offensive and there was an undercurrent strongly resembling anger on both sides. Of course it was an absurd thing, but Professor Van Dusen reiterated his willingness to undertake the escape and it was decided upon.

"To begin now," added Dr. Ransome.

"I'd prefer that it begin to-morrow," said The Thinking Machine, "because———"

"No, now," said Mr. Fielding, flatly. "You are arrested, figuratively, of course, without any warning locked in a cell with no chance to communicate with friends, and left there with identically the same care and attention that would be given to a man under sentence of death. Are you willing?"

"All right, now, then," said The Thinking Machine, and he arose.

"Say, the death-cell in Chisholm Prison."*

"The death-cell in Chisholm Prison."

---

* This is a fictional prison. Most of the Thinking Machine stories take place in the Boston area, and so it has been suggested that Charlestown State Prison was the model for Chisholm Prison. However, the dates of construction of the former prison do not match those of the "twenty years before" when Cell 13 had been built (see page 10), and in fact at least one prisoner had escaped from Charlestown in 1890.

"And what will you wear?"

"As little as possible," said The Thinking Machine. "Shoes, stockings, trousers and a shirt."

"You will permit yourself to be searched, of course?"

"I am to be treated precisely as all prisoners are treated," said The Thinking Machine. "No more attention and no less."

There were some preliminaries to be arranged in the matter of obtaining permission for the test, but all three were influential men and everything was done satisfactorily by telephone, albeit the prison commissioners, to whom the experiment was explained on purely scientific grounds, were sadly bewildered. Professor Van Dusen would be the most distinguished prisoner they had ever entertained.

When The Thinking Machine had donned those things which he was to wear during his incarceration he called the little old woman who was his housekeeper, cook and maid servant all in one.

"Martha," he said, "it is now twenty-seven minutes past nine o'clock. I am going away. One week from to-night, at half-past nine, these gentlemen and one, possibly two, others will take supper with me here. Remember Dr. Ransome is very fond of artichokes."

The three men were driven to Chisholm Prison, where the warden was awaiting them, having been informed of the matter by telephone. He understood merely that the eminent Professor Van Dusen was to be his prisoner, if he could keep him, for one week; that he had committed no crime, but that he was to be treated as all other prisoners were treated.

"Search him," instructed Dr. Ransome.

The Thinking Machine was searched. Nothing was found on him; the pockets of the trousers were empty; the white, stiff-bosomed shirt had no pocket. The shoes and stockings were removed, examined, then replaced. As he watched all these preliminaries—the rigid search and noted the pitiful, childlike physical weakness of the man, the colorless face, and the thin, white hands—Dr. Ransome almost regretted his part in the affair.

"Are you sure you want to do this?" he asked.

"Would you be convinced if I did not?" inquired The Thinking Machine in turn.

"No."

"All right. I'll do it."

What sympathy Dr. Ransome had was dissipated by the tone. It nettled him, and he resolved to see the experiment to the end; it would be a stinging reproof to egotism.

"It will be impossible for him to communicate with anyone outside?" he asked.

"Absolutely impossible," replied the warden. "He will not be permitted writing materials of any sort."

"And your jailers, would they deliver a message from him?"

"Not one word, directly or indirectly," said the warden. "You may rest assured of that. They will report anything he might say or turn over to me anything he might give them."

"That seems entirely satisfactory," said Mr. Fielding, who was frankly interested in the problem.

"Of course, in the event he fails," said Dr. Ransome, "and asks for his liberty, you understand you are to set him free?"

"I understand," replied the warden.

The Thinking Machine stood listening, but had nothing to say until this was all ended, then:

"I should like to make three small requests. You may grant them or not, as you wish."

"No special favors, now," warned Mr. Fielding.

"I am asking none," was the stiff response. "I would like to have some tooth powder—buy it yourself to see that it is tooth powder—and I should like to have one five-dollar and two ten-dollar bills."

Dr. Ransome, Mr. Fielding and the warden exchanged astonished glances. They were not surprised at the request for tooth powder, but were at the request for money.

"Is there any man with whom our friend would come in contact that he could bribe with twenty-five dollars?" asked Dr. Ransome of the warden.

"Not for twenty-five hundred dollars," was the positive reply.

"Well, let him have them," said Mr. Fielding. "I think they are harmless enough."

"And what is the third request?" asked Dr. Ransome.

"I should like to have my shoes polished."

Again the astonished glances were exchanged. This last request was the height of absurdity, so they agreed to it. These things all being attended to, The Thinking Machine was led back into the prison from which he had undertaken to escape.

"Here is Cell 13," said the warden, stopping three doors down the steel corridor. "This is where we keep condemned murderers. No one can leave it without my permission; and no one in it can communicate with the outside. I'll stake my reputation on that. It's only three doors back of my office and I can readily hear any unusual noise."

"Will this cell do, gentlemen?" asked The Thinking Machine. There was a touch of irony in his voice.

"Admirably," was the reply.

The heavy steel door was thrown open, there was a great scurrying and scampering of tiny feet, and The Thinking Machine passed into the gloom of the cell. Then the door was closed and double locked by the warden.

"What is that noise in there?" asked Dr. Ransome, through the bars.

"Rats—dozens of them," replied The Thinking Machine, tersely.

The three men, with final good-nights, were turning away when The Thinking Machine called:

"What time is it exactly, warden?"

"Eleven seventeen," replied the warden.

"Thanks. I will join you gentlemen in your office at half-past eight o'clock one week from to-night," said The Thinking Machine.

"And if you do not?"

"There is no 'if' about it."

II

Chisholm Prison was a great, spreading structure of granite, four stories in all, which stood in the center of acres of open space. It was surrounded by a wall of solid masonry eighteen feet high, and so smoothly finished inside and out as to offer no foothold to a climber, no matter how expert. Atop of this fence, as a further precaution, was a five-foot fence of steel rods, each terminating in a keen point. This fence in itself marked an absolute deadline between freedom and imprisonment, for, even if a man escaped from his cell, it would seem impossible for him to pass the wall.

The yard, which on all sides of the prison building was twenty-five feet wide, that being the distance from the building to the wall, was by day an exercise ground for those prisoners to whom was granted the boon of occasional semi-liberty. But that was not for those in Cell 13. At all times of the day there were armed guards in the yard, four of them, one patrolling each side of the prison building.

By night the yard was almost as brilliantly lighted as by day.

On each of the four sides was a great arc light which rose above the prison wall and gave to the guards a clear sight. The lights, too, brightly illuminated the spiked top of the wall. The wires which fed the arc lights ran up the side of the prison building on insulators and from the top story led out to the poles supporting the arc lights.

All these things were seen and comprehended by The Thinking Machine, who was only enabled to see out his closely barred cell window by standing on his bed. This was on the morning following his incarceration. He gathered, too, that the river lay over there beyond the wall somewhere, because he heard faintly the pulsation of a motor-boat and high up in the air saw a river bird. From that same direction came the shouts of boys at play and the occasional crack of a batted ball. He knew then that between the prison wall and the river was an open space, a playground.

Chisholm Prison was regarded as absolutely safe. No man had ever escaped from it. The Thinking Machine, from his perch on the bed, seeing what he saw, could readily understand why. The walls of the cell, though built he judged twenty years before, were perfectly solid, and the window bars of new iron had not a shadow of rust on them. The window itself, even with the bars out, would be a difficult mode of egress because it was small.

Yet, seeing these things, The Thinking Machine was not discouraged. Instead, he thoughtfully squinted at the great arc light—there was bright sunlight now—and traced with his eyes the wire which led from it to the building. That electric wire, he reasoned, must come down the side of the building not a great distance from his cell. That might be worth knowing.

Cell 13 was on the same floor with the offices of the prison— that is, not in the basement, nor yet upstairs. There were only four steps up to the office floor, therefore the level of the floor must be only three or four feet above the ground. He couldn't see the ground directly beneath his window, but he could see it further out toward the wall. It would be an easy drop from the window. Well and good.

Then The Thinking Machine fell to remembering how he had come to the cell. First, there was the outside guard's booth, a part of the wall. There were two heavily barred gates there, both of steel. At this gate was one man always on guard. He admitted persons to the prison after much clanking of keys and locks, and let them out when ordered to do so. The warden's office was in the prison building, and in order to reach that official from the prison yard one had to pass a gate of solid steel with only a peep-hole in it. Then coming from that inner office to Cell 13, where he was now, one must pass a heavy wooden door and two steel doors into the corridors of the prison; and always there was the double-locked door of Cell 13 to reckon with.

There were then, The Thinking Machine recalled, seven doors to be overcome before one could pass from Cell 13 into the outer world, a free man. But against this was the fact that he was rarely interrupted. A jailer appeared at his cell door at six in the morning with a breakfast of prison fare; he would come again at noon, and again at six in the afternoon. At nine o'clock at night would come the inspection tour. That would be all.

"It's admirably arranged, this prison system," was the mental tribute paid by The Thinking Machine. "I'll have to study it a little when I get out. I had no idea there was such great care exercised in the prisons."

There was nothing, positively nothing, in his cell, except his iron bed, so firmly put together that no man could tear it to pieces save with sledges or a file. He had neither of these. There was not even a chair, or a small table, or a bit of tin or crockery.

Nothing! The jailer stood by when he ate, then took away the wooden spoon and bowl which he had used.

One by one these things sank into the brain of The Thinking Machine. When the last possibility had been considered he began an examination of his cell. From the roof, down the walls on all sides, he examined the stones and the cement between them. He stamped over the floor carefully time after time, but it was cement, perfectly solid. After the examination he sat on the edge of the iron bed and was lost in thought for a long time. For Professor Augustus S. F. X. Van Dusen, The Thinking Machine, had something to think about.

He was disturbed by a rat, which ran across his foot, then scampered away into a dark corner of the cell, frightened at its own daring. After awhile The Thinking Machine, squinting steadily into the darkness of the corner where the rat had gone, was able to make out in the gloom many little beady eyes staring at him. He counted six pair, and there were perhaps others; he didn't see very well.

Then The Thinking Machine, from his seat on the bed, noticed for the first time the bottom of his cell door. There was an opening there of two inches between the steel bar and the floor. Still looking steadily at this opening, The Thinking Machine backed suddenly into the corner where he had seen the beady eyes. There was a great scampering of tiny feet, several squeaks of frightened rodents, and then silence.

None of the rats had gone out the door, yet there were none in the cell. Therefore there must be another way out of the cell, however small. The Thinking Machine, on hands and knees, started a search for this spot, feeling in the darkness with his long, slender fingers.

At last his search was rewarded. He came upon a small opening in the floor, level with the cement. It was perfectly round and somewhat larger than a silver dollar. This was the way the rats had gone. He put his fingers deep into the opening; it seemed to be a disused drainage pipe and was dry and dusty.

Having satisfied himself on this point, he sat on the bed again for an hour, then made another inspection of his surroundings through the small cell window. One of the outside guards stood directly opposite, beside the wall, and happened to be looking at the window of Cell 13 when the head of The Thinking Machine appeared. But the scientist didn't notice the guard.

Noon came and the jailer appeared with the prison dinner of repulsively plain food. At home The Thinking Machine merely ate to live; here he took what was offered without comment. Occasionally he spoke to the jailer who stood outside the door watching him.

"Any improvements made here in the last few years?" he asked.

"Nothing particularly," replied the jailer. "New wall was built four years ago."

"Anything done to the prison proper?"

"Painted the woodwork outside, and I believe about seven years ago a new system of plumbing was put in."

"Ah!" said the prisoner. "How far is the river over there?"

"About three hundred feet. The boys have a baseball ground between the wall and the river."

The Thinking Machine had nothing further to say just then, but when the jailer was ready to go he asked for some water.

"I get very thirsty here," he explained. "Would it be possible for you to leave a little water in a bowl for me?"

"I'll ask the warden," replied the jailer, and he went away.

Half an hour later he returned with water in a small earthen bowl.

"The warden says you may keep this bowl," he informed the

prisoner. "But you must show it to me when I ask for it. If it is broken, it will be the last."

"Thank you," said The Thinking Machine. "I shan't break it."

The jailer went on about his duties. For just the fraction of a second it seemed that The Thinking Machine wanted to ask a question, but he didn't.

Two hours later this same jailer, in passing the door of Cell No. 13, heard a noise inside and stopped. The Thinking Machine was down on his hands and knees in a corner of the cell, and from that same corner came several frightened squeaks. The jailer looked on interestedly.

"Ah, I've got you," he heard the prisoner say.

"Got what?" he asked, sharply.

"One of these rats," was the reply. "See?" And between the scientist's long fingers the jailer saw a small gray rat struggling. The prisoner brought it over to the light and looked at it closely. "It's a water rat," he said.

"Ain't you got anything better to do than to catch rats?" asked the jailer.

"It's disgraceful that they should be here at all," was the irritated reply. "Take this one away and kill it. There are dozens more where it came from."

The jailer took the wriggling, squirmy rodent and flung it down on the floor violently. It gave one squeak and lay still. Later he reported the incident to the warden, who only smiled.

Still later that afternoon the outside armed guard on the Cell 13 side of the prison looked up again at the window and saw the prisoner looking out. He saw a hand raised to the barred window and then something white fluttered to the ground, directly under the window of Cell 13. It was a little roll of linen, evidently of white shirting material, and tied around it was a five-dollar bill. The guard looked up at the window again, but the face had disappeared.

With a grim smile he took the little linen roll and the five-dollar bill to the warden's office. There together they deciphered something which was written on it with a queer sort of ink, frequently blurred. On the outside was this:

"Finder of this please deliver to Dr. Charles Ransome."

"Ah," said the warden, with a chuckle. "Plan of escape number one has gone wrong." Then, as an afterthought: "But why did he address it to Dr. Ransome?"

"And where did he get the pen and ink to write with?" asked the guard.

The warden looked at the guard and the guard looked at the warden. There was no apparent solution of that mystery. The warden studied the writing carefully, then shook his head.

"Well, let's see what he was going to say to Dr. Ransome," he said at length, still puzzled, and he unrolled the inner piece of linen.

"Well, if that—what—what do you think of that?" he asked, dazed.

The guard took the bit of linen and read this:

"Epa cseot d'net niiy awe htto n'si sih." "T."

III

The warden spent an hour wondering what sort of a cipher it was, and half an hour wondering why his prisoner should attempt to communicate with Dr. Ransome, who was the cause of him being there. After this the warden devoted some thought to the question of where the prisoner got writing materials, and what sort of writing materials he had. With the idea of illuminating this point, he examined the linen again. It was a torn part of a white shirt and had ragged edges.

Now it was possible to account for the linen, but what

the prisoner had used to write with was another matter. The warden knew it would have been impossible for him to have either pen or pencil, and, besides, neither pen nor pencil had been used in this writing. What, then? The warden decided to personally investigate. The Thinking Machine was his prisoner; he had orders to hold his prisoners; if this one sought to escape by sending cipher messages to persons outside, he would stop it, as he would have stopped it in the case of any other prisoner.

The warden went back to Cell 13 and found The Thinking Machine on his hands and knees on the floor, engaged in nothing more alarming than catching rats. The prisoner heard the warden's step and turned to him quickly.

"It's disgraceful," he snapped, "these rats. There are scores of them."

"Other men have been able to stand them," said the warden. "Here is another shirt for you—let me have the one you have on."

"Why?" demanded The Thinking Machine, quickly. His tone was hardly natural, his manner suggested actual perturbation.

"You have attempted to communicate with Dr. Ransome," said the warden severely. "As my prisoner, it is my duty to put a stop to it."

The Thinking Machine was silent for a moment.

"All right," he said, finally. "Do your duty."

The warden smiled grimly. The prisoner arose from the floor and removed the white shirt, putting on instead a striped convict shirt the warden had brought. The warden took the white shirt eagerly, and then and there compared the pieces of linen on which was written the cipher with certain torn places in the shirt. The Thinking Machine looked on curiously.

"The guard brought *you* those, then?" he asked.

"He certainly did," replied the warden triumphantly. "And that ends your first attempt to escape."

The Thinking Machine watched the warden as he, by comparison, established to his own satisfaction that only two pieces of linen had been torn from the white shirt.

"What did you write this with?" demanded the warden.

"I should think it a part of your duty to find out," said The Thinking Machine, irritably.

The warden started to say some harsh things, then restrained himself and made a minute search of the cell and of the prisoner instead. He found absolutely nothing; not even a match or toothpick which might have been used for a pen. The same mystery surrounded the fluid with which the cipher had been written. Although the warden left Cell 13 visibly annoyed, he took the torn shirt in triumph.

"Well, writing notes on a shirt won't get him out, that's certain," he told himself with some complacency. He put the linen scraps into his desk to await developments. "If that man escapes from that cell I'll—hang it—I'll resign."

On the third day of his incarceration The Thinking Machine openly attempted to bribe his way out. The jailer had brought his dinner and was leaning against the barred door, waiting, when The Thinking Machine began the conversation.

"The drainage pipes of the prison lead to the river, don't they?" he asked.

"Yes," said the jailer.

"I suppose they are very small?"

"Too small to crawl through, if that's what you're thinking about," was the grinning response.

There was silence until The Thinking Machine finished his meal. Then:

"You know I'm not a criminal, don't you?"

"Yes."

"And that I've a perfect right to be freed if I demand it?"

"Yes."

"Well, I came here believing that I could make my escape," said the prisoner, and his squint eyes studied the face of the jailer. "Would you consider a financial reward for aiding me to escape?"

The jailer, who happened to be an honest man, looked at the slender, weak figure of the prisoner, at the large head with its mass of yellow hair, and was almost sorry.

"I guess prisons like these were not built for the likes of you to get out of," he said, at last.

"But would you consider a proposition to help me get out?" the prisoner insisted, almost beseechingly.

"No," said the jailer, shortly.

"Five hundred dollars," urged The Thinking Machine. "I am not a criminal."

"No," said the jailer.

"A thousand?"

"No," again said the jailer, and he started away hurriedly to escape further temptation. Then he turned back. "If you should give me ten thousand dollars I couldn't get you out. You'd have to pass through seven doors, and I only have the keys to two."

Then he told the warden all about it.

"Plan number two fails," said the warden, smiling grimly. "First a cipher, then bribery."

When the jailer was on his way to Cell 13 at six o'clock, again bearing food to The Thinking Machine, he paused, startled by the unmistakable scrape, scrape of steel against steel. It stopped at the sound of his steps, then craftily the jailer, who was beyond the prisoner's range of vision, resumed his tramping, the sound being apparently that of a man going away from Cell 13. As a matter of fact he was in the same spot.

After a moment there came again the steady scrape, scrape, and the jailer crept cautiously on tiptoes to the door and peered between the bars. The Thinking Machine was standing on the iron bed working at the bars of the little window. He was using a file, judging from the backward and forward swing of his arms.

Cautiously the jailer crept back to the office, summoned the warden in person, and they returned to Cell 13 on tiptoes. The steady scrape was still audible. The warden listened to satisfy himself and then suddenly appeared at the door.

"Well?" he demanded, and there was a smile on his face.

The Thinking Machine glanced back from his perch on the bed and leaped suddenly to the floor, making frantic efforts to hide something. The warden went in, with hand extended.

"Give it up," he said.

"No," said the prisoner, sharply.

"Come, give it up," urged the warden. "I don't want to have to search you again."

"No," repeated the prisoner.

"What was it, a file?" asked the warden.

The Thinking Machine was silent and stood squinting at the warden with something very nearly approaching disappointment on his face—nearly, but not quite. The warden was almost sympathetic.

"Plan number three fails, eh?" he asked, good-naturedly. "Too bad, isn't it?"

The prisoner didn't say.

"Search him," instructed the warden.

The jailer searched the prisoner carefully. At last, artfully concealed in the waist band of the trousers, he found a piece of steel about two inches long, with one side curved like a half moon.

"Ah," said the warden, as he received it from the jailer. "From your shoe heel," and he smiled pleasantly.

The jailer continued his search and on the other side of the trousers waist band found another piece of steel identical with the first. The edges showed where they had been worn against the bars of the window.

"You couldn't saw a way through those bars with these," said the warden.

"I could have," said The Thinking Machine firmly.

"In six months, perhaps," said the warden, good-naturedly.

The warden shook his head slowly as he gazed into the slightly flushed face of his prisoner.

"Ready to give it up?" he asked.

"I haven't started yet," was the prompt reply.

Then came another exhaustive search of the cell. Carefully the two men went over it, finally turning out the bed and searching that. Nothing. The warden in person climbed upon the bed and examined the bars of the window where the prisoner had been sawing. When he looked he was amused.

"Just made it a little bright by hard rubbing," he said to the prisoner, who stood looking on with a somewhat crestfallen air. The warden grasped the iron bars in his strong hands and tried to shake them. They were immovable, set firmly in the solid granite. He examined each in turn and found them all satisfactory. Finally he climbed down from the bed.

"Give it up, Professor," he advised.

The Thinking Machine shook his head and the warden and jailer passed on again. As they disappeared down the corridor The Thinking Machine sat on the edge of the bed with his head in his hands.

"He's crazy to try to get out of that cell," commented the jailer.

"Of course he can't get out," said the warden. "But he's clever. I would like to know what he wrote that cipher with."

* * *

It was four o'clock next morning when an awful, heart-racking shriek of terror resounded through the great prison. It came from a cell, somewhere about the center, and its tone told a tale of horror, agony, terrible fear. The warden heard and with three of his men rushed into the long corridor leading to Cell 13.

IV

As they ran there came again that awful cry. It died away in a sort of wail. The white faces of prisoners appeared at cell doors upstairs and down, staring out wonderingly, frightened.

"It's that fool in Cell 13," grumbled the warden.

He stopped and stared in as one of the jailers flashed a lantern. "That fool in Cell 13" lay comfortably on his cot, flat on his back with his mouth open, snoring. Even as they looked there came again, the piercing cry, from somewhere above. The warden's face blanched a little as he started up the stairs. There on the top floor he found a man in Cell 43, directly above Cell 13, but two floors higher, cowering in a corner of his cell.

"What's the matter?" demanded the warden.

"Thank God you've come," exclaimed the prisoner, and he cast himself against the bars of his cell.

"What is it?" demanded the warden again.

He threw open the door and went in. The prisoner dropped on his knees and clasped the warden about the body. His face was white with terror, his eyes were widely distended, and he was shuddering. His hands, icy cold, clutched at the warden's.

"Take me out of this cell, please take me out," he pleaded.

"What's the matter with you, anyhow?" insisted the warden, impatiently.

"I heard something—something," said the prisoner, and his eyes roved nervously around the cell.

"What did you hear?"

"I—I can't tell you," stammered the prisoner. Then, in a sudden burst of terror: "Take me out of this cell—put me anywhere—but take me out of here."

The warden and the three jailers exchanged glances.

"Who is this fellow? What's he accused of?" asked the warden.

"Joseph Ballard," said one of the jailers. "He's accused of throwing acid in a woman's face. She died from it."

"But they can't prove it," gasped the prisoner. "They can't prove it. Please put me in some other cell."

He was still clinging to the warden, and that official threw his arms off roughly. Then for a time he stood looking at the cowering wretch, who seemed possessed of all the wild, unreasoning terror of a child.

"Look here, Ballard," said the warden, finally, "if you heard anything, I want to know what it was. Now tell me."

"I can't, I can't," was the reply. He was sobbing.

"Where did it come from?"

"I don't know. Everywhere—nowhere. I just heard it."

"What was it—a voice?"

"Please don't make me answer," pleaded the prisoner.

"You must answer," said the warden, sharply.

"It was a voice—but—but it wasn't human," was the sobbing reply.

"Voice, but not human?" repeated the warden, puzzled.

"It sounded muffled and—and far away—and ghostly," explained the man.

"Did it come from inside or outside the prison?"

"It didn't seem to come from anywhere—it was just here, here, everywhere. I heard it. I heard it."

For an hour the warden tried to get the story, but Ballard had become suddenly obstinate and would say nothing—only pleaded to be placed in another cell, or to have one of the jailers remain near him until daylight. These requests were gruffly refused.

"And see here," said the warden, in conclusion, "if there's any more of this screaming I'll put you in the padded cell."

Then the warden went his way, a sadly puzzled man. Ballard sat at his cell door until daylight, his face, drawn and white with terror, pressed against the bars, and looked out into the prison with wide, staring eyes.

That day, the fourth since the incarceration of The Thinking Machine, was enlivened considerably by the volunteer prisoner, who spent most of his time at the little window of his cell. He began proceedings by throwing another piece of linen down to the guard, who picked it up dutifully and took it to the warden. On it was written:

"Only three days more."

The warden was in no way surprised at what he read; he understood that The Thinking Machine meant only three days more of his imprisonment, and he regarded the note as a boast. But how was the thing written? Where had The Thinking Machine found this new piece of linen? Where? How? He carefully examined the linen. It was white, of fine texture, shirting material. He took the shirt which he had taken and carefully fitted the two original pieces of the linen to the torn places. This third piece was entirely superfluous; it didn't fit anywhere, and yet it was unmistakably the same goods.

"And where—where does he get anything to write with?" demanded the warden of the world at large.

Still later on the fourth day The Thinking Machine, through the window of his cell, spoke to the armed guard outside.

"What day of the month is it?" he asked.

"The fifteenth," was the answer.

The Thinking Machine made a mental astronomical calculation and satisfied himself that the moon would not rise until after nine o'clock that night. Then he asked another question:

"Who attends to those arc lights?"

"Man from the company."

"You have no electricians in the building?"

"No."

"I should think you could save money if you had your own man."

"None of my business," replied the guard.

The guard noticed The Thinking Machine at the cell window frequently during that day, but always the face seemed listless and there was a certain wistfulness in the squint eyes behind the glasses. After a while he accepted the presence of the leonine head as a matter of course. He had seen other prisoners do the same thing; it was the longing for the outside world.

That afternoon, just before the day guard was relieved, the head appeared at the window again, and The Thinking Machine's hand held something out between the bars. It fluttered to the ground and the guard picked it up. It was a five-dollar bill.

"That's for you," called the prisoner.

As usual, the guard took it to the warden. That gentleman looked at it suspiciously; he looked at everything that came from Cell 13 with suspicion.

"He said it was for me," explained the guard.

"It's a sort of a tip, I suppose," said the warden. "I see no particular reason why you shouldn't accept——"

Suddenly he stopped. He had remembered that The Thinking Machine had gone into Cell 13 with one five-dollar bill and two ten-dollar bills; twenty-five dollars in all. Now a five-dollar bill had been tied around the first pieces of linen that came from the cell. The warden still had it, and to convince himself he took it out and looked at it. It was five dollars; yet here was another five dollars, and The Thinking Machine had only had ten-dollar bills.

"Perhaps somebody changed one of the bills for him," he thought at last, with a sigh of relief.

But then and there he made up his mind. He would search Cell 13 as a cell was never before searched in this world. When a man could write at will, and change money, and do other wholly inexplicable things, there was something radically wrong with his prison. He planned to enter the cell at night—three o'clock would be an excellent time. The Thinking Machine must do all the weird things he did sometime. Night seemed the most reasonable.

Thus it happened that the warden stealthily descended upon Cell 13 that night at three o'clock. He paused at the door and listened. There was no sound save the steady, regular breathing of the prisoner. The keys unfastened the double locks with scarcely a clank, and the warden entered, locking the door behind him. Suddenly he flashed his dark-lantern* in the face of the recumbent figure.

If the warden had planned to startle The Thinking Machine he was mistaken, for that individual merely opened his eyes quietly, reached for his glasses and inquired, in a most matter-of-fact tone:

"Who is it?"

It would be useless to describe the search that the warden made. It was minute. Not one inch of the cell or the bed was

---

* The dark lantern was a modification of an ordinary gas or kerosene hand lantern that could be darkened while lit by a sliding shield that covered the light without extinguishing the flame. In this way, it was the predecessor of the electric hand torch or flashlight.

overlooked. He found the round hole in the floor, and with a flash of inspiration thrust his thick fingers into it. After a moment of fumbling there he drew up something and looked at it in the light of his lantern.

"Ugh!" he exclaimed.

The thing he had taken out was a rat—a dead rat. His inspiration fled as a mist before the sun. But he continued the search. The Thinking Machine, without a word, arose and kicked the rat out of the cell into the corridor.

The warden climbed on the bed and tried the steel bars in the tiny window. They were perfectly rigid; every bar of the door was the same.

Then the warden searched the prisoner's clothing, beginning at the shoes. Nothing hidden in them! Then the trousers waist band. Still nothing! Then the pockets of the trousers. From one side he drew out some paper money and examined it.

"Five one-dollar bills," he gasped.

"That's right," said the prisoner.

"But the—you had two tens and a five—what the—how do you do it?"

"That's my business," said The Thinking Machine.

"Did any of my men change this money for you—on your word of honor?"

The Thinking Machine paused just a fraction of a second.

"No," he said.

"Well, do you make it?" asked the warden. He was prepared to believe anything.

"That's my business," again said the prisoner.

The warden glared at the eminent scientist fiercely. He felt—he knew—that this man was making a fool of him, yet he didn't know how. If he were a real prisoner he would get the truth—but, then, perhaps, those inexplicable things which had happened would not have been brought before him so sharply. Neither of the men spoke for a long time, then suddenly the warden turned fiercely and left the cell, slamming the door behind him. He didn't dare to speak, then.

He glanced at the clock. It was ten minutes to four. He had hardly settled himself in bed when again came that heart-breaking shriek through the prison. With a few muttered words, which, while not elegant, were highly expressive, he relighted his lantern and rushed through the prison again to the cell on the upper floor.

Again Ballard was crushing himself against the steel door, shrieking, shrieking at the top of his voice. He stopped only when the warden flashed his lamp in the cell.

"Take me out, take me out," he screamed. "I did it, I did it, I killed her. Take it away."

"Take what away?" asked the warden.

"I threw the acid in her face—I did it—I confess. Take me out of here."

Ballard's condition was pitiable; it was only an act of mercy to let him out into the corridor. There he crouched in a corner, like an animal at bay, and clasped his hands to his ears. It took half an hour to calm him sufficiently for him to speak. Then he told incoherently what had happened. On the night before at four o'clock he had heard a voice—a sepulchral voice, muffled and wailing in tone.

"What did it say?" asked the warden, curiously.

"Acid—acid—acid!" gasped the prisoner. "It accused me. Acid! I threw the acid, and the woman died. Oh!" It was a long, shuddering wail of terror.

"Acid?" echoed the warden, puzzled. The case was beyond him.

"Acid. That's all I heard—that one word, repeated several times. There were other things, too, but I didn't hear them."

"That was last night, eh?" asked the warden. "What happened to-night—what frightened you just now?"

"It was the same thing," gasped the prisoner. "Acid—acid—acid!" He covered his face with his hands and sat shivering. "It was acid I used on her, but I didn't mean to kill her. I just heard the words. It was something accusing me—accusing me." He mumbled, and was silent.

"Did you hear anything else?"

"Yes—but I couldn't understand—only a little bit—just a word or two."

"Well, what was it?"

"I heard 'acid' three times, then I heard a long, moaning sound, then—then—I heard 'No. 8 hat.' I heard that twice."

"No. 8 hat," repeated the warden. "What the devil—No. 8 hat? Accusing voices of conscience have never talked about No. 8 hats, so far as I ever heard."

"He's insane," said one of the jailers, with an air of finality.

"I believe you," said the warden. "He must be. He probably heard something and got frightened. He's trembling now. No. 8 hat! What the————"

V

When the fifth day of The Thinking Machine's imprisonment rolled around the warden was wearing a hunted look. He was anxious for the end of the thing. He could not help but feel that his distinguished prisoner had been amusing himself. And if this were so, The Thinking Machine had lost none of his sense of humor. For on this fifth day he flung down another linen note to the outside guard, bearing the words: "Only two days more." Also he flung down half a dollar.

Now the warden knew—he *knew*—that the man in Cell 13

didn't have any half dollars—he *couldn't* have any half dollars, no more than he could have pen and ink and linen, and yet he did have them. It was a condition, not a theory; that is one reason why the warden was wearing a hunted look.

That ghastly, uncanny thing, too, about "Acid" and "No. 8 hat" clung to him tenaciously. They didn't mean anything, of course, merely the ravings of an insane murderer who had been driven by fear to confess his crime, still there were so many things that "didn't mean anything" happening in the prison now since The Thinking Machine was there.

On the sixth day the warden received a postal stating that Dr. Ransome and Mr. Fielding would be at Chisholm Prison on the following evening, Thursday, and in the event Professor Van Dusen had not yet escaped—and they presumed he had not because they had not heard from him—they would meet him there.

"In the event he had not yet escaped!" The warden smiled grimly. Escaped!

The Thinking Machine enlivened this day for the warden with three notes. They were on the usual linen and bore generally on the appointment at half-past eight o'clock Thursday night, which appointment the scientist had made at the time of his imprisonment.

On the afternoon of the seventh day the warden passed Cell 13 and glanced in. The Thinking Machine was lying on the iron bed, apparently sleeping lightly. The cell appeared precisely as it always did from a casual glance. The warden would swear that no man was going to leave it between that hour—it was then four o'clock—and half-past eight o'clock that evening.

On his way back past the cell the warden heard the steady breathing again, and coming close to the door looked in. He wouldn't have done so if The Thinking Machine had been look-ing, but now—well, it was different.

A ray of light came through the high window and fell on the face of the sleeping man. It occurred to the warden for the first time that his prisoner appeared haggard and weary. Just then The Thinking Machine stirred slightly and the warden hurried on up the corridor guiltily. That evening after six o'clock he saw the jailer.

"Everything all right in Cell 13?" he asked.

"Yes, sir," replied the jailer. "He didn't eat much, though."

It was with a feeling of having done his duty that the warden received Dr. Ransome and Mr. Fielding shortly after seven o'clock. He intended to show them the linen notes and lay before them the full story of his woes, which was a long one. But before this came to pass the guard from the river side of the prison yard entered the office.

"The arc light in my side of the yard won't light," he informed the warden.

"Confound it, that man's a hoodoo," thundered the official. "Everything has happened since he's been here."

The guard went back to his post in the darkness, and the warden 'phoned to the electric light company.

"This is Chisholm Prison," he said through the 'phone. "Send three or four men down here quick, to fix an arc light."

The reply was evidently satisfactory, for the warden hung up the receiver and passed out into the yard. While Dr. Ransome and Mr. Fielding sat waiting the guard at the outer gate came in with a special delivery letter. Dr. Ransome happened to notice the address, and, when the guard went out, looked at the letter more closely.

"By George!" he exclaimed.

"What is it?" asked Mr. Fielding.

Silently the doctor offered the letter. Mr. Fielding examined it closely.

"Coincidence," he said. "It must be."

It was nearly eight o'clock when the warden returned to his office. The electricians had arrived in a wagon, and were now at work. The warden pressed the buzz-button communicating with the man at the outer gate in the wall.

"How many electricians came in?" he asked, over the short 'phone. "Four? Three workmen in jumpers and overalls and the manager? Frock coat and silk hat? All right. Be certain that only four go out. That's all."

He turned to Dr. Ransome and Mr. Fielding. "We have to be careful here—particularly," and there was broad sarcasm in his tone, "since we have scientists locked up."

The warden picked up the special delivery letter carelessly, and then began to open it.

"When I read this I want to tell you gentlemen something about how—— Great Cæsar!" he ended, suddenly, as he glanced at the letter. He sat with mouth open, motionless, from astonishment.

"What is it?" asked Mr. Fielding.

"A special delivery letter from Cell 13," gasped the warden. "An invitation to supper."

"What?" and the two others arose, unanimously.

The warden sat dazed, staring at the letter for a moment, then called sharply to a guard outside in the corridor.

"Run down to Cell 13 and see if that man's in there."

The guard went as directed, while Dr. Ransome and Mr. Fielding examined the letter.

"It's Van Dusen's handwriting; there's no question of that," said Dr. Ransome. "I've seen too much of it."

Just then the buzz on the telephone from the outer gate

sounded, and the warden, in a semi-trance, picked up the receiver.

"Hello! Two reporters, eh? Let 'em come in." He turned suddenly to the doctor and Mr. Fielding. "Why, the man *can't* be out. He must be in his cell."

Just at that moment the guard returned.

"He's still in his cell, sir," he reported. "I saw him. He's lying down."

"There, I told you so," said the warden, and he breathed freely again. "But how did he mail that letter?"

There was a rap on the steel door which led from the jail yard into the warden's office.

"It's the reporters," said the warden. "Let them in," he instructed the guard; then to the two other gentlemen: "Don't say anything about this before them, because I'd never hear the last of it."

The door opened, and the two men from the front gate entered.

"Good-evening, gentlemen," said one. That was Hutchinson Hatch; the warden knew him well.

"Well?" demanded the other, irritably. "I'm here."

That was The Thinking Machine.

He squinted belligerently at the warden, who sat with mouth agape. For the moment that official had nothing to say. Dr. Ransome and Mr. Fielding were amazed, but they didn't know what the warden knew. They were only amazed; he was paralyzed. Hutchinson Hatch, the reporter, took in the scene with greedy eyes.

"How—how—how did you do it?" gasped the warden, finally.

"Come back to the cell," said The Thinking Machine, in the irritated voice which his scientific associates knew so well.

The warden, still in a condition bordering on trance, led the way.

"Flash your light in there," directed The Thinking Machine.

The warden did so. There was nothing unusual in the appearance of the cell, and there—there on the bed lay the figure of The Thinking Machine. Certainly! There was the yellow hair! Again the warden looked at the man beside him and wondered at the strangeness of his own dreams.

With trembling hands he unlocked the cell door and The Thinking Machine passed inside.

"See here," he said.

He kicked at the steel bars in the bottom of the cell door and three of them were pushed out of place. A fourth broke off and rolled away in the corridor.

"And here, too," directed the erstwhile prisoner as he stood on the bed to reach the small window. He swept his hand across the opening and every bar came out.

"What's this in the bed?" demanded the warden, who was slowly recovering.

"A wig," was the reply. "Turn down the cover."

The warden did so. Beneath it lay a large coil of strong rope, thirty feet or more, a dagger, three files, ten feet of electric wire, a thin, powerful pair of steel pliers, a small tack hammer with its handle, and—and a Derringer pistol.

"How did you do it?" demanded the warden.

"You gentlemen have an engagement to supper with me at half-past nine o'clock," said The Thinking Machine. "Come on, or we shall be late."

"But how did you do it?" insisted the warden.

"Don't ever think you can hold any man who can use his brain," said The Thinking Machine. "Come on; we shall be late."

VI

It was an impatient supper party in the rooms of Professor Van Dusen and a somewhat silent one. The guests were Dr. Ransome, Albert Fielding, the warden, and Hutchinson Hatch, reporter. The meal was served to the minute, in accordance with Professor Van Dusen's instructions of one week before; Dr. Ransome found the artichokes delicious. At last the supper was finished and The Thinking Machine turned full on Dr. Ransome and squinted at him fiercely.

"Do you believe it now?" he demanded.

"I do," replied Dr. Ransome.

"Do you admit that it was a fair test?"

"I do."

With the others, particularly the warden, he was waiting anxiously for the explanation.

"Suppose you tell us how———" began Mr. Fielding.

"Yes, tell us how," said the warden.

The Thinking Machine readjusted his glasses, took a couple of preparatory squints at his audience, and began the story. He told it from the beginning logically; and no man ever talked to more interested listeners.

"My agreement was," he began, "to go into a cell, carrying nothing except what was necessary to wear, and to leave that cell within a week. I had never seen Chisholm Prison. When I went into the cell I asked for tooth powder, two ten and one five-dollar bills, and also to have my shoes blacked. Even if these requests had been refused it would not have mattered seriously. But you agreed to them.

"I knew there would be nothing in the cell which you thought I might use to advantage. So when the warden locked the door on me I was apparently helpless, unless I could turn three seemingly innocent things to use. They were things which would have been permitted any prisoner under sentence of death, were they not, warden?"

"Tooth powder and polished shoes, yes, but not money," replied the warden.

"Anything is dangerous in the hands of a man who knows how to use it," went on The Thinking Machine. "I did nothing that first night but sleep and chase rats." He glared at the warden. "When the matter was broached I knew I could do nothing that night, so suggested next day. You gentlemen thought I wanted time to arrange an escape with outside assistance, but this was not true. I knew I could communicate with whom I pleased, when I pleased."

The warden stared at him a moment, then went on smoking solemnly.

"I was aroused next morning at six o'clock by the jailer with my breakfast," continued the scientist. "He told me dinner was at twelve and supper at six. Between these times, I gathered, I would be pretty much to myself. So immediately after breakfast I examined my outside surroundings from my cell window. One look told me it would be useless to try to scale the wall, even should I decide to leave my cell by the window, for my purpose was to leave not only the cell, but the prison. Of course, I could have gone over the wall, but it would have taken me longer to lay my plans that way. Therefore, for the moment, I dismissed all idea of that.

"From this first observation I knew the river was on that side of the prison, and that there was also a playground there. Subsequently these surmises were verified by a keeper. I knew then one important thing—that anyone might approach the prison wall from that side if necessary without attracting any particular attention. That was well to remember. I remembered it.

"But the outside thing which most attracted my attention was the feed wire to the arc light which ran within a few feet— probably three or four—of my cell window. I knew that would be valuable in the event I found it necessary to cut off that arc light."

"Oh, you shut it off to-night, then?" asked the warden.

"Having learned all I could from that window," resumed The Thinking Machine, without heeding the interruption, "I considered the idea of escaping through the prison proper. I recalled just how I had come into the cell, which I knew would be the only way. Seven doors lay between me and the outside. So, also for the time being, I gave up the idea of escaping that way. And I couldn't go through the solid granite walls of the cell."

The Thinking Machine paused for a moment and Dr. Ransome lighted a new cigar. For several minutes there was silence, then the scientific jail-breaker went on:

"While I was thinking about these things a rat ran across my foot. It suggested a new line of thought. There were at least half a dozen rats in the cell—I could see their beady eyes. Yet I had noticed none come under the cell door. I frightened them purposely and watched the cell door to see if they went out that way. They did not, but they were gone. Obviously they went another way. Another way meant another opening.

"I searched for this opening and found it. It was an old drain pipe, long unused and partly choked with dirt and dust. But this was the way the rats had come. They came from somewhere. Where? Drain pipes usually lead outside prison grounds. This one probably led to the river, or near it. The rats must therefore come from that direction. If they came a part of the way, I reasoned that they came all the way, because it was extremely unlikely that a solid iron or lead pipe would have any hole in it except at the exit.

"When the jailer came with my luncheon he told me two important things, although he didn't know it. One was that a new system of plumbing had been put in the prison seven years before; another that the river was only three hundred feet away. Then I knew positively that the pipe was a part of an old system; I knew, too, that it slanted generally toward the river. But did the pipe end in the water or on land?

"This was the next question to be decided. I decided it by catching several of the rats in the cell. My jailer was surprised to see me engaged in this work. I examined at least a dozen of them. They were perfectly dry; they had come through the pipe, and, most important of all, they were *not house rats, but field rats*. The other end of the pipe was on land, then, outside the prison walls. So far, so good.

"Then, I knew that if I worked freely from this point I must attract the warden's attention in another direction. You see, by telling the warden that I had come there to escape you made the test more severe, because I had to trick him by false scents."

The warden looked up with a sad expression in his eyes.

"The first thing was to make him think I was trying to communicate with you, Dr. Ransome. So I wrote a note on a piece of linen I tore from my shirt, addressed it to Dr. Ransome, tied a five-dollar bill around it and threw it out the window. I knew the guard would take it to the warden, but I rather hoped the warden would send it as addressed. Have you that first linen note, warden?"

The warden produced the cipher.

"What the deuce does it mean, anyhow?" he asked.

"Read it backward, beginning with the 'T' signature and disregard the division into words," instructed The Thinking Machine.

The warden did so.

"T-h-i-s, this," he spelled, studied it a moment, then read it off, grinning:

"This is not the way I intend to escape."

"Well, now what do you think o' that?" he demanded, still grinning.

"I knew that would attract your attention, just as it did," said The Thinking Machine, "and if you really found out what it was it would be a sort of gentle rebuke."

"What did you write it with?" asked Dr. Ransome, after he had examined the linen and passed it to Mr. Fielding.

"This," said the erstwhile prisoner, and he extended his foot. On it was the shoe he had worn in prison, though the polish was gone—scraped off clean. "The shoe blacking, moistened with water, was my ink; the metal tip of the shoe lace made a fairly good pen."

The warden looked up and suddenly burst into a laugh, half of relief, half of amusement.

"You're a wonder," he said, admiringly. "Go on."

"That precipitated a search of my cell by the warden, as I had intended," continued The Thinking Machine. "I was anxious to get the warden into the habit of searching my cell, so that finally, constantly finding nothing, he would get disgusted and quit. This at last happened, practically."

The warden blushed.

"He then took my white shirt away and gave me a prison shirt. He was satisfied that those two pieces of the shirt were all that was missing. But while he was searching my cell I had another piece of that same shirt, about nine inches square, rolled into a small ball in my mouth."

"Nine inches of that shirt?" demanded the warden. "Where did it come from?"

"The bosoms of all stiff white shirts are of triple thickness," was the explanation. "I tore out the inside thickness, leaving the bosom only two thicknesses. I knew you wouldn't see it. So much for that."

There was a little pause, and the warden looked from one to another of the men with a sheepish grin.

"Having disposed of the warden for the time being by giving him something else to think about, I took my first serious step toward freedom," said Professor Van Dusen. "I knew, within reason, that the pipe led somewhere to the playground outside; I knew a great many boys played there; I knew that rats came into my cell from out there. Could I communicate with some one outside with these things at hand?

"First was necessary, I saw, a long and fairly reliable thread, so—but here," he pulled up his trousers legs and showed that the tops of both stockings, of fine, strong lisle,* were gone. "I unraveled those—after I got them started it wasn't difficult— and I had easily a quarter of a mile of thread that I could depend on.

"Then on half of my remaining linen I wrote, laboriously enough I assure you, a letter explaining my situation to this gentleman here," and he indicated Hutchinson Hatch. "I knew he would assist me—for the value of the newspaper story. I tied firmly to this linen letter a ten-dollar bill—there is no surer way of attracting the eye of anyone—and wrote on the linen: 'Finder of this deliver to Hutchinson Hatch, *Daily American*, who will give another ten dollars for the information.'

"The next thing was to get this note outside on that playground where a boy might find it. There were two ways, but I chose the best. I took one of the rats—I became adept in catching them—tied the linen and money firmly to one leg, fastened

---

* A smooth cotton thread, often used in hosiery.

my lisle thread to another, and turned him loose in the drain pipe. I reasoned that the natural fright of the rodent would make him run until he was outside the pipe and then out on earth he would probably stop to gnaw off the linen and money.

"From the moment the rat disappeared into that dusty pipe I became anxious. I was taking so many chances. The rat might gnaw the string, of which I held one end; other rats might gnaw it; the rat might run out of the pipe and leave the linen and money where they would never be found; a thousand other things might have happened. So began some nervous hours, but the fact that the rat ran on until only a few feet of the string remained in my cell made me think he was outside the pipe. I had carefully instructed Mr. Hatch what to do in case the note reached him. The question was: Would it reach him?

"This done, I could only wait and make other plans in case this one failed. I openly attempted to bribe my jailer, and learned from him that he held the keys to only two of seven doors between me and freedom. Then I did something else to make the warden nervous. I took the steel supports out of the heels of my shoes and made a pretense of sawing the bars of my cell window. The warden raised a pretty row about that. He developed, too, the habit of shaking the bars of my cell window to see if they were solid. They were—then."

Again the warden grinned. He had ceased being astonished.

"With this one plan I had done all I could and could only wait to see what happened," the scientist went on. "I couldn't know whether my note had been delivered or even found, or whether the mouse had gnawed it up. And I didn't dare to draw back through the pipe that one slender thread which connected me with the outside.

"When I went to bed that night I didn't sleep, for fear there would come the slight signal twitch at the thread which was to tell me that Mr. Hatch had received the note. At half-past three o'clock, I judge, I felt this twitch, and no prisoner actually under sentence of death ever welcomed a thing more heartily."

The Thinking Machine stopped and turned to the reporter. "You'd better explain just what you did," he said.

"The linen note was brought to me by a small boy who had been playing baseball," said Mr. Hatch. "I immediately saw a big story in it, so I gave the boy another ten dollars, and got several spools of silk, some twine, and a roll of light, pliable wire. The professor's note suggested that I have the finder of the note show me just where it was picked up, and told me to make my search from there, beginning at two o'clock in the morning. If I found the other end of the thread I was to twitch it gently three times, then a fourth.

"I began the search with a small bulb electric light.* It was an hour and twenty minutes before I found the end of the drain pipe, half hidden in weeds. The pipe was very large there, say twelve inches across. Then I found the end of the lisle thread, twitched it as directed and immediately I got an answering twitch.

"Then I fastened the silk to this and Professor Van Dusen began to pull it into his cell. I nearly had heart disease for fear the string would break. To the end of the silk I fastened the twine, and when that had been pulled in I tied on the wire. Then that was drawn into the pipe and we had a substantial line, which rats couldn't gnaw, from the mouth of the drain into the cell."

The Thinking Machine raised his hand and Hatch stopped.

"All this was done in absolute silence," said the scientist. "But

---

* Invented in 1886 by German inventor Carl Gassner, the first dry cell batteries were marketed for consumer use in 1896 by an American company. Only three years later, English inventor David Misell applied them to create a handheld "flashlight," or electric torch, in which three batteries powered a small incandescent lamp.

when the wire reached my hand I could have shouted. Then we tried another experiment, which Mr. Hatch was prepared for. I tested the pipe as a speaking tube. Neither of us could hear very clearly, but I dared not speak loud for fear of attracting attention in the prison. At last I made him understand what I wanted immediately. He seemed to have great difficulty in understanding when I asked for nitric acid,* and I repeated the word 'acid' several times.

"Then I heard a shriek from a cell above me. I knew instantly that some one had overheard, and when I heard you coming, Mr. Warden, I feigned sleep. If you had entered my cell at that moment that whole plan of escape would have ended there. But you passed on. That was the nearest I ever came to being caught.

"Having established this improvised trolley it is easy to see how I got things in the cell and made them disappear at will. I merely dropped them back into the pipe. You, Mr. Warden, could not have reached the connecting wire with your fingers; they are too large. My fingers, you see, are longer and more slender. In addition I guarded the top of that pipe with a rat—you remember how."

"I remember," said the warden, with a grimace.

"I thought that if any one were tempted to investigate that hole the rat would dampen his ardor. Mr. Hatch could not send me anything useful through the pipe until next night, although he did send me change for ten dollars as a test, so I proceeded with other parts of my plan. Then I evolved the method of escape, which I finally employed.

"In order to carry this out successfully it was necessary for

---

* Nitric acid (HNO_3) was discovered centuries earlier, and beginning in 1905, it was commercially produced in great quantities by applying an electric arc to air, producing nitrogen oxide, then nitrogen dioxide, and eventually, by bubbling the latter through water, nitric acid. Commonly used as an oxidizing agent, it is highly corrosive.

the guard in the yard to get accustomed to seeing me at the cell window. I arranged this by dropping linen notes to him, boastful in tone, to make the warden believe, if possible, one of his assistants was communicating with the outside for me. I would stand at my window for hours gazing out, so the guard could see, and occasionally I spoke to him. In that way I learned that the prison had no electricians of its own, but was dependent upon the lighting company if anything should go wrong.

"That cleared the way to freedom perfectly. Early in the evening of the last day of my imprisonment, when it was dark, I planned to cut the feed wire which was only a few feet from my window, reaching it with an acid-tipped wire I had. That would make that side of the prison perfectly dark while the electricians were searching for the break. That would also bring Mr. Hatch into the prison yard.

"There was only one more thing to do before I actually began the work of setting myself free. This was to arrange final details with Mr. Hatch through our speaking tube. I did this within half an hour after the warden left my cell on the fourth night of my imprisonment. Mr. Hatch again had serious difficulty in understanding me, and I repeated the word 'acid' to him several times, and later the words: 'Number eight hat'—that's my size—and these were the things which made a prisoner upstairs confess to murder, so one of the jailers told me next day. This prisoner heard our voices, confused of course, through the pipe, which also went to his cell. The cell directly over me was not occupied, hence no one else heard.

"Of course the actual work of cutting the steel bars out of the window and door was comparatively easy with nitric acid, which I got through the pipe in thin bottles, but it took time. Hour after hour on the fifth and sixth and seventh days the guard below was looking at me as I worked on the bars of the window

with the acid on a piece of wire. I used the tooth powder to prevent the acid spreading. I looked away abstractedly as I worked
and each minute the acid cut deeper into the metal. I noticed
that the jailers always tried the door by shaking the upper part,
never the lower bars, therefore I cut the lower bars, leaving them
hanging in place by thin strips of metal. But that was a bit of
dare-deviltry. I could not have gone that way so easily."

The Thinking Machine sat silent for several minutes.

"I think that makes everything clear," he went on. "Whatever
points I have not explained were merely to confuse the warden
and jailers. These things in my bed I brought in to please Mr.
Hatch, who wanted to improve the story. Of course, the wig was
necessary in my plan. The special delivery letter I wrote and
directed in my cell with Mr. Hatch's fountain pen, then sent it
out to him and he mailed it. That's all, I think."

"But your actually leaving the prison grounds and then
coming in through the outer gate to my office?" asked the
warden.

"Perfectly simple," said the scientist. "I cut the electric light
wire with acid, as I said, when the current was off. Therefore
when the current was turned on the arc didn't light. I knew
it would take some time to find out what was the matter and
make repairs. When the guard went to report to you the yard
was dark. I crept out the window—it was a tight fit, too—
replaced the bars by standing on a narrow ledge and remained
in a shadow until the force of electricians arrived. Mr. Hatch was
one of them.

"When I saw him I spoke and he handed me a cap, a jumper
and overalls, which I put on within ten feet of you, Mr. Warden,
while you were in the yard. Later Mr. Hatch called me, presumably as a workman, and together we went out the gate to
get something out of the wagon. The gate guard let us pass out

readily as two workmen who had just passed in. We changed our clothing and reappeared, asking to see you. We saw you. That's all."

There was silence for several minutes. Dr. Ransome was first to speak.

"Wonderful!" he exclaimed. "Perfectly amazing."

"How did Mr. Hatch happen to come with the electricians?" asked Mr. Fielding.

"His father is manager of the company," replied The Thinking Machine.

"But what if there had been no Mr. Hatch outside to help?"

"Every prisoner has one friend outside who would help him escape if he could."

"Suppose—just suppose—there had been no old plumbing system there?" asked the warden, curiously.

"There were two other ways out," said The Thinking Machine, enigmatically.

Ten minutes later the telephone bell rang. It was a request for the warden.

"Light all right, eh?" the warden asked, through the 'phone. "Good. Wire cut beside Cell 13? Yes, I know. One electrician too many? What's that? Two came out?"

The warden turned to the others with a puzzled expression.

"He only let in four electricians, he has let out two and says there are three left."

"I was the odd one," said The Thinking Machine.

"Oh," said the warden. "I see." Then through the 'phone: "Let the fifth man go. He's all right."

THE SCARLET THREAD*

I

The Thinking Machine—Professor Augustus S. F. X. Van Dusen, Ph.D., LL.D., F.R.S., M.D., etc., scientist and logician—listened intently and without comment to a weird, seemingly inexplicable story. Hutchinson Hatch, reporter, was telling it. The bowed figure of the savant lay at ease in a large chair. The enormous head with its bushy yellow hair was thrown back, the thin, white fingers were pressed tip to tip and the blue eyes, narrowed to mere slits, squinted aggressively upward. The scientist was in a receptive mood.

"From the beginning, every fact you know," he had requested.

"It's all out in the Back Bay," the reporter explained. "There is a big apartment house there, a fashionable establishment, in a side street, just off Commonwealth Avenue. It is five stories in all, and is cut up into small suites, of two and three rooms with bath. These suites are handsomely, even luxuriously furnished, and are occupied by people who can afford to pay big rents. Generally these are young unmarried men, although in several

---

* First published in *Boston American*, December 12, 1905.

cases they are husband and wife. It is a house of every modern improvement, elevator service, hall boys, liveried door men, spacious corridors and all that. It has both the gas and electric systems of lighting.* Tenants are at liberty to use either or both.

"A young broker, Weldon Henley, occupies one of the handsomest of these suites, being on the second floor, in front. He has met with considerable success in the Street.† He is a bachelor and lives there alone. There is no personal servant. He dabbles in photography as a hobby, and is said to be remarkably expert.

"Recently there was a report that he was to be married this Winter to a beautiful Virginia girl who has been visiting Boston from time to time, a Miss Lipscomb—Charlotte Lipscomb, of Richmond. Henley has never denied or affirmed this rumor, although he has been asked about it often. Miss Lipscomb is impossible of access even when she visits Boston. Now she is in Virginia, I understand, but will return to Boston later in the season."

The reporter paused, lighted a cigarette and leaned forward in his chair, gazing steadily into the inscrutable eyes of the scientist.

"When Henley took the suite he requested that all the electric lighting apparatus be removed from his apartments," he went on. "He had taken a long lease of the place, and this was done. Therefore he uses only gas for lighting purposes, and he usually keeps one of his gas jets burning low all night."

---

* Boston (in which the "Back Bay" neighborhood may be found) was not the first American city to adopt electric lighting. That was Cleveland, which installed twelve electric lights around its central plaza, Public Square, in 1879. However, by 1882, electric lamps began to appear in Boston's Scollay Square, and in 1909, the city began to replace all of the gaslit streetlights, beginning with the roadways in commercial districts. Conversion of residential streets and private residences occurred more slowly.

† A nickname for the financial district; in Boston, it is bounded on one side by State Street, where we will find the offices of Mr. Henley.

"Bad, bad for his health," commented the scientist.

"Now comes the mystery of the affair," the reporter went on. "It was five weeks or so ago Henley retired as usual—about midnight. He locked his door on the inside—he is positive of that—and awoke about four o'clock in the morning nearly asphyxiated by gas. He was barely able to get up and open the window to let in the fresh air. The gas jet he had left burning was out, and the suite was full of gas."

"Accident, possibly," said The Thinking Machine. "A draught through the apartments; a slight diminution of gas pressure; a hundred possibilities."

"So it was presumed," said the reporter. "Of course it would have been impossible for————"

"Nothing is impossible," said the other, tartly. "Don't say that. It annoys me exceedingly."

"Well, then, it seems highly improbable that the door had been opened or that anyone came into the room and did this deliberately," the newspaper man went on, with a slight smile. "So Henley said nothing about this; attributed it to accident. The next night he lighted his gas as usual, but he left it burning a little brighter. The same thing happened again."

"Ah," and The Thinking Machine changed his position a little. "The second time."

"And again he awoke just in time to save himself," said Hatch. "Still he attributed the affair to accident, and determined to avoid a recurrence of the affair by doing away with the gas at night. Then he got a small night lamp and used this for a week or more."

"Why does he have a light at all?" asked the scientist, testily.

"I can hardly answer that," replied Hatch. "I may say, however, that he is of a very nervous temperament, and gets up frequently during the night. He reads occasionally when he can't sleep. In addition to that he has slept with a light going all his life; it's a habit."

"Go on."

"One night he looked for the night lamp, but it had disappeared—at least he couldn't find it—so he lighted the gas again. The fact of the gas having twice before gone out had been dismissed as a serious possibility. Next morning at five o'clock a bell boy, passing through the hall, smelled gas and made a quick investigation. He decided it came from Henley's place, and rapped on the door. There was no answer. It ultimately developed that it was necessary to smash in the door. There on the bed they found Henley unconscious with the gas pouring into the room from the jet which he had left lighted. He was revived in the air, but for several hours was deathly sick."

"Why was the door smashed in?" asked The Thinking Machine. "Why not unlocked?"

"It was done because Henley had firmly barred it," Hatch explained. "He had become suspicious, I suppose, and after the second time he always barred his door and fastened every window before he went to sleep. There may have been a fear that some one used a key to enter."

"Well?" asked the scientist. "After that?"

"Three weeks or so elapsed, bringing the affair down to this morning," Hatch went on. "Then the same thing happened a little differently. For instance, after the third time the gas went out Henley decided to find out for himself what caused it, and so expressed himself to a few friends who knew of the mystery. Then, night after night, he lighted the gas as usual and kept watch. It was never disturbed during all that time, burning steadily all night. What sleep he got was in daytime.

"Last night Henley lay awake for a time; then, exhausted and tired, fell asleep. This morning early he awoke; the room was filled with gas again. In some way my city editor heard of it and asked me to look into the mystery."

That was all. The two men were silent for a long time, and finally The Thinking Machine turned to the reporter.

"Does anyone else in the house keep gas going all night?" he asked.

"I don't know," was the reply. "Most of them, I know, use electricity."

"Nobody else has been overcome as he has been?"

"No. Plumbers have minutely examined the lighting system all over the house and found nothing wrong."

"Does the gas in the house all come through the same meter?"

"Yes, so the manager told me. This meter, a big one, is just off the engine room. I supposed it possible that some one shut it off there on these nights long enough to extinguish the lights all over the house, then turned it on again. That is, presuming that it was done purposely. Do you think it was an attempt to kill Henley?"

"It might be," was the reply. "Find out for me just who in the house uses gas; also if anyone else leaves a light burning all night; also what opportunity anyone would have to get at the meter, and then something about Henley's love affair with Miss Lipscomb. Is there anyone else? If so, who? Where does he live? When you find out these things come back here."

* * *

That afternoon at one o'clock Hatch returned to the apartments of The Thinking Machine, with excitement plainly apparent on his face.

"Well?" asked the scientist.

"A French girl, Louise Regnier, employed as a maid by Mrs.

Standing in the house, was found dead in her room on the third floor to-day at noon," Hatch explained quickly. "It looks like suicide."

"How?" asked The Thinking Machine.

"The people who employed her—husband and wife—have been away for a couple of days," Hatch rushed on. "She was in the suite alone. This noon she had not appeared, there was an odor of gas and the door was broken in. Then she was found dead."

"With the gas turned on?"

"With the gas turned on. She was asphyxiated."

"Dear me, dear me," exclaimed the scientist. He arose and took up his hat. "Let's go see what this is all about."

II

When Professor Van Dusen and Hatch arrived at the apartment house they had been preceded by the medical examiner and the police. Detective Mallory, whom both knew, was moving about in the apartment where the girl had been found dead. The body had been removed and a telegram sent to her employers in New York.

"Too late," said Mallory, as they entered.

"What was it, Mr. Mallory?" asked the scientist.

"Suicide," was the reply. "No question of it. It happened in this room," and he led the way into the third room of the suite. "The maid, Miss Regnier, occupied this, and was here alone last night. Mr. and Mrs. Standing, her employers, have gone to New York for a few days. She was left alone, and killed herself."

Without further questioning The Thinking Machine went

* Mallory is the only police official who appears in the Thinking Machine tales.

over to the bed, from which the girl's body had been taken, and, stooping beside it, picked up a book. It was a novel by "The Duchess."* He examined this critically, then, standing on a chair, he examined the gas jet. This done, he stepped down and went to the window of the little room. Finally The Thinking Machine turned to the detective.

"Just how much was the gas turned on?" he asked.

"Turned on full," was the reply.

"Were both the doors of the room closed?"

"Both, yes."

"Any cotton, or cloth, or anything of the sort stuffed in the cracks of the window?"

"No. It's a tight-fitting window, anyway. Are you trying to make a mystery out of this?"

"Cracks in the doors stuffed?" The Thinking Machine went on.

"No." There was a smile about the detective's lips.

The Thinking Machine, on his knees, examined the bottom of one of the doors, that which led into the hall. The lock of this door had been broken when employees burst into the room. Having satisfied himself here and at the bottom of the other door, which connected with the bedroom adjoining, The Thinking Machine again climbed on a chair and examined the doors at the top.

"Both transoms closed, I suppose?" he asked.

"Yes," was the reply. "You can't make anything but suicide out of it," explained the detective. "The medical examiner has given that as his opinion—and everything I find indicates it."

"All right," broke in The Thinking Machine abruptly. "Don't let us keep you."

---

* Margaret Wolfe Hungerford (1855–1897) was an Irish writer of light romantic fiction. In the United States, her work appeared under the pen name "The Duchess."

After awhile Detective Mallory went away. Hatch and the scientist went down to the office floor, where they saw the manager. He seemed to be greatly distressed, but was willing to do anything he could in the matter.

"Is your night engineer perfectly trustworthy?" asked The Thinking Machine.

"Perfectly," was the reply. "One of the best and most reliable men I ever met. Alert and wide-awake."

"Can I see him a moment? The night man, I mean?"

"Certainly," was the reply. "He's downstairs. He sleeps there. He's probably up by this time. He sleeps usually till one o'clock in the daytime, being up all night."

"Do you supply gas for your tenants?"

"Both gas and electricity are included in the rent of the suites. Tenants may use one or both."

"And the gas all comes through one meter?"

"Yes, one meter. It's just off the engine room."

"I suppose there's no way of telling just who in the house uses gas?"

"No. Some do and some don't. I don't know."

This was what Hatch had told the scientist. Now together they went to the basement, and there met the night engineer, Charles Burlingame, a tall, powerful, clean-cut man, of alert manner and positive speech. He gazed with a little amusement at the slender, almost childish figure of The Thinking Machine and the grotesquely large head.

"You are in the engine room or near it all night every night?" began The Thinking Machine.

"I haven't missed a night in four years," was the reply.

"Anybody ever come here to see you at night?"

"Never. It's against the rules."

"The manager or a hall boy?"

"Never."

"In the last two months?" The Thinking Machine persisted.

"Not in the last two years," was the positive reply. "I go on duty every night at seven o'clock, and I am on duty until seven in the morning. I don't believe I've seen anybody in the basement here with me between those hours for a year at least."

The Thinking Machine was squinting steadily into the eyes of the engineer, and for a time both were silent. Hatch moved about the scrupulously clean engine room and nodded to the day engineer, who sat leaning back against the wall. Directly in front of him was the steam gauge.

"Have you a fireman?" was The Thinking Machine's next question.

"No. I fire myself," said the night man.*

"Here's the coal," and he indicated a bin within half a dozen feet of the mouth of the boiler.

"I don't suppose you ever had occasion to handle the gas meter?" insisted The Thinking Machine.

"Never touched it in my life," said the other. "I don't know anything about meters, anyway."

"And you never drop off to sleep at night for a few minutes when you get lonely? Doze, I mean?"

The engineer grinned good-naturedly.

"Never had any desire to, and besides I wouldn't have the chance," he explained. "There's a time check here,"—and he indicated it. "I have to punch that every half hour all night to prove that I have been awake."

"Dear me, dear me," exclaimed The Thinking Machine, irritably. He went over and examined the time check—a revolving

---

* The night man means that he stokes the boiler himself, by shoveling coal into it when needed.

paper disk with hours marked on it, made to move by the action of a clock, the face of which showed in the middle.

"Besides there's the steam gauge to watch," went on the engineer. "No engineer would dare go to sleep. There might be an explosion."

"Do you know Mr. Weldon Henley?" suddenly asked The Thinking Machine.

"Who?" asked Burlingame.

"Weldon Henley?"

"No-o," was the slow response. "Never heard of him. Who is he?"

"One of the tenants, on the second floor, I think."

"Lord, I don't know any of the tenants. What about him?"

"When does the inspector come here to read the meter?"

"I never saw him. I presume in daytime, eh Bill?" and he turned to the day engineer.

"Always in daytime—usually about noon," said Bill from his corner.

"Any other entrance to the basement except this way—and you could see anyone coming here this way I suppose?"

"Sure I could see 'em. There's no other entrance to the cellar except the coal hole in the sidewalk in front."

"Two big electric lights in front of the building, aren't there?"

"Yes. They go all night."

A slightly puzzled expression crept into the eyes of The Thinking Machine. Hatch knew from the persistency of the questions that he was not satisfied; yet he was not able to fathom or to understand all the queries. In some way they had to do with the possibility of some one having access to the meter.

"Where do you usually sit at night here?" was the next question.

"Over there where Bill's sitting. I always sit there."

The Thinking Machine crossed the room to Bill, a typical, grimy-handed man of his class.

"May I sit there a moment?" he asked.

Bill arose lazily, and The Thinking Machine sank down into the chair. From this point he could see plainly through the opening into the basement proper—there was no door—the gas meter of enormous proportions through which all the gas in the house passed. An electric light in the door made it bright as daylight. The Thinking Machine noted these things, arose, nodded his thanks to the two men and, still with the puzzled expression on his face, led the way upstairs. There the manager was still in his office.

"I presume you examine and know that the time check in the engineer's room is properly punched every half hour during the night?" he asked.

"Yes. I examine the dial every day—have them here, in fact, each with the date on it."

"May I see them?"

Now the manager was puzzled. He produced the cards, one for each day, and for half an hour The Thinking Machine studied them minutely. At the end of that time, when he arose and Hatch looked at him inquiringly, he saw still the perplexed expression.

After urgent solicitation, the manager admitted them to the apartments of Weldon Henley. Mr. Henley himself had gone to his office in State Street. Here The Thinking Machine did several things which aroused the curiosity of the manager, one of which was to minutely study the gas jets. Then The Thinking Machine opened one of the front windows and glanced out into the street. Below fifteen feet was the sidewalk; above was the solid front of the building, broken only by a flagpole which, properly roped, extended from the hall window of the next floor above out over the sidewalk a distance of twelve feet or so.

"Ever use that flagpole?" he asked the manager.

"Rarely," said the manager. "On holidays sometimes—Fourth of July and such times. We have a big flag for it."

From the apartments The Thinking Machine led the way to the hall, up the stairs and to the flagpole. Leaning out of this window, he looked down toward the window of the apartments he had just left. Then he inspected the rope of the flagpole, drawing it through his slender hands slowly and carefully. At last he picked off a slender thread of scarlet and examined it.

"Ah," he exclaimed. Then to Hatch: "Let's go, Mr. Hatch. Thank you," this last to the manager, who had been a puzzled witness.

Once on the street, side by side with The Thinking Machine, Hatch was bursting with questions, but he didn't ask them. He knew it would be useless. At last The Thinking Machine broke the silence.

"That girl, Miss Regnier, *was murdered!*" he said suddenly, positively. "There have been four attempts to murder Henley."

"How?" asked Hatch, startled.

"By a scheme so simple that neither you nor I nor the police have ever heard of it being employed," was the astonishing reply. *"It is perfectly horrible in its simplicity."*

"What was it?" Hatch insisted, eagerly.

"It would be futile to discuss that now," was the rejoinder. "There has been murder. We know how. Now the question is—who? What person would have a motive to kill Henley?"

III

There was a pause as they walked on.

"Where are we going?" asked Hatch finally.

"Come up to my place and let's consider this matter a bit further," replied The Thinking Machine.

Not another word was spoken by either until half an hour later, in the small laboratory. For a long time the scientist was thoughtful—deeply thoughtful. Once he took down a volume from a shelf and Hatch glanced at the title. It was "Gases: Their Properties." After awhile he returned this to the shelf and took down another, on which the reporter caught the title, "Anatomy."

"Now, Mr. Hatch," said The Thinking Machine in his perpetually crabbed voice, "we have a most remarkable riddle. It gains this remarkable aspect from its very simplicity. It is not, however, necessary to go into that now. I will make it clear to you when we know the motives.

"As a general rule, the greatest crimes never come to light because the greatest criminals, their perpetrators, are too clever to be caught. Here we have what I might call a great crime committed with a subtle simplicity that is wholly disarming, and a greater crime even than this was planned. This was to murder Weldon Henley. The first thing for you to do is to see Mr. Henley and warn him of his danger. Asphyxiation will not be attempted again, but there is a possibility of poison, a pistol shot, a knife, anything almost. As a matter of fact, he is in great peril.

"Superficially, the death of Miss Regnier, the maid, looks to be suicide. Instead it is the fruition of a plan which has been tried time and again against Henley. There is a possibility that Miss Regnier was not an intentional victim of the plot, but the fact remains that she was murdered. Why? Find the motive for the plot to murder Mr. Henley and you will know why."

The Thinking Machine reached over to the shelf, took a book, looked at it a moment, then went on:

"The first question to determine positively is: Who hated Weldon Henley sufficiently to desire his death? You say he is a successful man in the Street. Therefore there is a possibility that some enemy there is at the bottom of the affair, yet it seems hardly probable. If by his operations Mr. Henley ever happened to wreck another man's fortune find this man and find out all about him. He may be the man. There will be innumerable questions arising from this line of inquiry to a man of your resources. Leave none of them unanswered.

"On the other hand there is Henley's love affair. Had he a rival who might desire his death? Had he any rival? If so, find out all about him. He may be the man who planned all this. Here, too, there will be questions arising which demand answers. Answer them—all of them—fully and clearly before you see me again.

"Was Henley ever a party to a liaison of any kind? Find that out, too. A vengeful woman or a discarded sweetheart of a vengeful woman, you know, will go to any extreme. The rumor of his engagement to Miss—Miss———"

"Miss Lipscomb," Hatch supplied.

"The rumor of his engagement to Miss Lipscomb might have caused a woman whom he had once been interested in or who was once interested in him to attempt his life. The subtler murders—that is, the ones which are most attractive as problems—are nearly always the work of a cunning woman. I know nothing about women myself," he hastened to explain; "but Lombroso has taken that attitude.* Therefore, see if there is a woman."

Most of these points Hatch had previously seen—seen with the unerring eye of a clever newspaper reporter—yet there were several which had not occurred to him. He nodded his understanding.

---

* Cesare Lombroso, an influential early Italian criminologist, along with his assistant Guglielmo Ferrero, published *La donna delinquente* (*Criminal Woman, the Prostitute, and the Normal Woman*) in 1893. Using Darwinian theories, Lombroso argued that criminal women were more cunning and dangerous than men, and demonstrated statistically that crimes committed by women were more likely to be savage and premeditated.

"Now the center of the affair, of course," The Thinking Machine continued, "is the apartment house where Henley lives. The person who attempted his life either lives there or has ready access to the place, and frequently spends the night there. This is a vital question for you to answer. I am leaving all this to you because you know better how to do these things than I do. That's all, I think. When these things are all learned come back to me."

The Thinking Machine arose as if the interview were at an end, and Hatch also arose, reluctantly. An idea was beginning to dawn in his mind.

"Does it occur to you that there is any connection whatever between Henley and Miss Regnier?" he asked.

"It is possible," was the reply. "I had thought of that. If there is a connection it is not apparent yet."

"Then how—how was it she—she was killed, or killed herself, whichever may be true, and——"

"The attempt to kill Henley killed her. That's all I can say now."

"That all?" asked Hatch, after a pause.

"No. Warn Mr. Henley immediately that he is in grave danger. Remember the person who has planned this will probably go to any extreme. I don't know Mr. Henley, of course, but from the fact that he always had a light at night I gather that he is a timid sort of man—not necessarily a coward, but a man lacking in stamina—therefore, one who might better disappear for a week or so until the mystery is cleared up. Above all, impress upon him the importance of the warning."

The Thinking Machine opened his pocketbook and took from it the scarlet thread which he had picked from the rope of the flagpole.

"Here, I believe, is the real clew to the problem," he explained to Hatch. "What does it seem to be?"

Hatch examined it closely.

"I should say a strand from a Turkish bath robe," was his final judgment.

"Possibly. Ask some cloth expert what he makes of it, then if it sounds promising look into it. Find out if by any possibility it can be any part of any garment worn by any person in the apartment house."

"But it's so slight———" Hatch began.

"I know," the other interrupted, tartly. "It's slight, but I believe it is a part of the wearing apparel of the person, man or woman, who has four times attempted to kill Mr. Henley and who did kill the girl. Therefore, it is important."

Hatch looked at him quickly.

"Well, how—in what manner—did it come where you found it?"

"Simple enough," said the scientist. "It is a wonder that there were not more pieces of it—that's all."

Perplexed by his instructions, but confident of results, Hatch left The Thinking Machine. What possible connection could this tiny bit of scarlet thread, found on a flagpole, have with some one shutting off the gas in Henley's rooms? How did any one go into Henley's rooms to shut off the gas? How was it Miss Regnier was dead? What was the manner of her death?

A cloth expert in a great department store turned his knowledge on the tiny bit of scarlet for the illumination of Hatch, but he could go no further than to say that it seemed to be part of a Turkish bath robe.

"Man or woman's?" asked Hatch.

"The material from which bath robes are made is the same for both men and women," was the reply. "I can say nothing else. Of course there's not enough of it to even guess at the pattern of the robe."

Then Hatch went to the financial district and was ushered into the office of Weldon Henley, a slender, handsome man of thirty-two or three years, pallid of face and nervous in manner. He still showed the effect of the gas poisoning, and there was even a trace of a furtive fear—fear of something, he himself didn't know what—in his actions.

Henley talked freely to the newspaper man of certain things, but of other things was resentfully reticent. He admitted his engagement to Miss Lipscomb, and finally even admitted that Miss Lipscomb's hand had been sought by another man, Regnault Cabell, formerly of Virginia.

"Could you give me his address?" asked Hatch.

"He lives in the same apartment house with me—two floors above," was the reply.

Hatch was startled; startled more than he would have cared to admit.

"Are you on friendly terms with him?" he asked.

"Certainly," said Henley. "I won't say anything further about this matter. It would be unwise for obvious reasons."

"I suppose you consider that this turning on of the gas was an attempt on your life?"

"I can't suppose anything else."

Hatch studied the pallid face closely as he asked the next question.

"Do you know Miss Regnier was found dead to-day?"

"Dead?" exclaimed the other, and he arose. "Who—what—who is she?"

It seemed a distinct effort for him to regain control of himself.

The reporter detailed then the circumstances of the finding of the girl's body, and the broker listened without comment. From that time forward all the reporter's questions were either parried or else met with a flat refusal to answer. Finally Hatch repeated to him the warning which he had from The Thinking Machine, and feeling that he had accomplished little, went away.

At eight o'clock that night—a night of complete darkness—Henley was found unconscious, lying in a little used walk in the Common. There was a bullet hole through his left shoulder, and he was bleeding profusely. He was removed to the hospital, where he regained consciousness for just a moment.

"Who shot you?" he was asked.

"None of your business," he replied, and lapsed into unconsciousness.

IV

Entirely unaware of this latest attempt on the life of the broker, Hutchinson Hatch steadily pursued his investigations. They finally led him to an intimate friend of Regnault Cabell. The young Southerner had apartments on the fourth floor of the big house off Commonwealth Avenue, directly over those Henley occupied, but two flights higher up. This friend was a figure in the social set of the Back Bay. He talked to Hatch freely of Cabell.

"He's a good fellow," he explained, "one of the best I ever met, and comes of one of the best families Virginia ever had—a true F. F. V.* He's pretty quick tempered and all that, but an excellent chap, and everywhere he has gone here he has made friends."

"He used to be in love with Miss Lipscomb of Virginia, didn't he?" asked Hatch, casually.

---

* The so-called "First Families" of Virginia were the descendants of the early English colonists (excluding, as might be expected, illegitimate children and those descended from enslaved women). Many of the First Families claimed Native American heritage from the marriage of Powhatan woman Pocahontas and Englishman John Rolfe. Though there were doubtless other relationships between Native Americans and White colonists, Pocahontas's line was celebrated because she became a Christian and married her partner.

"Used to be?" the other repeated with a laugh. "He is in love with her. But recently he understood that she was engaged to Weldon Henley, a broker—you may have heard of him?—and that, I suppose, has dampened his ardor considerably. As a matter of fact, Cabell took the thing to heart. He used to know Miss Lipscomb in Virginia—she comes from another famous family there—and he seemed to think he had a prior claim on her."

Hatch heard all these things as any man might listen to gossip, but each additional fact was sinking into his mind, and each additional fact led his suspicions on deeper into the channel they had chosen.

"Cabell is pretty well to do," his informant went on, "not rich as we count riches in the North, but pretty well to do, and I believe he came to Boston because Miss Lipscomb spent so much of her time here. She is a beautiful young woman of twenty-two and extremely popular in the social world everywhere, particularly in Boston. Then there was the additional fact that Henley was here."

"No chance at all for Cabell?" Hatch suggested.

"Not the slightest," was the reply. "Yet despite the heartbreak he had, he was the first to congratulate Henley on winning her love. And he meant it, too."

"What's his attitude toward Henley now?" asked Hatch. His voice was calm, but there was an underlying tense note imperceptible to the other.

"They meet and speak and move in the same set. There's no love lost on either side, I don't suppose, but there is no trace of any ill feeling."

"Cabell doesn't happen to be a vindictive sort of man?"

"Vindictive?" and the other laughed. "No. He's like a big boy, forgiving, and all that; hot-tempered, though. I could imagine him in a fit of anger making a personal matter of it with Henley, but I don't think he ever did."

The mind of the newspaper man was rapidly focusing on one point; the rush of thoughts, questions and doubts silenced him for a moment. Then:

"How long has Cabell been in Boston?"

"Seven or eight months—that is, he has had apartments here for that long—but he has made several visits South. I suppose it's South. He has a trick of dropping out of sight occasionally. I understand that he intends to go South for good very soon. If I'm not mistaken, he is trying now to rent his suite."

Hatch looked suddenly at his informant; an idea of seeing Cabell and having a legitimate excuse for talking to him had occurred to him.

"I'm looking for a suite," he volunteered at last. "I wonder if you would give me a card of introduction to him? We might get together on it."

Thus it happened that half an hour later, about ten minutes past nine o'clock, Hatch was on his way to the big apartment house. In the office he saw the manager.

"Heard the news?" asked the manager.

"No," Hatch replied. "What is it?"

"Somebody's shot Mr. Henley as he was passing through the Common early to-night."

Hatch whistled his amazement.

"Is he dead?"

"No, but he is unconscious. The hospital doctors say it is a nasty wound, but not necessarily dangerous."

"Who shot him? Do they know?"

"He knows, but he won't say."

Amazed and alarmed by this latest development, an accurate fulfillment of The Thinking Machine's prophecy, Hatch stood thoughtful for a moment, then recovering his composure a little asked for Cabell.

"I don't think there's much chance of seeing him," said the manager. "He's going away on the midnight train—going South, to Virginia."

"Going away to-night?" Hatch gasped.

"Yes; it seems to have been rather a sudden determination. He was talking to me here half an hour or so ago, and said something about going away. While he was here the telephone boy told me that Henley had been shot; they had 'phoned from the hospital to inform us. Then Cabell seemed greatly agitated. He said he was going away to-night, if he could catch the midnight train, and now he's packing."

"I suppose the shooting of Henley upset him considerably?" the reporter suggested.

"Yes, I guess it did," was the reply. "They moved in the same set and belonged to the same clubs."

The manager sent Hatch's card of introduction to Cabell's apartments. Hatch went up and was ushered into a suite identical with that of Henley's in every respect save in minor details of furnishings. Cabell stood in the middle of the floor, with his personal belongings scattered about the room; his valet, evidently a Frenchman, was busily engaged in packing.

Cabell's greeting was perfunctorily cordial; he seemed agitated. His face was flushed and from time to time he ran his fingers through his long, brown hair. He stared at Hatch in a preoccupied fashion, then they fell into conversation about the rent of the apartments.

"I'll take almost anything reasonable," Cabell said hurriedly. "You see, I am going away to-night, rather more suddenly than I had intended, and I am anxious to get the lease off my hands. I pay two hundred dollars a month for these just as they are."

"May I look them over?" asked Hatch.

He passed from the front room into the next. Here, on a bed, was piled a huge lot of clothing, and the valet, with deft fingers, was brushing and folding, preparatory to packing. Cabell was directly behind him.

"Quite comfortable, you see," he explained. "There's room enough if you are alone. Are you?"

"Oh, yes," Hatch replied.

"This other room here," Cabell explained, "is not in very tidy shape now. I have been out of the city for several weeks, and—What's the matter?" he demanded suddenly.

Hatch had turned quickly at the words and stared at him, then recovered himself with a start.

"I beg your pardon," he stammered. "I rather thought I saw you in town here a week or so ago—of course I didn't know you—and I was wondering if I could have been mistaken."

"Must have been," said the other easily. "During the time I was away a Miss———, a friend of my sister's, occupied the suite. I'm afraid some of her things are here. She hasn't sent for them as yet. She occupied this room, I think; when I came back a few days ago she took another place and all her things haven't been removed."

"I see," remarked Hatch, casually. "I don't suppose there's any chance of her returning here unexpectedly if I should happen to take her apartments?"

"Not the slightest. She knows I am back, and thinks I am to remain. She was to send for these things."

Hatch gazed about the room ostentatiously. Across a trunk lay a Turkish bath robe with a scarlet stripe in it. He was anxious to get hold of it, to examine it closely. But he didn't dare to, then. Together they returned to the front room.

"I rather like the place," he said, after a pause, "but the price is———"

"Just a moment," Cabell interrupted. "Jean, before you finish packing that suit case be sure to put my bath robe in it. It's in the far room."

Then one question was settled for Hatch. After a moment the valet returned with the bath robe, which had been in the far room. It was Cabell's bath robe. As Jean passed the reporter an end of the robe caught on a corner of the trunk, and, stopping, the reporter unfastened it. A tiny strand of thread clung to the metal; Hatch detached it and stood idly twirling it in his fingers.

"As I was saying," he resumed, "I rather like the place, but the price is too much. Suppose you leave it in the hands of the manager of the house—"

"I had intended doing that," the Southerner interrupted.

"Well, I'll see him about it later," Hatch added.

With a cordial, albeit preoccupied, handshake, Cabell ushered him out. Hatch went down in the elevator with a feeling of elation; a feeling that he had accomplished something. The manager was waiting to get into the lift.

"Do you happen to remember the name of the young lady who occupied Mr. Cabell's suite while he was away?" he asked.

"Miss Austin," said the manager, "but she's not young. She was about forty-five years old, I should judge."

"Did Mr. Cabell have his servant Jean with him?"

"Oh, no," said the manager. "The valet gave up the suite to Miss Austin entirely, and until Mr. Cabell returned occupied a room in the quarters we have for our own employees."

"Was Miss Austin ailing any way?" asked Hatch. "I saw a large number of medicine bottles upstairs."

"I don't know what was the matter with her," replied the manager, with a little puzzled frown. "She certainly was not a woman of sound mental balance—that is, she was eccentric, and all that. I think rather it was an act of charity for Mr. Cabell to let her have the suite in his absence. Certainly we didn't want her."

Hatch passed out and burst in eagerly upon The Thinking Machine in his laboratory.

"Here," he said, and triumphantly he extended the tiny scarlet strand which he had received from The Thinking Machine, and the other of the identical color which came from Cabell's bath robe. "Is that the same?"

The Thinking Machine placed them under the microscope and examined them immediately. Later he submitted them to a chemical test.

"It is the same," he said, finally.

"Then the mystery is solved," said Hatch, conclusively.

V

The Thinking Machine stared steadily into the eager, exultant eyes of the newspaper man until Hatch at last began to fear that he had been precipitate. After awhile, under close scrutiny, the reporter began to feel convinced that he had made a mistake—he didn't quite see where, but it must be there, and the exultant manner passed. The voice of The Thinking Machine was like a cold shower.

"Remember, Mr. Hatch," he said, critically, "that unless every possible question has been considered one cannot boast of a solution. Is there any possible question lingering yet in your mind?"

The reporter silently considered that for a moment, then:

"Well, I have the main facts, anyway. There may be one or two minor questions left, but the principal ones are answered."

"Then tell me, to the minutest detail, what you have learned, what has happened."

Professor Van Dusen sank back in his old, familiar pose in the large arm chair and Hatch related what he had learned and what he surmised. He related, too, the peculiar circumstances surrounding the wounding of Henley, and right on down to the beginning and end of the interview with Cabell in the latter's apartments. The Thinking Machine was silent for a time, then there came a host of questions.

"Do you know where the woman—Miss Austin—is now?" was the first.

"No," Hatch had to admit.

"Or her precise mental condition?"

"No."

"Or her exact relationship to Cabell?"

"No."

"Do you know, then, what the valet, Jean, knows of the affair?"

"No, not that," said the reporter, and his face flushed under the close questioning. "He was out of the suite every night."

"Therefore might have been the very one who turned on the gas," the other put in testily.

"So far as I can learn, nobody could have gone into that room and turned on the gas," said the reporter, somewhat aggressively. "Henley barred the doors and windows and kept watch, night after night."

"Yet the moment he was exhausted and fell asleep the gas was turned on to kill him," said The Thinking Machine; "thus we see that *he was watched more closely than he watched*."

"I see what you mean now," said Hatch, after a long pause.

"I should like to know what Henley and Cabell and the valet knew of the girl who was found dead," The Thinking Machine suggested. "Further, I should like to know if there was a good-sized mirror—not one set in a bureau or dresser—either in

Henley's room or the apartments where the girl was found. Find out this for me and—never mind. I'll go with you."

The scientist left the room. When he returned he wore his coat and hat. Hatch arose mechanically to follow. For a block or more they walked along, neither speaking. The Thinking Machine was the first to break the silence:

"You believe Cabell is the man who attempted to kill Henley?"

"Frankly, yes," replied the newspaper man.

"Why?"

"Because he had the motive—disappointed love."

"How?"

"I don't know," Hatch confessed. "The doors of the Henley suite were closed. I don't see how anybody passed them."

"And the girl? Who killed her? How? Why?"

Disconsolately Hatch shook his head as he walked on. The Thinking Machine interpreted his silence aright.

"Don't jump at conclusions," he advised sharply. "You are confident Cabell was to blame for this—and he might have been, I don't know yet—but you can suggest nothing to show how he did it. I have told you before that imagination is half of logic."

At last the lights of the big apartment house where Henley lived came in sight. Hatch shrugged his shoulders. He had grave doubts—based on what he knew—whether The Thinking Machine would be able to see Cabell. It was nearly eleven o'clock and Cabell was to leave for the South at midnight.

"Is Mr. Cabell here?" asked the scientist of the elevator boy.

"Yes, just about to go, though. He won't see anyone."

"Hand him this note," instructed The Thinking Machine, and he scribbled something on a piece of paper. "He'll see us."

The boy took the paper and the elevator shot up to the fourth floor. After awhile he returned.

"He'll see you," he said.

"Is he unpacking?"

"After he read your note twice he told his valet to unpack," the boy replied.

"Ah, I thought so," said The Thinking Machine.

With Hatch, mystified and puzzled, following, The Thinking Machine entered the elevator to step out a second or so later on the fourth floor. As they left the car they saw the door of Cabell's apartment standing open; Cabell was in the door. Hatch traced a glimmer of anxiety in the eyes of the young man.

"Professor Van Dusen?" Cabell inquired.

"Yes," said the scientist. "It was of the utmost importance that I should see you, otherwise I should not have come at this time of night."

With a wave of his hand Cabell passed that detail.

"I was anxious to get away at midnight," he explained, "but, of course, now I shan't go, in view of your note. I have ordered my valet to unpack my things, at least until tomorrow."

The reporter and the scientist passed into the luxuriously furnished apartments. Jean, the valet, was bending over a suit case as they entered, removing some things he had been carefully placing there. He didn't look back or pay the least attention to the visitors.

"This is your valet?" asked The Thinking Machine.

"Yes," said the young man.

"French, isn't he?"

"Yes."

"Speak English at all?"

"Very badly," said Cabell. "I use French when I talk to him."

"Does he know that you are accused of murder?" asked The Thinking Machine, in a quiet, conversational tone.

The effect of the remark on Cabell was startling. He staggered back a step or so as if he had been struck in the face, and a crimson flush overspread his brow. Jean, the valet, straightened up suddenly and looked around. There was a queer expression, too, in his eyes; an expression which Hatch could not fathom.

"Murder?" gasped Cabell, at last.

"Yes, he speaks English all right," remarked The Thinking Machine. "Now, Mr. Cabell, will you please tell me just who Miss Austin is, and where she is, and her mental condition? Believe me, it may save you a great deal of trouble. What I said in the note is not exaggerated."

The young man turned suddenly and began to pace back and forth across the room. After a few minutes he paused before The Thinking Machine, who stood impatiently waiting for an answer.

"I'll tell you, yes," said Cabell, firmly. "Miss Austin is a middle-aged woman whom my sister befriended several times—was, in fact, my sister's governess when she was a child. Of late years she has not been wholly right mentally, and has suffered a great deal of privation. I had about concluded arrangements to put her in a private sanitarium. I permitted her to remain in these rooms in my absence, South. I did not take Jean—he lived in the quarters of the other employees of the place, and gave the apartment entirely to Miss Austin. It was simply an act of charity."

"What was the cause of your sudden determination to go South to-night?" asked the scientist.

"I won't answer that question," was the sullen reply.

There was a long, tense silence. Jean, the valet, came and went several times.

"How long has Miss Austin known Mr. Henley?"

"Presumably since she has been in these apartments," was the reply.

"Are you sure *you* are not Miss Austin?" demanded the scientist.

The question was almost staggering, not only to Cabell, but to Hatch. Suddenly, with flaming face, the young Southerner leaped forward as if to strike down The Thinking Machine.

"That won't do any good," said the scientist, coldly. "Are you sure you are not Miss Austin?" he repeated.

"Certainly I am not Miss Austin," responded Cabell, fiercely.

"Have you a mirror in these apartments about twelve inches by twelve inches?" asked The Thinking Machine, irrelevantly.

"I—I don't know," stammered the young man. "I—have we, Jean?"

"*Oui,*" replied the valet.

"Yes," snapped The Thinking Machine. "Talk English, please. May I see it?"

The valet, without a word but with a sullen glance at the questioner, turned and left the room. He returned after a moment with the mirror. The Thinking Machine carefully examined the frame, top and bottom and on both sides. At last he looked up; again the valet was bending over a suit case.

"Do you use gas in these apartments?" the scientist asked suddenly.

"No," was the bewildered response. "What is all this, anyway?"

Without answering, The Thinking Machine drew a chair up under the chandelier where the gas and electric fixtures were and began to finger the gas tips. After awhile he climbed down and passed into the next room, with Hatch and Cabell, both hopelessly mystified, following. There the scientist went through the same process of fingering the gas jets. Finally, one of the gas tips came out in his hand.

"Ah," he exclaimed, suddenly, and Hatch knew the note of triumph in it. The jet from which the tip came was just on a level with his shoulder, set between a dressing table and a window. He leaned over and squinted at the gas pipe closely. Then he returned to the room where the valet was.

"Now, Jean," he began, in an even, calm voice, "please tell me *if you did or did not kill Miss Regnier purposely?*"

"I don't know what you mean," said the servant sullenly, angrily, as he turned on the scientist.

"You speak very good English now," was The Thinking Machine's terse comment. "Mr. Hatch, lock the door and use this 'phone to call the police."

Hatch turned to do as he was bid and saw a flash of steel in young Cabell's hand, which was drawn suddenly from a hip pocket. It was a revolver. The weapon glittered in the light, and Hatch flung himself forward. There was a sharp report, and a bullet was buried in the floor.

VI

Then came a fierce, hard fight for possession of the revolver. It ended with the weapon in Hatch's hand, and both he and Cabell blowing from the effort they had expended. Jean, the valet, had turned at the sound of the shot and started toward the door leading into the hall. The Thinking Machine had stepped in front of him, and now stood there with his back to the door. Physically he would have been a child in the hands of the valet, yet there was a look in his eyes which stopped him.

"Now, Mr. Hatch," said the scientist quietly, a touch of

irony in his voice, "hand me the revolver, then 'phone for Detective Mallory to come here immediately. Tell him we have a murderer—and if he can't come at once get some other detective whom you know."

"Murderer!" gasped Cabell.

Uncontrollable rage was blazing in the eyes of the valet, and he made as if to throw The Thinking Machine aside, despite the revolver, when Hatch was at the telephone. As Jean started forward, however, Cabell stopped him with a quick, stern gesture. Suddenly the young Southerner turned on The Thinking Machine; but it was with a question.

"What does it all mean?" he asked, bewildered.

"It means that that man there," and The Thinking Machine indicated the valet by a nod of his head, "is a murderer—that he killed Louise Regnier; that he shot Weldon Henley on Boston Common, and that, with the aid of Miss Regnier, he had four times previously attempted to kill Mr. Henley. Is he coming, Mr. Hatch?"

"Yes," was the reply. "He says he'll be here directly."

"Do you deny it?" demanded The Thinking Machine of the valet.

"I've done nothing," said the valet sullenly. "I'm going out of here."

Like an infuriated animal he rushed forward. Hatch and Cabell seized him and bore him to the floor. There, after a frantic struggle, he was bound and the other three men sat down to wait for Detective Mallory. Cabell sank back in his chair with a perplexed frown on his face. From time to time he glanced at Jean. The flush of anger which had been on the valet's face was gone now; instead there was the pallor of fear.

"Won't you tell us?" pleaded Cabell impatiently.

"When Detective Mallory comes and takes his prisoner," said The Thinking Machine.

Ten minutes later they heard a quick step in the hall outside and Hatch opened the door. Detective Mallory entered and looked from one to another inquiringly.

"That's your prisoner, Mr. Mallory," said the scientist, coldly. "I charge him with the murder of Miss Regnier, whom you were so confident committed suicide; I charge him with five attempts on the life of Weldon Henley, four times by gas poisoning, in which Miss Regnier was his accomplice, and once by shooting. He is the man who shot Mr. Henley."

The Thinking Machine arose and walked over to the prostrate man, handing the revolver to Hatch. He glared down at Jean fiercely.

"Will you tell how you did it or shall I?" he demanded.

His answer was a sullen, defiant glare. He turned and picked up the square mirror which the valet had produced previously.

"That's where the screw was, isn't it?" he asked, as he indicated a small hole in the frame of the mirror. Jean stared at it and his head sank forward hopelessly. "And this is the bath robe you wore, isn't it?" he demanded again, and from the suit case he pulled out the garment with the scarlet stripe.

"I guess you got me all right," was the sullen reply.

"It might be better for you if you told the story then?" suggested The Thinking Machine.

"You know so much about it, tell it yourself."

"Very well," was the calm rejoinder. "I will. If I make any mistake you will correct me."

For a long time no one spoke. The Thinking Machine had dropped back into a chair and was staring through his thick glasses at the ceiling; his finger tips were pressed tightly together. At last he began:

"Will you tell how you did it or shall I?"

"There are certain trivial gaps which only the imagination can supply until the matter is gone into more fully. I should have supplied these myself, but the arrest of this man, Jean, was precipitated by the attempted hurried departure of Mr. Cabell for the South to-night, and I did not have time to go into the case to the fullest extent.

"Thus, we begin with the fact that there were several clever attempts made to murder Mr. Henley. This was by putting out the gas which he habitually left burning in his room. It happened four times in all; thus proving that it was an attempt to kill him. If it had been only once it might have been accident, even twice it might have been accident, but the same accident does not happen four times at the same time of night.

"Mr. Henley finally grew to regard the strange extinguishing of the gas as an effort to kill him, and carefully locked and barred his door and windows each night. He believed that some one came into his apartments and put out the light, leaving the gas flow. This, of course, was not true. Yet the gas was put out. How? My first idea, a natural one, was that it was turned off for an instant at the meter, when the light would go out, then turned on again. This, I convinced myself, was not true. Therefore still the question—how?

"It is a fact—I don't know how widely known it is—but it is a fact that every gas light in this house might be extinguished at the same time from this room without leaving it. How? Simply by removing the gas jet tip and blowing into the gas pipe. It would not leave a jet in the building burning. It is due to the fact that the lung power is greater than the pressure of the gas in the pipes, and forces it out.

"Thus we have the method employed to extinguish the light in Mr. Henley's rooms, and all the barred and locked doors and windows would not stop it. At the same time it threatened the life of every other person in the house—that is, every other person who used gas. It was probably for this reason that the attempt was always made late at night, I should say three or four o'clock. That's when it was done, isn't it?" he asked suddenly of the valet.

Staring at The Thinking Machine in open-mouthed astonishment the valet nodded his acquiescence before he was fully aware of it.

"Yes, that's right," The Thinking Machine resumed complacently. "This was easily found out—comparatively. The next question was how was a watch kept on Mr. Henley? It would have done no good to extinguish the gas before he was asleep, or to have turned it on when he was not in his rooms. It might have led to a speedy discovery of just how the thing was done.

"There's a spring lock on the door of Mr. Henley's apartment. Therefore it would have been impossible for anyone to peep through the keyhole. There are no cracks through which one might see. How was this watch kept? How was the plotter to satisfy himself positively of the time when Mr. Henley was asleep? How was it the gas was put out at no time of the score or more nights Mr. Henley himself kept watch? Obviously he was watched through a window.

"No one could climb out on the window ledge and look into Mr. Henley's apartments. No one could see into that apartment from the street—that is, could see whether Mr. Henley was asleep or even in bed. They could see the light. Watch was kept with the aid offered by the flagpole, supplemented with a mirror—this mirror. A screw was driven into the frame—it has been removed now—it was swung on the flagpole rope and pulled out to the end of the pole, facing the building. To a man standing in the hall window of the third floor it offered precisely the angle necessary to reflect the interior of Mr. Henley's suite, possibly even showed him in bed through a narrow opening in the curtain. There is no shade on the windows of that suite; heavy curtains instead. Is that right?"

Again the prisoner was surprised into a mute acquiescence.

"I saw the possibility of these things, and I saw, too, that at three or four o'clock in the morning it would be perfectly possible for a person to move about the upper halls of this house without being seen. If he wore a heavy bath robe, with a hood, say, no one would recognize him even if he were seen, and besides the garb would not cause suspicion. This bath robe has a hood.

"Now, in working the mirror back and forth on the flagpole at night a tiny scarlet thread was pulled out of the robe and clung to the rope. I found this thread; later Mr. Hatch found an identical thread in these apartments. Both came from that bath robe. Plain logic shows that the person who blew down the gas pipes worked the mirror trick; the person who worked the mirror trick left the thread; the thread comes back to the bath robe—that bath robe there," he pointed dramatically. "Thus the person who desired Henley's death was in these apartments, or had easy access to them."

He paused a moment and there was a tense silence. A great light was coming to Hatch, slowly but surely. The brain that had followed all this was unlimited in possibilities.

"Even before we traced the origin of the crime to this room," went on the scientist, quietly now, "attention had been attracted here, particularly to you, Mr. Cabell. It was through the love affair, of which Miss Lipscomb was the center. Mr. Hatch learned that you and Henley had been rivals for her hand. It was that, even before this scarlet thread was found, which indicated that you might have some knowledge of the affair, directly or indirectly.

"You are not a malicious or revengeful man, Mr. Cabell. But you are hot-tempered—extremely so. You demonstrated that just now, when, angry and not understanding, but feeling that your honor was at stake, you shot a hole in the floor."

"What?" asked Detective Mallory.

"A little accident," explained The Thinking Machine quickly. "Not being a malicious or revengeful man, you are not the man to deliberately go ahead and make elaborate plans for the murder of Henley. In a moment of passion you might have killed him—but never deliberately as the result of premeditation. Besides you were out of town. Who was then in these apartments? Who had access to these apartments? Who might have used your bath robe? Your valet, possibly Miss Austin. Which? Now, let's see how we reached this conclusion which led to the valet.

"Miss Regnier was found dead. It was not suicide. How did I know? Because she had been reading with the gas light at its full. If she had been reading by the gas light, how was it then that it went out and suffocated her before she could arise and shut it off? Obviously she must have fallen asleep over her book and left the light burning.

"If she was in this plot to kill Henley, why did she light the jet in her room? There might have been some slight defect in the electric bulb in her room which she had just discovered. Therefore she lighted the gas, intending to extinguish it—turn it off entirely—later. But she fell asleep. Therefore when the valet here blew into the pipe, intending to kill Mr. Henley, he unwittingly killed the woman he loved—Miss Regnier. It was perfectly possible, meanwhile, that she did not know of the attempt to be made that particular night, although she had participated in the others, knowing that Henley had night after night sat up to watch the light in his rooms.

"The facts, as I knew them, showed no connection between Miss Regnier and this man at that time—nor any connection between Miss Regnier and Henley. It might have been that the person who blew the gas out of the pipe from these rooms knew nothing whatever of Miss Regnier, just as he didn't know who else he might have killed in the building.

"But I had her death and the manner of it. I had eliminated you, Mr. Cabell. Therefore there remained Miss Austin and the valet. Miss Austin was eccentric—insane, if you will. Would she have any motive for killing Henley? I could imagine none. Love? Probably not. Money? They had nothing in common on that ground. What? Nothing that I could see. Therefore, for the moment, I passed Miss Austin by, after asking you, Mr. Cabell, if you were Miss Austin.

"What remained? The valet. Motive? Several possible ones, one or two probable. He is French, or says he is. Miss Regnier is French. Therefore I had arrived at the conclusion that they knew each other as people of the same nationality will in a house of this sort. And remember, I had passed by Mr. Cabell and Miss Austin, so the valet was the only one left; he could use the bath robe.

"Well, the motive. Frankly that was the only difficult point in the entire problem—difficult because there were so many possibilities. And each possibility that suggested itself suggested also a woman. Jealousy? There must be a woman. Hate? Probably a woman. Attempted extortion? With the aid of a woman. No other motive which would lead to so elaborate a plot of murder would come forward. Who was the woman? Miss Regnier.

"Did Miss Regnier know Henley? Mr. Hatch had reason to believe he knew her because of his actions when informed of her death. Knew her how? People of such relatively different planes of life can know each other—or do know each other— only on one plane. Henley is a typical young man, fast, I dare say, and liberal. Perhaps, then, there had been a liaison. When I saw this possibility I had my motives—all of them—jealousy, hate and possibly attempted extortion as well.

"What was more possible than Mr. Henley and Miss Regnier had been acquainted? All liaisons are secret ones. Suppose she had been cast off because of the engagement to a young woman of Henley's own level? Suppose she had confided in the valet here? Do you see? Motives enough for any crime, however diabolical. The attempts on Henley's life possibly followed an attempted extortion of money. The shot which wounded Henley was fired by this man, Jean. Why? Because the woman who had cause to hate Henley was dead. Then the man? He was alive and vindictive. Henley knew who shot him, and knew why, but he'll never say it publicly. He can't afford to. It would ruin him. I think probably that's all. Do you want to add anything?" he asked of the valet.

"No," was the fierce reply. "I'm sorry I didn't kill him, that's all. It was all about as you said, though God knows how you found it out," he added, desperately.

"Are you a Frenchman?"

"I was born in New York, but lived in France for eleven years. I first knew Louise there."

Silence fell upon the little group. Then Hatch asked a question:

"You told me, Professor, that there would be no other attempt to kill Henley by extinguishing the gas. How did you know that?"

"Because one person—the wrong person—had been killed that way," was the reply. "For this reason it was hardly likely that another attempt of that sort would be made. You had no intention of killing Louise Regnier, had you, Jean?"

"No, God help me, no."

"It was all done in these apartments," The Thinking Machine added, turning to Cabell, "at the gas jet from which I took the tip. It had been only loosely replaced and the metal was tarnished where the lips had dampened it."

"It must take great lung power to do a thing like that," remarked Detective Mallory.

"You would be amazed to know how easily it is done," said the scientist. "Try it some time."

The Thinking Machine arose and picked up his hat; Hatch did the same. Then the reporter turned to Cabell.

"Would you mind telling me why you were so anxious to get away to-night?" he asked.

"Well, no," Cabell explained, and there was a rush of red to his face. "It's because I received a telegram from Virginia—Miss Lipscomb, in fact. Some of Henley's past had come to her knowledge and the telegram told me that the engagement was broken. On top of this came the information that Henley had been shot and—I was considerably agitated."

The Thinking Machine and Hatch were walking along the street.

"What did you write in the note you sent to Cabell that made him start to unpack?" asked the reporter, curiously.

"There are some things that it wouldn't be well for everyone to know," was the enigmatic response. "Perhaps it would be just as well for you to overlook this little omission."

"Of course, of course," replied the reporter, wonderingly.

THE MAN WHO WAS LOST*

I

Here are the facts in the case as they were known in the beginning to Professor Augustus S. F. X. Van Dusen, scientist and logician. After hearing a statement of the problem from the lips of its principal he declared it to be one of the most engaging that had ever come to his attention, and———

But let me begin at the beginning:

* * *

The Thinking Machine was in the small laboratory of his modest apartments at two o'clock in the afternoon. Martha, the scientist's only servant, appeared at the door with a puzzled expression on her wrinkled face.

"A gentleman to see you, sir," she said.

"Name?" inquired The Thinking Machine, without turning.

"He—he didn't give it, sir," she stammered.

"I have told you always, Martha, to ask names of callers."

---

* First published in *Boston American*, December 19, 1905.

"I did ask his name, sir, and—and he said he didn't know it."

The Thinking Machine was never surprised, yet now he turned on Martha in perplexity and squinted at her fiercely through his thick glasses.

"Don't know his own name?" he repeated. "Dear me! How careless! Show the gentleman into the reception-room immediately."

With no more introduction to the problem than this, therefore, The Thinking Machine passed into the other room. A stranger arose and came forward. He was tall, of apparently thirty-five years, clean shaven and had the keen, alert face of a man of affairs. He would have been handsome had it not been for dark rings under the eyes and the unusual white of his face. He was immaculately dressed from top to toe; altogether a man who would attract attention.

For a moment he regarded the scientist curiously; perhaps there was a trace of well-bred astonishment in his manner. He gazed curiously at the enormous head, with its shock of yellow hair, and noted, too, the droop in the thin shoulders. Thus for a moment they stood, face to face, the tall stranger making The Thinking Machine dwarf-like by comparison.

"Well?" asked the scientist.

The stranger turned as if to pace back and forth across the room, then instead dropped into a chair which the scientist indicated.

"I have heard a great deal about you, Professor," he began, in a well-modulated voice, "and at last it occurred to me to come to you for advice. I am in a most remarkable position—and I'm not insane. Don't think that, please. But unless I see some way out of this amazing predicament I shall be. As it is now, my nerves have gone; I am not myself."

"Your story? What is it? How can I help you?"

"I am lost, hopelessly lost," the stranger resumed. "I know neither my home, my business, nor even my name. I know nothing whatever of myself or my life; what it was or what it might have been previous to four weeks ago. I am seeking light on my identity. Now, if there is any fee————"

"Never mind that," the scientist put in, and he squinted steadily into the eyes of the visitor. "What *do* you know? From the time you remember things tell me all of it."

He sank back into his chair, squinting steadily upward. The stranger arose, paced back and forth across the room several times and then dropped into his chair again.

"It's perfectly incomprehensible," he said. "It's precisely as if I, full grown, had been born into a world of which I knew nothing except its language. The ordinary things, chairs, tables and such things, are perfectly familiar, but who I am, where I came from, why I came—of these I have no idea. I will tell you just as my impressions came to me when I awoke one morning, four weeks ago.

"It was eight or nine o'clock, I suppose. I was in a room. I knew instantly it was a hotel, but had not the faintest idea of how I got there, or of ever having seen the room before. I didn't even know my own clothing when I started to dress. I glanced out of my window; the scene was wholly strange to me.

"For half an hour or so I remained in my room, dressing and wondering what it meant. Then, suddenly, in the midst of my other worries, it came home to me that I didn't know my own name, the place where I lived nor anything about myself. I didn't know what hotel I was in. In terror I looked into a mirror. The face reflected at me was not one I knew. It didn't seem to be the face of a stranger; it was merely not a face that I knew.

"The thing was unbelievable. Then I began a search of my clothing for some trace of my identity. I found nothing whatever that would enlighten me—not a scrap of paper of any kind, no personal or business card."

"Have a watch?" asked The Thinking Machine.

"No."

"Any money?"

"Yes, money," said the stranger. "There was a bundle of more than ten thousand dollars in my pocket, in one-hundred-dollar bills. Whose it is or where it came from I don't know. I have been living on it since, and shall continue to do so, but I don't know if it is mine. I knew it was money when I saw it, but did not recollect ever having seen any previously."

"Any jewelry?"

"These cuff buttons," and the stranger exhibited a pair which he drew from his pocket.

"Go on."

"I finally finished dressing and went down to the office. It was my purpose to find out the name of the hotel and who I was. I knew I could learn some of this from the hotel register without attracting any attention or making anyone think I was insane. I had noted the number of my room. It was twenty-seven.

"I looked over the hotel register casually. I saw I was at the Hotel Yarmouth in Boston. I looked carefully down the pages until I came to the number of my room. Opposite this number was a name—John Doane, but where the name of the city should have been there was only a dash."

"You realize that it is perfectly possible that John Doane is your name?" asked The Thinking Machine.

"Certainly," was the reply. "But I have no recollection of ever having heard it before. This register showed that I had arrived at the hotel the night before—or rather that John Doane had arrived and been assigned to Room 27, and I was the John Doane, presumably. From that moment to this the hotel people have known me as John Doane, as have other people whom I have met during the four weeks since I awoke."

"Did the handwriting recall nothing?"

"Nothing whatever."

"Is it anything like the handwriting you write now?"

"Identical, so far as I can see."

"Did you have any baggage or checks for baggage?"

"No. All I had was the money and this clothing I stand in. Of course, since then I have bought necessities."

Both were silent for a long time and finally the stranger—Doane—arose and began pacing nervously again.

"That a tailor-made suit?" asked the scientist.

"Yes," said Doane, quickly. "I know what you mean. Tailor-made garments have linen strips sewed inside the pockets on which are the names of the manufacturers and the name of the man for whom the clothes were made, together with the date. I looked for those. They had been removed, cut out."

"Ah!" exclaimed The Thinking Machine suddenly. "No laundry marks on your linen either, I suppose?"

"No. It was all perfectly new."

"Name of the maker on it?"

"No. That had been cut out, too."

Doane was pacing back and forth across the reception-room; the scientist lay back in his chair.

"Do you know the circumstances of your arrival at the hotel?" he asked at last.

"Yes. I asked, guardedly enough, you may be sure, hinting to the clerk that I had been drunk so as not to make him think I was insane. He said I came in about eleven o'clock at night, without any baggage, paid for my room with a one-hundred-dollar bill, which he changed, registered and went upstairs. I said nothing that he recalls beyond making a request for a room."

"The name Doane is not familiar to you?"

"No."

"You can't recall a wife or children?"

"No."

"Do you speak any foreign language?"

"No."

"Is your mind clear now? Do you remember things?"

"I remember perfectly every incident since I awoke in the hotel," said Doane. "I seem to remember with remarkable clearness, and somehow I attach the gravest importance to the most trivial incidents."

The Thinking Machine arose and motioned to Doane to sit down. He dropped back into a seat wearily. Then the scientist's long, slender fingers ran lightly, deftly through the abundant black hair of his visitor. Finally they passed down from the hair and along the firm jaws; thence they went to the arms, where they pressed upon good, substantial muscles. At last the hands, well shaped and white, were examined minutely. A magnifying glass was used to facilitate this examination. Finally The Thinking Machine stared into the quick-moving, nervous eyes of the stranger.

"Any marks at all on your body?" he asked at last.

"No," Doane responded. "I had thought of that and sought for an hour for some sort of mark. There's nothing—nothing." The eyes glittered a little and finally, in a burst of nervousness, he struggled to his feet. "My God!" he exclaimed. "Is there nothing you can do? What is it all, anyway?"

"Seems to be a remarkable form of aphasia,"* replied The

---

* Aphasia is a loss of the ability to understand speech or to speak, viewed in literature of the day as an impairment of intelligence. Aphasia is recognized today as the result of brain damage. Probably a more accurate diagnosis for Doane would have been amnesia—a loss of memory—for Doane has no problems with language.

Thinking Machine. "That's not an uncommon disease among people whose minds and nerves are overwrought. You've simply lost yourself—lost your identity. If it is aphasia, you will recover in time. When, I don't know."

"And meantime?"

"Let me see the money you found."

With trembling hands Doane produced a large roll of bills, principally hundreds, many of them perfectly new. The Thinking Machine examined them minutely, and finally made some memoranda on a slip of paper. The money was then returned to Doane.

"Now, what shall I do?" asked the latter.

"Don't worry," advised the scientist. "I'll do what I can."

"And—tell me who and what I am?"

"Oh, I can find that out all right," remarked The Thinking Machine. "But there's a possibility that you wouldn't recall even if I told you all about yourself."

II

When John Doane of Nowhere—to all practical purposes— left the home of The Thinking Machine he bore instructions of divers kinds. First he was to get a large map of the United States and study it closely, reading over and pronouncing aloud the name of every city, town and village he found. After an hour of this he was to take a city directory and read over the names, pronouncing them aloud as he did so. Then he was to make out a list of the various professions and higher commercial pursuits, and pronounce these. All these things were calculated, obviously, to arouse the sleeping brain. After Doane had gone The Thinking Machine called up Hutchinson Hatch, reporter, on the 'phone.

"Come up immediately," he requested. "There's something that will interest you."

"A mystery?" Hatch inquired, eagerly.

"One of the most engaging problems that has ever come to my attention," replied the scientist.

It was only a question of a few minutes before Hatch was ushered in. He was a living interrogation point, and repressed a rush of questions with a distinct effort. The Thinking Machine finally told what he knew.

"Now it seems to be," said The Thinking Machine, and he emphasized the "seems," "it seems to be a case of aphasia. You know, of course, what that is. The man simply doesn't know himself. I examined him closely. I went over his head for a sign of a possible depression, or abnormality. It didn't appear. I examined his muscles. He has biceps of great power, is evidently now or has been athletic. His hands are white, well cared for and have no marks on them. They are not the hands of a man who has ever done physical work. The money in his pocket tends to confirm the fact that he is not of that sphere.

"Then what is he? Lawyer? Banker? Financier? What? He might be either, yet he impressed me as being rather of the business than the professional school. He has a good, square-cut jaw—the jaw of a fighting man—and his poise gives one the impression that whatever he has been doing he has been foremost in it. Being foremost in it, he would naturally drift to a city, a big city. He is typically a city man.

"Now, please, to aid me, communicate with your correspondents in the large cities and find if such a name as John Doane appears in any directory. Is he at home now? Has he a family? All about him."

"Do you believe that John Doane is his name?" asked the reporter.

"No reason why it shouldn't be," said The Thinking Machine. "Yet it might not be."

"How about inquiries in this city?"

"He can't well be a local man," was the reply. "He has been wandering about the streets for four weeks, and if he had lived here he would have met some one who knew him."

"But the money?"

"I'll probably be able to locate him through that," said The Thinking Machine. "The matter is not at all clear to me now, but it occurs to me that he is a man of consequence, and that it was possibly necessary for some one to get rid of him for a time."

"Well, if it's plain aphasia, as you say," the reporter put in, "it seems rather difficult to imagine that the attack came at a moment when it was necessary to get rid of him."

"I say it *seems* like aphasia," said the scientist, crustily. "There are known drugs which will produce the identical effect if properly administered."

"Oh," said Hatch. He was beginning to see.

"There is one drug particularly, made in India, and not unlike hasheesh. In a case of this kind anything is possible. To-morrow I shall ask you to take Mr. Doane down through the financial district, as an experiment. When you go there I want you particularly to get him to the sound of the 'ticker.'* It will be an interesting experiment."

The reporter went away and The Thinking Machine sent a telegram to the Blank National Bank of Butte, Montana:†

---

* The ticker-tape machine, a telegraphic device used to transmit news or, more particularly in this case, by financial houses to transmit information regarding market activity.

† There was no Blank National Bank in Butte, Montana, but First National Bank was chartered there in 1881 and Silver Bow National Bank (of Butte City) was chartered in 1890.

"To whom did you issue hundred-dollar bills, series B, numbering 846380 to 846395 inclusive? Please answer."[*]

It was ten o'clock next day when Hatch called on The Thinking Machine. There he was introduced to John Doane, the man who was lost. The Thinking Machine was asking questions of Mr. Doane when Hatch was ushered in.

"Did the map recall nothing?"

"Nothing."

"Montana, Montana, Montana," the scientist repeated monotonously; "think of it. Butte, Montana."

Doane shook his head hopelessly, sadly.

"Cowboy, cowboy. Did you ever see a cowboy?"

Again the head shake.

"Coyote—something like a wolf—coyote. Don't you recall ever having seen one?"

"I'm afraid it's hopeless," remarked the other.

There was a note of more than ordinary irritation in The Thinking Machine's voice when he turned to Hatch.

"Mr. Hatch, will you walk through the financial district with Mr. Doane?" he asked. "Please go to the places I suggested."

So it came to pass that the reporter and Doane went out together, walking through the crowded, hurrying, bustling financial district. The first place visited was a private room where market quotations were displayed on a blackboard. Mr. Doane was interested, but the scene seemed to suggest nothing.

He looked upon it all as any stranger might have done. After

---

[*] National banks issued their own National Bank Notes in various denominations, backed typically by US bonds; these ceased to be issued after 1935 when the US Treasury took over the issuance of Federal Reserve Notes and other forms of currency. The First National Bank of Butte printed 1,933 sheets of $100 bills in 1902, and the Silver Bow National Bank printed 1,140 sheets that year as well.

a time they passed out. Suddenly a man came running toward them—evidently a broker.

"What's the matter?" asked another.

"Montana copper's gone to smash," was the reply.

"Copper! Copper!" gasped Doane suddenly.

Hatch looked around quickly at his companion. Doane's face was a study. On it was half realization and a deep perplexed wrinkle, a glimmer even of excitement.

"Copper!" he repeated.

"Does the word mean anything to you?" asked Hatch quickly. "Copper—metal, you know."

"Copper, copper, copper," the other repeated. Then, as Hatch looked, the queer expression faded; there came again utter hopelessness.

There are many men with powerful names who operate in the Street—some of them in copper. Hatch led Doane straight to the office of one of these men and there introduced him to a partner in the business.

"We want to talk about copper a little," Hatch explained, still eying his companion.

"Do you want to buy or sell?" asked the broker.

"Sell," said Doane suddenly. "Sell, sell, sell copper. That's it—copper."

He turned to Hatch, stared at him dully a moment, a deathly pallor came over his face, then, with upraised hands, fell senseless.

III

Still unconscious, the man of mystery was removed to the home of The Thinking Machine and there stretched out on a sofa. The Thinking Machine was bending over him, this time in his capacity of physician, making an examination. Hatch stood by, looking on curiously.

"I never saw anything like it," Hatch remarked. "He just threw up his hands and collapsed. He hasn't been conscious since."

"It may be that when he comes to he will have recovered his memory, and in that event he will have absolutely no recollection whatever of you and me," explained The Thinking Machine.

Doane moved a little at last, and under a stimulant the color began to creep back into his pallid face.

"Just what was said, Mr. Hatch, before he collapsed?" asked the scientist.

Hatch explained, repeating the conversation as he remembered it.

"And he said 'sell,'" mused The Thinking Machine. "In other words, he thinks—or imagines he knows—that copper is to drop. I believe the first remark he heard was that copper had gone to smash—down, I presume that means?"

"Yes," the reporter replied.

Half an hour later John Doane sat up on the couch and looked about the room.

"Ah, Professor," he remarked. "I fainted, didn't I?"

The Thinking Machine was disappointed because his patient had not recovered memory with consciousness. The remark showed that he was still in the same mental condition—the man who was lost.

"Sell copper, sell, sell, sell," repeated The Thinking Machine, commandingly.

"Yes, yes, sell," was the reply.

The reflection of some great mental struggle was on Doane's face; he was seeking to recall something which persistently eluded him.

"Copper, copper," the scientist repeated, and he exhibited a penny.

"Yes, copper," said Doane. "I know. A penny."

"Why did you say sell copper?"

"I don't know," was the weary reply. "It seemed to be an unconscious act entirely. I don't know."

He clasped and unclasped his hands nervously and sat for a long time dully staring at the floor. The fight for memory was a dramatic one.

"It seemed to me," Doane explained after awhile, "that the word copper touched some responsive chord in my memory, then it was lost again. Some time in the past, I think, I must have had something to do with copper."

"Yes," said The Thinking Machine, and he rubbed his slender fingers briskly. "Now you are coming around again."

His remarks were interrupted by the appearance of Martha at the door with a telegram. The Thinking Machine opened it hastily. What he saw perplexed him again.

"Dear me! Most extraordinary!" he exclaimed.

"What is it?" asked Hatch, curiously.

The scientist turned to Doane again.

"Do you happen to remember Preston Bell?" he demanded, emphasizing the name explosively.

"Preston Bell?" the other repeated, and again the mental struggle was apparent on his face. "Preston Bell!"

"Cashier of the Blank National Bank of Butte, Montana?" urged the other, still in an emphatic tone. "Cashier Bell?"

He leaned forward eagerly and watched the face of his patient; Hatch unconsciously did the same. Once there was almost realization, and seeing it The Thinking Machine sought to bring back full memory.

"Bell, cashier, copper," he repeated, time after time.

The flash of realization which had been on Doane's face passed, and there came infinite weariness—the weariness of one who is ill.

"I don't remember," he said at last. "I'm very tired."

"Stretch out there on the couch and go to sleep," advised The Thinking Machine, and he arose to arrange a pillow. "Sleep will do you more good than anything else right now. But before you lie down, let me have, please, a few of those hundred-dollar bills you found."

Doane extended the roll of money, and then slept like a child. It was uncanny to Hatch, who had been a deeply interested spectator.

The Thinking Machine ran over the bills and finally selected fifteen of them—bills that were new and crisp. They were of an issue by the Blank National Bank of Butte, Montana. The Thinking Machine stared at the money closely, then handed it to Hatch.

"Does that look like counterfeit to you?" he asked.

"Counterfeit?" gasped Hatch. "Counterfeit?" he repeated. He took the bills and examined them. "So far as I can see they seem to be good," he went on, "though I have never had enough experience with one-hundred-dollar bills to qualify as an expert."

"Do you know an expert?"

"Yes."

"See him immediately. Take fifteen bills and ask him to pass on them, each and every one. Tell him you have reason— excellent reason—to believe that they are counterfeit. When he gives his opinion come back to me."

Hatch went away with the money in his pocket. Then The Thinking Machine wrote another telegram, addressed to Preston Bell, cashier of the Butte Bank. It was as follows:

"Please send me full details of the manner in which money previously described was lost, with names of all persons who might
have had any knowledge of the matter. Highly important to your
bank and to justice. Will communicate in detail on receipt of your
answer."

Then, while his visitor slept, The Thinking Machine quietly removed his shoes and examined them. He found, almost
worn away, the name of the maker. This was subjected to close
scrutiny under the magnifying glass, after which The Thinking
Machine arose with a perceptible expression of relief on his face.

"Why didn't I think of that before?" he demanded of himself.

Then other telegrams went into the West. One was to a
custom shoemaker in Denver, Colorado:

"To what financier or banker have you sold within three months
a pair of shoes, Senate brand,˙ calfskin blucher, number eight, D
last? Do you know John Doane?"

A second telegram went to the Chief of Police of Denver. It
was:

"Please wire if any financier, banker or business man has been
out of your city for five weeks or more, presumably on business
trip. Do you know John Doane?"

Then The Thinking Machine sat down to wait. At last the
door bell rang and Hatch entered. "Well?" demanded the scientist, impatiently.

"The expert declares those are not counterfeit," said Hatch.

---

* This appears to be a fictional brand of shoes. A "blucher" is a high shoe or half-boot,
the exact design varying with fashion.

Now The Thinking Machine was surprised. It was shown clearly by the quick lifting of the eyebrows, by the sudden snap of his jaws, by a quick forward movement of the yellow head.

"Well, well, well!" he exclaimed at last. Then again: "Well, well!"

"What is it?"

"See here," and The Thinking Machine took the hundred-dollar bills in his own hands. "These bills, perfectly new and crisp, were issued by the Blank National Bank of Butte, and the fact that they are in proper sequence would indicate that they were issued to one individual at the same time, probably recently. There can be no doubt of that. The numbers run from 846380 to 846395, all series B."

"I see," said Hatch.

"Now read that," and the scientist extended to the reporter the telegram Martha had brought in just before Hatch had gone away. Hatch read this:

"Series B, hundred-dollar bills 846380 to 846395 issued by this bank are not in existence. Were destroyed by fire, together with twenty-seven others of the same series. Government has been asked to grant permission to reissue these numbers.

"PRESTON BELL, CASHIER."

The reporter looked up with a question in his eyes. "It means," said The Thinking Machine, "that this man is either a thief or the victim of some sort of financial jugglery."

"In that case is he what he pretends to be—a man who doesn't know himself?" asked the reporter.

"That remains to be seen."

IV

Event followed event with startling rapidity during the next few hours. First came a message from the Chief of Police of Denver. No capitalist or financier of consequence was out of Denver at the moment, so far as his men could ascertain. Longer search might be fruitful. He did not know John Doane. One John Doane in the directory was a teamster.

Then from the Blank National Bank came another telegram signed "Preston Bell, Cashier," reciting the circumstances of the disappearance of the hundred-dollar bills. The Blank National Bank had moved into a new structure; within a week there had been a fire which destroyed it. Several packages of money, including one package of hundred-dollar bills, among them those specified by The Thinking Machine, had been burned. President Harrison of the bank immediately made affidavit to the Government that these bills were left in his office.

The Thinking Machine studied this telegram carefully and from time to time glanced at it while Hatch made his report. This was as to the work of the correspondents who had been seeking John Doane.

They found many men of the name and reported at length on each. One by one The Thinking Machine heard the reports, then shook his head.

Finally he reverted again to the telegram, and after consideration sent another—this time to the Chief of Police of Butte. In it he asked these questions:

"Has there ever been any financial trouble in Blank National Bank? Was there an embezzlement or shortage at any time? What is reputation of President Harrison? What is reputation of Cashier Bell? Do you know John Doane?"

In due course of events the answer came. It was brief and to the point. It said:

"Harrison recently embezzled $175,000 and disappeared. Bell's reputation excellent; now out of city. Don't know John Doane. If you have any trace of Harrison, wire quick."

This answer came just after Doane awoke, apparently greatly refreshed, but himself again—that is, himself in so far as he was still lost. For an hour The Thinking Machine pounded him with questions—questions of all sorts, serious, religious and at times seemingly silly. They apparently aroused no trace of memory, save when the name Preston Bell was mentioned; then there was the strange, puzzled expression on Doane's face.

"Harrison—do you know him?" asked the scientist. "President of the Blank National Bank of Butte?"

There was only an uncomprehending stare for an answer. After a long time of this The Thinking Machine instructed Hatch and Doane to go for a walk. He had still a faint hope that some one might recognize Doane and speak to him. As they wandered aimlessly on two persons spoke to him. One was a man who nodded and passed on.

"Who was that?" asked Hatch quickly. "Do you remember ever having seen him before?"

"Oh, yes," was the reply. "He stops at my hotel. He knows me as Doane."

It was just a few minutes before six o'clock when, walking slowly, they passed a great office building. Coming toward them was a well-dressed, active man of thirty-five years or so. As he approached he removed a cigar from his lips.

"Hello, Harry!" he exclaimed, and reached for Doane's hand.

"Hello," said Doane, but there was no trace of recognition in his voice.

"How's Pittsburg?" asked the stranger.*

"Oh, all right, I guess," said Doane, and there came new wrinkles of perplexity in his brow. "Allow me, Mr.—Mr.—really I have forgotten your name————"

"Manning," laughed the other.

"Mr. Hatch, Mr. Manning."

The reporter shook hands with Manning eagerly; he saw now a new line of possibilities suddenly revealed. Here was a man who knew Doane as Harry—and then Pittsburg, too.

"Last time I saw you was in Pittsburg, wasn't it?" Manning rattled on, as he led the way into a nearby café. "By George, that was a stiff game that night! Remember that jack full I held? It cost me nineteen hundred dollars," he added, ruefully.

"Yes, I remember," said Doane, but Hatch knew that he did not. And meanwhile a thousand questions were surging through the reporter's brain.

"Poker hands as expensive as that are liable to be long remembered," remarked Hatch, casually. "How long ago was that?"

"Three years, wasn't it, Harry?" asked Manning.

"All of that, I should say," was the reply.

"Twenty hours at the table," said Manning, and again he laughed cheerfully. "I was woozy when we finished."

Inside the café they sought out a table in a corner. No one else was near. When the waiter had gone, Hatch leaned over and looked Doane straight in the eyes.

---

* There are numerous towns named Pittsburg, including one in California and one in Kansas, as well as, of course, the major city of Pittsburgh in Pennsylvania. Curiously, from 1891 to 1911, the federal government referred to the Pennsylvania city without its "h." There is a "Lincoln Club Drive" in Pittsburgh, and adding that clue to the small size of the other towns, we may conclude that a "millionaire's club" populated by "iron men" would be found most likely in Pennsylvania.

"Shall I ask some questions?" he inquired.

"Yes, yes," said the other eagerly.

"What—what is it?" asked Manning.

"It's a remarkably strange chain of circumstances," said Hatch, in explanation. "This man whom you call Harry, we know as John Doane. What is his real name? Harry what?"

Manning stared at the reporter for a moment in amazement, then gradually a smile came to his lips.

"What are you trying to do?" he asked. "Is this a joke?"

"No, my God, man, can't you see?" exclaimed Doane, fiercely. "I'm ill, sick, something. I've lost my memory, all of my past. I don't remember anything about myself. What is my name?"

"Well, by George!" exclaimed Manning. "By George! I don't believe I know your full name. Harry—Harry—what?"

He drew from his pocket several letters and half a dozen scraps of paper and ran over them. Then he looked carefully through a worn notebook.

"I don't know," he confessed. "I had your name and address in an old notebook, but I suppose I burned it. I remember, though, I met you in the Lincoln Club in Pittsburg three years ago. I called you Harry because everyone was calling everyone else by his first name. Your last name made no impression on me at all. By George!" he concluded, in a new burst of amazement.

"What were the circumstances, exactly?" asked Hatch.

"I'm a traveling man," Manning explained. "I go everywhere. A friend gave me a card to the Lincoln Club in Pittsburg and I went there. There were five or six of us playing poker, among them Mr.—Mr. Doane here. I sat at the same table with him for twenty hours or so, but I can't recall his last name to save me. It isn't Doane, I'm positive. I have an excellent memory for faces, and I know you're the man. Don't you remember me?"

"I haven't the slightest recollection of ever having seen you before in my life," was Doane's slow reply. "I have no recollection of ever having been in Pittsburg—no recollection of anything."

"Do you know if Mr. Doane is a resident of Pittsburg?" Hatch inquired. "Or was he there as a visitor, as you were?"

"Couldn't tell you to save my life," replied Manning. "Lord, it's amazing, isn't it? You don't remember me? You called me Bill all evening."

The other man shook his head.

"Well, say, is there anything I can do for you?"

"Nothing, thanks," said Doane. "Only tell me my name, and who I am."

"Lord, I don't know."

"What sort of a club is the Lincoln?" asked Hatch.

"It's a sort of a millionaire's club," Manning explained. "Lots of iron men belong to it. I had considerable business with them—that's what took me to Pittsburg."

"And you are absolutely positive this is the man you met there?"

"Why, I know it. I never forget faces; it's my business to remember them."

"Did he say anything about a family?"

"Not that I recall. A man doesn't usually speak of his family at a poker table."

"Do you remember the exact date or the month?"

"I think it was in January or February possibly," was the reply. "It was bitterly cold and the snow was all smoked up. Yes, I'm positive it was in January, three years ago."

After awhile the men separated. Manning was stopping at the Hotel Teutonic* and willingly gave his name and permanent address to Hatch, explaining at the same time that he would be in

---

* A fictional Boston hotel.

the city for several days and was perfectly willing to help in any way he could. He took also the address of The Thinking Machine.

From the café Hatch and Doane returned to the scientist. They found him with two telegrams spread out on a table before him. Briefly Hatch told the story of the meeting with Manning, while Doane sank down with his head in his hands. The Thinking Machine listened without comment.

"Here," he said, at the conclusion of the recital, and he offered one of the telegrams to Hatch. "I got the name of a shoemaker from Mr. Doane's shoe and wired to him in Denver, asking if he had a record of the sale. This is the answer. Read it aloud."

Hatch did so.

"Shoes such as described made nine weeks ago for Preston Bell, cashier Blank National Bank of Butte. Don't know John Doane."

"Well—what———" Doane began, bewildered.

"*It means that you are Preston Bell*," said Hatch, emphatically.

"No," said The Thinking Machine, quickly. "It means that there is only a strong probability of it."

* * *

The door bell rang. After a moment Martha appeared.

"A lady to see you, sir," she said.

"Her name?"

"Mrs. John Doane."

"Gentlemen, kindly step into the next room," requested The Thinking Machine.

Together Hatch and Doane passed through the door. There was an expression of—of—no man may say what—on Doane's face as he went.

"Show her in here, Martha," instructed the scientist.

There was a rustle of silk in the hall, the curtains on the door were pulled apart quickly and a richly gowned woman rushed into the room.

"My husband? Is he here?" she demanded, breathlessly. "I went to the hotel; they said he came here for treatment. Please, please, is he here?"

"A moment, madam," said The Thinking Machine. He stepped to the door through which Hatch and Doane had gone, and said something. One of them appeared in the door. It was Hutchinson Hatch.

"John, John, my darling husband," and the woman flung her arms about Hatch's neck. "Don't you know me?"

With blushing face Hatch looked over her shoulder into the eyes of The Thinking Machine, who stood briskly rubbing his hands. Never before in his long acquaintance with the scientist had Hatch seen him smile.

V

For a time there was silence, broken only by sobs, as the woman clung frantically to Hatch, with her face buried on his shoulder. Then:

"Don't you remember me?" she asked again and again. "Your wife? Don't you remember me?"

Hatch could still see the trace of a smile on the scientist's face, and said nothing.

"You are positive this gentleman is your husband?" inquired The Thinking Machine, finally.

"Oh, I know," the woman sobbed. "Oh, John, don't you remember me?" She drew away a little and looked deeply into the reporter's eyes. "Don't you remember me, John?"

"Can't say that I ever saw you before," said Hatch, truthfully enough. "I—I—fact is————"

"Mr. Doane's memory is wholly gone now," explained The Thinking Machine. "Meanwhile, perhaps you would tell me something about him. He is my patient. I am particularly interested."

The voice was soothing; it had lost for the moment its perpetual irritation. The woman sat down beside Hatch. Her face, pretty enough in a bold sort of way, was turned to The Thinking Machine inquiringly. With one hand she stroked that of the reporter.

"Where are you from?" began the scientist. "I mean where is the home of John Doane?"

"In Buffalo," she replied, glibly. "Didn't he even remember that?"

"And what's his business?"

"His health has been bad for some time and recently he gave up active business," said the woman. "Previously he was connected with a bank."

"When did you see him last?"

"Six weeks ago. He left the house one day and I have never heard from him since. I had Pinkerton men* searching and at last

---

* The Pinkerton National Detective Agency, with its striking logo of an eye and the motto "We never sleep," was the most famous private detective agency in the world. Founded by the Scot Allan Pinkerton in 1850, the agency claimed credit for foiling an assassination attempt on President-elect Abraham Lincoln in 1861 and was engaged by Lincoln to spy on the Confederacy in the Civil War. By the 1870s, the agency was deeply involved in labor unrest, always on the side of management, and took an active role in putting down the "Molly Maguires" (a secret labor organization) in violent disputes in the Pennsylvania coal mines. A number of popular true-crime narratives appeared under the Allan Pinkerton byline, including such sensational titles as The Detective and the Somnambulist (1875) and The Rail-Road Forger and the Detectives (1881). The most famous of these was The Molly Maguires and the Detectives (1877), the basis for Arthur Conan Doyle's The Valley of Fear (1917), featuring Sherlock Holmes.

they reported he was at the Yarmouth Hotel. I came on immediately. And now we shall go back to Buffalo." She turned to Hatch with a languishing glance. "Shall we not, dear?"

"Whatever Professor Van Dusen thinks best," was the equivocal reply.

Slowly the glimmer of amusement was passing out of the squint eyes of The Thinking Machine; as Hatch looked he saw a hardening of the lines of the mouth. There was an explosion coming. He knew it. Yet when the scientist spoke his voice was more velvety than ever.

"Mrs. Doane, do you happen to be acquainted with a drug which produces temporary loss of memory?"

She stared at him, but did not lose her self-possession.

"No," she said finally. "Why?"

"You know, of course, that this man is *not* your husband?"

This time the question had its effect. The woman arose suddenly, stared at the two men, and her face went white.

"Not?—not?—what do you mean?"

"I mean," and the voice reassumed its tone of irritation, "I mean that I shall send for the police and give you in their charge unless you tell me the truth about this affair. Is that perfectly clear to you?"

The woman's lips were pressed tightly together. She saw that she had fallen into some sort of a trap; her gloved hands were clenched fiercely; the pallor faded and a flush of anger came.

"Further, for fear you don't quite follow me even now," explained The Thinking Machine, "I will say that I know all about this copper deal of which this so-called John Doane was the victim. *I know his condition now.* If you tell the truth you may escape prison—if you don't, there is a long term, not only for you, but for your fellow-conspirators. Now will you talk?"

"No," said the woman. She arose as if to go out.

"Never mind that," said The Thinking Machine. "You had better stay where you are. You will be locked up at the proper moment. Mr. Hatch, please 'phone for Detective Mallory."

Hatch arose and passed into the adjoining room.

"You tricked me," the woman screamed suddenly, fiercely.

"Yes," the other agreed, complacently. "Next time be sure you know your own husband. Meanwhile where is Harrison?"

"Not another word," was the quick reply.

"Very well," said the scientist, calmly. "Detective Mallory will be here in a few minutes. Meanwhile I'll lock this door."

"You have no right———" the woman began.

Without heeding the remark, The Thinking Machine passed into the adjoining room. There for half an hour he talked earnestly to Hatch and Doane. At the end of that time he sent a telegram to the manager of the Lincoln Club in Pittsburg, as follows:

"Does your visitors' book show any man, registered there in the month of January three years ago, whose first name is Harry or Henry? If so, please wire name and description, also name of man whose guest he was."

This telegram was dispatched. A few minutes later the door bell rang and Detective Mallory entered.

"What is it?" he inquired.

"A prisoner for you in the next room," was the reply. "A woman. I charge her with conspiracy to defraud a man who for the present we will call John Doane. That may or may not be his name."

"What do you know about it?" asked the detective.

"A great deal now—more after awhile. I shall tell you then. Meanwhile take this woman. You gentlemen, I should suggest, might go out somewhere this evening. If you drop by afterwards there may be an answer to a few telegrams which will make this matter clear."

Protestingly the mysterious woman was led away by Detective Mallory; and Doane and Hatch followed shortly after. The next act of The Thinking Machine was to write a telegram addressed to Mrs. Preston Bell, Butte, Montana. Here it is:

> "Your husband suffering temporary mental trouble here. Can you come on immediately? Answer."

When the messenger boy came for the telegram he found a man on the stoop. The Thinking Machine received the telegram, and the man, who gave to Martha the name of Manning, was announced.

"Manning, too," mused the scientist. "Show him in."

"I don't know if you know why I am here," explained Manning.

"Oh, yes," said the scientist. "You have remembered Doane's name. What is it, please?"

Manning was too frankly surprised to answer and only stared at the scientist.

"Yes, that's right," he said finally, and he smiled. "His name is Pillsbury. I recall it now."

"And what made you recall it?"

"I noticed an advertisement in a magazine with the name in large letters. It instantly came to me that that was Doane's real name."

"Thanks," remarked the scientist. "And the woman—who is she?"

"What woman?" asked Manning.

"Never mind, then. I am deeply obliged for your information. I don't suppose you know anything else about it?"

"No," said Manning. He was a little bewildered, and after awhile went away.

For an hour or more The Thinking Machine sat with finger tips pressed together staring at the ceiling. His meditations were interrupted by Martha.

"Another telegram, sir."

The Thinking Machine took it eagerly. It was from the manager of the Lincoln Club in Pittsburg:

"Henry C. Carney, Harry Meltz, Henry Blake, Henry W. Tolman, Harry Pillsbury, Henry Calvert and Henry Louis Smith all visitors to club in month you name. Which do you want to learn more about?"

It took more than an hour for The Thinking Machine to establish long-distance connection by 'phone with Pittsburg. When he had finished talking he seemed satisfied.

"Now," he mused. "The answer from Mrs. Preston."

It was nearly midnight when that came. Hatch and Doane had returned from a theater and were talking to the scientist when the telegram was brought in.

"Anything important?" asked Doane, anxiously.

"Yes," said the scientist, and he slipped a finger beneath the flap of the envelope. "It's clear now. It was an engaging problem from first to last, and now————"

He opened the telegram and glanced at it; then with bewilderment on his face and mouth slightly open he sank down at the table and leaned forward with his head on his arms. The message fluttered to the table and Hatch read this:

"Man in Boston can't be my husband. He is now in Honolulu. I received cablegram from him to-day.

"Mrs. Preston Bell."

VI

It was thirty-six hours later that the three men met again. The Thinking Machine had abruptly dismissed Hatch and Doane the last time. The reporter knew that something wholly unexpected had happened. He could only conjecture that this had to do with Preston Bell. When the three met again it was in Detective Mallory's office at police headquarters. The mysterious woman who had claimed Doane for her husband was present, as were Mallory, Hatch, Doane and The Thinking Machine.

"Has this woman given any name?" was the scientist's first question.

"Mary Jones," replied the detective, with a grin.

"And address?"

"No."

"Is her picture in the Rogues' Gallery?"*

"No. I looked carefully."

"Anybody called to ask about her?"

"A man—yes. That is, he didn't ask about her—he merely asked some general questions, which now we believe were to find out about her."

The Thinking Machine arose and walked over to the woman. She looked up at him defiantly.

"There has been a mistake made, Mr. Mallory," said the scientist. "It's my fault entirely. Let this woman go. I am sorry to have done her so grave an injustice."

Instantly the woman was on her feet, her face radiant. A look of disgust crept into Mallory's face.

---

* A collection of images of known criminals. The first was established by Allan Pinkerton in 1855. Official forces soon adopted the idea, and the Detective Bureau of the New York Police Department had one by 1857. NYPD Inspector Thomas Byrnes popularized the term in his 1886 book, *Professional Criminals of America*, in which he reproduced some of the photographs.

"I can't let her go now without arraignment," the detective growled. "It ain't regular."

"You must let her go, Mr. Mallory," commanded The Thinking Machine, and over the woman's shoulder the detective saw an astonishing thing. The Thinking Machine winked. It was a decided, long, pronounced wink.

"Oh, all right," he said, "but it ain't regular at that."

The woman passed out of the room hurriedly, her silken skirts rustling loudly. She was free again. Immediately she disappeared, The Thinking Machine's entire manner changed.

"Put your best man to follow her," he directed rapidly. "Let him go to her home and arrest the man who is with her as her husband. Then bring them both back here, after searching their rooms for money."

"Why—what—what is all this?" demanded Mallory, amazed.

"The man who inquired for her, who is with her, is wanted for a $175,000 embezzlement in Butte, Montana. Don't let your man lose sight of her."

The detective left the room hurriedly. Ten minutes later he returned to find The Thinking Machine leaning back in his chair with eyes upturned. Hatch and Doane were waiting, both impatiently.

"Now, Mr. Mallory," said the scientist, "I shall try to make this matter as clear to you as it is to me. By the time I finish I expect your man will be back here with this woman and the embezzler. His name is Harrison; I don't know hers. I can't believe she is Mrs. Harrison, yet he has, I suppose, a wife. But here's the story. It is the chaining together of fact after fact; a necessary logical sequence to a series of incidents, which are, separately, deeply puzzling."

The detective lighted a cigar and the others disposed themselves comfortably to listen.

"This gentleman came to me," began The Thinking Machine, "with a story of loss of memory. He told me that he knew neither his name, home, occupation, nor anything whatever about himself. At the moment it struck me as a case for a mental expert; still I was interested. It seemed to be a remarkable case of aphasia, and I so regarded it until he told me that he had $10,000 in bills, that he had no watch, that everything which might possibly be of value in establishing his identity had been removed from his clothing. This included even the names of the makers of his linen. That showed intent, deliberation.

"Then I knew it could *not* be aphasia. That disease strikes a man suddenly as he walks the street, as he sleeps, as he works, but never gives any desire to remove traces of one's identity. On the contrary, a man is still apparently sound mentally—he has merely forgotten something—and usually his first desire is to find out who he is. This gentleman had that desire, and in trying to find some clew he showed a mind capable of grasping at every possible opportunity. Nearly every question I asked had been anticipated. Thus I recognized that he must be a more than usually astute man.

"But if not aphasia, what was it? What caused his condition? A drug? I remembered that there was such a drug in India, not unlike hasheesh. Therefore for the moment I assumed a drug. It gave me a working basis. Then what did I have? A man of striking mentality who was the victim of some sort of plot, who had been drugged until he lost himself, and in that way disposed of. The handwriting might be the same, for handwriting is rarely affected by a mental disorder; it is a physical function.

"So far, so good. I examined his head for a possible accident. Nothing. His hands were white and in no way calloused. Seeking to reconcile the fact that he had been a man of strong mentality, with all other things a financier or banker, occurred to me. The same things might have indicated a lawyer, but the poise of this man, his elaborate care in dress, all these things made me think him the financier rather than the lawyer.

"Then I examined some money he had when he awoke. Fifteen or sixteen of the hundred-dollar bills were new and in sequence. They were issued by a national bank. To whom? The possibilities were that the bank would have a record. I wired, asking about this, and also asked Mr. Hatch to have his correspondents make inquiries in various cities for a John Doane. It was not impossible that John Doane was his name. Now I believe it will be safe for me to say that when he registered at the hotel he was drugged, his own name slipped his mind, and he signed John Doane—the first name that came to him. That is *not* his name.

"While waiting for an answer from the bank I tried to arouse his memory by referring to things in the West. It appeared possible that he might have brought the money from the West with him. Then, still with the idea that he was a financier, I sent him to the financial district. There was a result. The word 'copper' aroused him so that he fainted after shouting, 'Sell copper, sell, sell, sell.'

"In a way my estimate of the man was confirmed. He was or had been in a copper deal, selling copper in the market, or planning to do so. I know nothing of the intricacies of the stock market. But there came instantly to me the thought that a man who would faint away in such a case must be vitally interested as well as ill. Thus I had a financier, in a copper deal, drugged as result of a conspiracy. Do you follow me, Mr. Mallory?"

"Sure," was the reply.

"At this point I received a telegram from the Butte bank telling me that the hundred-dollar bills I asked about had been burned. This telegram was signed 'Preston Bell, Cashier.' If that were true, the bills this man had were counterfeit. There were no ifs about that. I asked him if he knew Preston Bell. It was the only name of a person to arouse him in any way. A man knows his own name better than anything in the world. Therefore was it his? For a moment I presumed it was.

"Thus the case stood: Preston Bell, cashier of the Butte bank, had been drugged, was the victim of a conspiracy, which was probably a part of some great move in copper. But if this man were *Preston Bell*, how came the signature there? Part of the office regulation? It happens hundreds of times that a name is so used, particularly on telegrams.

"Well, this man who was lost—Doane, or Preston Bell— went to sleep in my apartments. At that time I believed it fully possible that he was a counterfeiter, as the bills were supposedly burned, and sent Mr. Hatch to consult an expert. I also wired for details of the fire loss in Butte and names of persons who had any knowledge of the matter. This done, I removed and examined this gentleman's shoes for the name of the maker. I found it. The shoes were of fine quality, probably made to order for him.

"Remember, at this time I believed this gentleman to be Preston Bell, for reasons I have stated. I wired to the maker or retailer to know if he had a record of a sale of the shoes, describing them in detail, to any financier or banker. I also wired to the Denver police to know if any financier or banker had been away from there for four or five weeks. Then came the somewhat startling information, through Mr. Hatch, that the hundred-dollar bills were genuine. That answer meant that Preston Bell—as I had begun to think of him—was either a thief or the victim of some sort of financial conspiracy."

During the silence which followed every eye was turned on the man who was lost—Doane or Preston Bell. He sat staring straight ahead of him with hands nervously clenched. On his face was written the sign of a desperate mental struggle. He was still trying to recall the past.

"Then," The Thinking Machine resumed, "I heard from the Denver police. There was no leading financier or banker out of the city so far as they could learn hurriedly. It was not conclusive, but it aided me. Also I received another telegram from Butte, signed Preston Bell, telling me the circumstances of the supposed burning of the hundred-dollar bills. It did not show that they were burned at all; it was merely an assumption that they had been. They were last seen in President Harrison's office."

"Harrison, Harrison, Harrison," repeated Doane.

"Vaguely I could see the possibility of something financially wrong in the bank. Possibly Harrison, even Mr. Bell here, knew of it. Banks do not apply for permission to reissue bills unless they are positive of the original loss. Yet here were the bills. Obviously some sort of jugglery. I wired to the police of Butte, asking some questions. The answer was that Harrison had embezzled $175,000 and had disappeared. Now I knew he had part of the missing, supposedly burned, bills with him. It was obvious. Was Bell also a thief?

"The same telegram said that Mr. Bell's reputation was of the best, and he was out of the city. That confirmed my belief that it was an office rule to sign telegrams with the cashier's name, and further made me positive that this man was Preston Bell. The chain of circumstances was complete. It was two and two—inevitable result, four.

"Now, what was the plot? Something to do with copper, and there was an embezzlement. Then, still seeking a man who knew Bell personally, I sent him out walking with Hatch. I had done so before. Suddenly another figure came into the mystery—a confusing one at the moment. This was a Mr. Manning, who knew Doane, or Bell, as Harry—something; met him in Pittsburg three years ago, in the Lincoln Club.

"It was just after Mr. Hatch told me of this man that I received a telegram from the shoemaker in Denver. It said that he had made a shoe such as I described within a few months for Preston Bell. I had asked if a sale had been made to a financier or banker; I got the name back by wire.

"At this point a woman appeared to claim John Doane as her husband. With no definite purpose, save general precaution, I asked Mr. Hatch to see her first. She imagined he was Doane and embraced him, calling him John. Therefore she was a fraud. She did not know John Doane, or Preston Bell, by sight. Was she acting under the direction of some one else? If so, whose?"

There was a pause as The Thinking Machine readjusted himself in the chair. After a time he went on:

"There are shades of emotion, intuition, call it what you will, so subtle that it is difficult to express them in words. As I had instinctively associated Harrison with Bell's present condition I instinctively associated this woman with Harrison. For not a word of the affair had appeared in a newspaper; only a very few persons knew of it. Was it possible that the stranger Manning was backing the woman in an effort to get the $10,000? That remained to be seen. I questioned the woman; she would say nothing. She is clever, but she blundered badly in claiming Mr. Hatch for a husband."

The reporter blushed modestly.

"I asked her flatly about a drug. She was quite calm and her manner indicated that she knew nothing of it. Yet I presume she did. Then I sprung the bombshell, and she saw she had made a mistake. I gave her over to Detective Mallory and she was locked up. This done, I wired to the Lincoln Club in Pittsburg to find out about this mysterious 'Harry' who had come into the case.

I was so confident then that I also wired to Mrs. Bell in Butte, presuming that there was a Mrs. Bell, asking about her husband.

"Then Manning came to see me. I knew he came because he had remembered the name he knew you by," and The Thinking Machine turned to the central figure in this strange entanglement of identity, "although he seemed surprised when I told him as much. He knew you as Harry Pillsbury. I asked him who the woman was. His manner told me that he knew nothing whatever of her. Then it came back to her as an associate of Harrison, your enemy for some reason, and I could see it in no other light. It was her purpose to get hold of you and possibly keep you a prisoner, at least until some gigantic deal in which copper figured was disposed of. That was what I surmised.

"Then another telegram came from the Lincoln Club in Pittsburg. The name of Harry Pillsbury appeared as a visitor in the book in January, three years ago. It was you—Manning is not the sort of man to be mistaken—and then there remained only one point to be solved as I then saw the case. That was an answer from Mrs. Preston Bell, if there was a Mrs. Bell. She would know where her husband was."

Again there was silence. A thousand things were running through Bell's mind. The story had been told so pointedly, and was so vitally a part of him, that semi-recollection was again on his face.

"That telegram said that Preston Bell was in Honolulu; that the wife had received a cable dispatch that day. Then, frankly, I was puzzled; so puzzled, in fact, that the entire fabric I had constructed seemed to melt away before my eyes. It took me hours to readjust it. I tried it all over in detail, and then the theory which would reconcile every fact in the case was evolved. That theory is right—as right as that two and two make four. It's logic."

It was half an hour later when a detective entered and spoke to Detective Mallory aside.

"Fine!" said Mallory. "Bring 'em in."

Then there reappeared the woman who had been a prisoner and a man of fifty years.

"Harrison!" exclaimed Bell, suddenly. He staggered to his feet with outstretched hands. "Harrison! I know! I know!"

"Good, good, very good," said The Thinking Machine.

Bell's nervously twitching hands were reaching for Harrison's throat when he was pushed aside by Detective Mallory. He stood pallid for a moment, then sank down on the floor in a heap. He was senseless. The Thinking Machine made a hurried examination.

"Good!" he remarked again. "When he recovers he will remember everything except what has happened since he has been in Boston. Meanwhile, Mr. Harrison, we know all about the little affair of the drug, the battle for new copper workings in Honolulu, and your partner there has been arrested. Your drug didn't do its work well enough. Have you anything to add?"

The prisoner was silent.

"Did you search his rooms?" asked The Thinking Machine of the detective who had made the double arrest.

"Yes, and found this."

It was a large roll of money. The Thinking Machine ran over it lightly—$70,000—scanning the numbers of the bills. At last he held forth half a dozen. They were among the twenty-seven reported to have been burned in the bank fire in Butte.

Harrison and the woman were led away. Subsequently it developed that he had been systematically robbing the bank of which he was president for years; was responsible for the fire, at which time he had evidently expected to make a great haul; and that the woman was not his wife. Following his arrest this entire story came out; also the facts of the gigantic copper deal, in which he had rid himself of Bell, who was his partner, and had sent another man to Honolulu in Bell's name to buy up options on some valuable copper property there. This confederate in Honolulu had sent the cable dispatches to the wife in Butte. She accepted them without question.

It was a day or so later that Hatch dropped in to see The Thinking Machine and asked a few questions.

"How did Bell happen to have that $10,000?"

"It was given to him, probably, because it was safer to have him rambling about the country, not knowing who he was, than to kill him."

"And how did he happen to be here?"

"That question may be answered at the trial."

"And how did it come that Bell was once known as Harry Pillsbury?"

"Bell is a director in United States Steel, I have since learned. There was a secret meeting of this board in Pittsburg three years ago. He went incog.* to attend that meeting and was introduced at the Lincoln Club as Harry Pillsbury."

"Oh!" exclaimed Hatch.

---

* Incognito, that is, concealing his identity.

THE GREAT AUTO MYSTERY[*]

I

With a little laugh of sheer light-heartedness on her lips and a twinkle in her blue eyes, Marguerite Melrose bound on a grotesque automobile mask,[†] and stuffed the last strand of her recalcitrant hair beneath her veil. The pretty face was hidden from mouth to brow; and her curls were ruthlessly imprisoned under a cap held in place by the tightly tied veil.

"It's perfectly hideous, isn't it?" she demanded of her companions.

Jack Curtis laughed.

"Well," he remarked, quizzically, "it's just as well that we *know* you are pretty."

"We could never discover it as you are now," added Charles Reid. "Can't see enough of your face to tell whether you are white or black."

The girl's red lips were pursed into a pout, which

---

* First published in *Boston American*, November 21, 1905.

† The wearing of masks while driving was common in the early twentieth century, in light of the open architecture of vehicles and the lack of paved roads; a tremendous amount of dust was blown into the car when traveling at high speed.

ungraciously hid her white teeth, as she considered the matter seriously.

"I think I'll take it off," she said at last.

"Don't," Curtis warned her. "On a good road The Green Dragon only hits the tall places."

"Tear your hair off," supplemented Reid. "When Jack lets her loose it's just a pszzzzt!—and wherever you're going you're there."

"Not on a night as dark as this?" protested the girl, quickly.

"I've got lights like twin locomotives," Curtis assured her, smilingly. "It's perfectly safe. Don't get nervous."

He tied on his own mask with its bleary goggles, while Reid did the same. The Green Dragon, a low, gasoline car of racing build,* stood panting impatiently, awaiting them at a side door of the hotel. Curtis assisted Miss Melrose into the front seat and climbed in beside her, while Reid sat behind in the tonneau.† There was a preparatory quiver, the car jerked a little and then began to move.

The three persons in it were Marguerite Melrose, an actress who had attracted attention in the West five years before by her great beauty and had afterwards, by her art, achieved a distinct place; Jack Curtis, a friend since childhood, when both lived in San Francisco and attended the same school, and Charles Reid, his chum, son of a mine owner at Denver.

The unexpected meeting of the three in Boston had been a source of mutual pleasure. It had been two years since they had

---

* Gasoline as contrasted with steam or electricity. Before the Ford Model T swept America beginning in 1908, only about a quarter of the eight thousand or so vehicles on the road had internal combustion engines powered by gasoline. Most were steam-driven. For several years, the Stanley Steamer was the racing car of choice. In 1906, the Stanley Rocket broke the world speed record for a mile course five times in Daytona Beach with its best performance being a top speed of 127 miles per hour.

† An open rear passenger compartment.

seen one another in Denver, where Miss Melrose was playing. Now she was in Boston, pursuing certain vocal studies before returning West for her next season.

Reid was in Boston to lay siege to the heart of a young woman of society, Miss Elizabeth Dow, whom he first met in San Francisco. She was only nineteen years old, but despite this he had begun a siege and his ardor had never cooled, even after Miss Dow returned East. In Boston, he had heard, she looked with favor upon another man, Morgan Mason, poor but of excellent family, and frantically Reid had rushed, like Lochinvar out of the West,* to find the rumor true.

Curtis was one who never had anything to do save seek excitement in a new and novel way. He had come East with Reid. They had been together constantly since their arrival in Boston. He was of a different type from Reid in that his wealth was distinctly a burden, a thing which left him with nothing to do, and opened illimitable possibilities of dissipation. The pace he led was one which caused other young men to pause and think.

Warm-hearted and perfectly at home with both Curtis and Reid, Miss Melrose, the actress, frequently took occasion to scold them. It was charming to be scolded by Miss Melrose, so much so in fact that it was worth while sinning again. Since she had appeared on the horizon Curtis had devoted a great deal of time to her; Reid had his own difficulties trying to make Miss Dow change her mind.

The Green Dragon with its three passengers ran slowly down from the Hotel Yarmouth, where Miss Melrose was stopping,

---

* A fictional romanticized knight and hero of the 1808 epic poem *Marmion* by Sir Walter Scott. The knight sweeps into a wedding, snatches up the bride-to-be, and rides away with her on his horse. Lochinvar's section of the poem begins, "O young Lochinvar is come out of the west…"

toward the Common, twisting and winding tortuously through the crowd of vehicles. It was half-past six o'clock in the evening.

"Cut across here to Commonwealth Avenue," Miss Melrose suggested. She remembered something and her bright blue eyes sparkled beneath the disfiguring mask. "I know a delightful old-fashioned inn out this way. It would be an ideal place to stop for supper. I was there once five years ago when I was in Boston."

"How far?" asked Reid.

"Fifteen or twenty miles," was the reply.

"Right," said Curtis. "Here we go."

Soon after they were skimming along Commonwealth Avenue, which at that time of day is practically given over to automobilists, past the Vendome, the Somerset and on over the flat, smooth road. It was perfectly light now, because the electric lights were about them; but there was no moon above, and once in the country it would be dark going.

Curtis was intent on his machine; Reid was thoughtful for a time, but after awhile leaned over and talked to Miss Melrose.

"I heard something to-day that might interest you," he remarked.

"What is it?" she asked.

"Don MacLean is in Boston."

"I heard that," she replied, casually.

"Who is he?" asked Curtis.

"A man who is frantically in love with Marguerite," said Reid, with a smile.

"Charlie!" the girl reproved, and a flush crept into her face. "It was never anything very serious."

Curtis looked at her curiously for a moment, then his eyes turned again to the road ahead.

"I don't suppose it's very serious if a man proposes to a girl seven times, is it?" Reid asked, banteringly.

"Did he do that?" asked Curtis, quickly.

"He merely made a fool of himself and me," replied the actress, with spirit, speaking to Curtis. "He was—in love with me, I suppose, but his family objected because I was on the stage and threatened to disinherit him, and all that sort of thing. So—it ended it. Not that I ever considered the matter seriously anyway," she added.

There was silence again as The Green Dragon plunged into the darkness of the country, the two brilliant lights ahead showing every dip and rise in the road. After awhile Curtis spoke again.

"He's now in Boston?"

"Yes," said the girl. "At least, I've heard so," she added, quickly.

Then the conversation ran into other channels, and Curtis, busy with the great machine and the innumerable levers which made it do this or do that or do the other, dropped out of it. Reid and Miss Melrose talked on, but the whirr of the car as it gained speed made talking unsatisfactory and finally the girl gave herself up to the pure delight of high speed; a dangerous pleasure which sets the nerves atingle and makes one greedy for more.

"Do you smell gasoline?" Curtis asked suddenly, turning to the others.

"Believe I do," said Reid.

"Confound it! If I've sprung a leak in my tank it will be the deuce," Curtis growled amiably.

"Do you think you've got enough to get to the inn?" asked Miss Melrose. "It can't be more than five or six miles now."

"I'll run on until we stop," said Curtis. "We might be able to stir up some along here somewhere. I suppose they are prepared for autos."

At last lights showed ahead, many lights glimmering through the trees.

"I suppose that's the inn now," said Curtis. "Is it?" he asked of the girl.

"Really, I don't know, but I have an impression that it isn't. The one I mean seems farther out than this and it seems to me we passed one on the way. However, I don't remember very well."

"We'll stop and get some gasoline, anyhow," said Curtis.

Puffing and snorting odorously The Green Dragon came to a standstill in front of an old house which stood back twenty feet or more from the road. It was lighted up, and from inside they could hear the cheery rattle of dishes and see white-aproned waiters moving about. Above the door was a sign, "Monarch Inn."

"Is this the place?" asked Reid.

"Oh, no," replied Miss Melrose. "The inn I spoke of was back from the road three or four hundred feet through a grove."

Curtis leaped out, and evidently dropped something from his pocket as he did so, for he stopped and felt around for a moment. Then he examined his tank.

"It's a leak," he said, in irritation. "I haven't more than half a gallon left. These people must have some gasoline. Wait a few minutes."

Miss Melrose and Reid still sat in the car as he started away toward the house. Almost at the veranda he turned and called back:

"Charlie, I dropped something there when I jumped out. Get down and strike a match and see if you can find it. Don't go near that gasoline tank with the match."

He disappeared inside the house. Reid climbed out and struck several matches. Finally he found what was lost and thrust it into an outside pocket. Miss Melrose was gazing away down the road at two brilliant lights coming toward them rapidly.

"Rather chilly," Reid said, as he straightened up. "Want a cup of coffee or something?"

"Thanks, no," the girl replied.

"I think I'll run in and scare up some sort of a hot drink, if you'll excuse me?"

"Now, Charlie, don't," the girl asked, suddenly. "I don't like it."

"Oh, one won't hurt," he replied, lightly.

"I shan't speak to you when you come out," she insisted, half banteringly.

"Oh, yes, you will." He laughed, and passed into the house.

Miss Melrose tossed her pretty head impatiently and turned to watch the approaching lights. They were blinding as they drew nearer, clearly revealing her figure, in its tan auto coat, to the occupant of the other car. The newcomer stopped and then she heard whoever was in it—she couldn't see—speaking to her.

"Would you mind turning your car a little so I can run in off the road?"

"I don't know how," she replied, helplessly.

There was a little pause. The occupant of the other car was leaning forward, looking at her closely.

"Is that you, Marguerite?" he asked finally.

"Yes," she replied. "Who is that? Don?"

"Yes."

A man's figure leaped out of the other machine and came toward her.

* * *

Curtis appeared beside The Green Dragon with a huge can of gasoline twenty minutes later. The two occupants of the car were clearly silhouetted against the sky, and Reid, leaning back in the tonneau, was smoking.

"Find it?" he asked.

"Yes," growled Curtis. And he began the work of repairing the leak and refilling his tank. It took only five minutes or so, and then he climbed up into the car.

"Cold, Marguerite?" he asked.

"She won't speak," said Reid, leaning forward a little. "She's angry because I went inside to get a hot Scotch."

"Wish I had one myself," said Curtis.

"Let's wait till we get to the next place," Reid interposed. "A little supper and trimmings will put all of us in a better humor."

Without answering, Curtis threw a lever, and the car pulled out. Two automobiles which had been standing when they arrived were still waiting for their owners. Annoyed at the delay, Curtis put on full speed. Finally Reid leaned forward and spoke to the girl.

"In a good humor?" he asked.

She gave no sign of having heard, and Reid placed his hand on her shoulder as he repeated the question. Still there was no answer.

"Make her talk to you, Jack," he suggested to Curtis.

"What's the matter, Marguerite?" asked Curtis, as he glanced around.

Still there was no answer, and he slowed up the car a little. Then he took her arm and shook it gently. There was no response.

"What *is* the matter with her?" he demanded. "Has she fainted?"

Again he shook her, this time more vigorously than before.

"Marguerite," he called.

Then his hand sought her face; it was deathly cold, clammy

even about the chin. The upper part was still covered by the mask. For the third time he shook her, then, really frightened, apparently, he caught at her gloved wrist and brought the car to a standstill. There was no trace of a pulse; the wrist was cold as death.

"She must be ill—very ill," he said in some agitation. "Is there a doctor near here?"

Reid was leaning over the senseless body now, having raised up in the tonneau, and when he spoke there seemed to be fear in his tone.

"Better run on as fast as you can to the inn ahead," he instructed Curtis. "It's nearer than the one we just left. There may be a doctor there."

Curtis grabbed frantically at the lever and the car shot ahead suddenly through the dark. In three minutes the lights of the second inn were in sight. The two men leaped from the car simultaneously and raced for the house.

"A doctor, quick," Curtis breathlessly demanded of a waiter.

"Next door."

Without waiting for further instructions, Curtis and Reid ran to the auto, lifted the girl in their arms and took her to a house which stood just a few feet away. There, after much clamoring, they aroused some one. Was the doctor in? Yes. Would he hurry? Yes.

The door opened and the men laid the girl's body on a couch in the hall. Dr. Leonard appeared. He was an old fellow, grizzled, with keen, kindly eyes and rigid mouth.

"What's the matter?" he asked.

"Think she's dead," replied Curtis.

The doctor adjusted his glasses rather hurriedly.

"Who is she?" he asked, as he bent over the still figure and fumbled about the throat and breast.

"Miss Marguerite Melrose, an actress," explained Curtis, hurriedly.

"What's the matter with her?" demanded Reid, fiercely.

The doctor still bent over the figure. In the dim lamplight Curtis and Reid stood waiting anxiously, impatiently, with white faces. At last the doctor straightened up.

"What is it?" demanded Curtis.

"She's dead," was the reply.

"Great God!" exclaimed Reid. "How?" Curtis seemed speechless.

"This," said the doctor, and he exhibited a long knife, damp with blood. "Stabbed through the heart."

Curtis stared at him, at the knife, then at the inert figure, and lastly at the dead white of her face where it showed beneath the mask.

"Look, Jack!" exclaimed Reid, suddenly. "The knife!"

Curtis looked again, then sank down on the couch beside the body.

"Oh, my God! It's horrible!" he said.

II

To Hutchinson Hatch and half a dozen other reporters, Dr. Leonard, at his home late that night, told the story of the arrival of Jack Curtis and Charles Reid with the body of the girl, and the succeeding events so far as he knew them. The police and Medical Examiner Francis had preceded the newspaper men, and the body had been removed to a nearby village.

"They came here in great excitement," Dr. Leonard explained. "They brought the body in with them, the man Curtis lifting her by the shoulders and the man Reid at the feet. They placed the body on this couch. I asked them who she was, and they told me she was Marguerite Melrose, an actress. That's all that was said of her identity.

"Then I made an examination of the body, seeking a trace of life. There was none, although the body was not then entirely cold. In examining her heart my hand struck the knife which had killed her—a heavy weapon, evidently used for rough work, with a blade of six or seven inches. 1 drew the knife out. Of course, knowing that it had pierced her heart, any idea of doing anything to save her was beyond question.

"One of the men, Curtis, seemed greatly excited about this knife after Reid called his attention to it. Curtis took the knife out of my hand and examined it closely, then asked if he might keep it. I told him it would have to be turned over to the medical examiner. He argued about it, and finally, to settle the argument, I took it out of his hand. Reid explained to Curtis that it was necessary for me to keep the knife, and finally Curtis seemed to agree to it.

"Then I suggested that the police be notified. I did this myself by telephone, the men remaining with me all the time. I asked if they could throw any light on the tragedy, but neither could. Curtis said he had been out searching for a man who had the keys to a shed where some gasoline was locked up, and it took fifteen or twenty minutes to find him. As soon as he got the gasoline he returned to the auto.

"Reid and Miss Melrose were at this time in the auto, he said. What had happened while he had been away Curtis didn't know. Reid said he, too, had stepped out of the automobile, and after exchanging a few words with Miss Melrose went into the inn. There he remained fifteen minutes or so, because inside he saw a woman he knew and spoke to her. He declared that any one of three waiters could verify his statement that he was in the Monarch Inn.

Curtis looked again, then sank down on the couch beside the body.

"After I had notified the police Curtis grew very uneasy in his actions—it didn't occur to me at the moment, but now I recall that it was so—and suggested to Reid that they go on to Boston and send out detectives—special Pinkerton men. I tried to dissuade them, but they went away. I couldn't stop them. They gave me their cards, however. They are at the Hotel Teutonic, and told me they could be seen there at any time. The medical examiner and the police came afterwards. I told them, and one of the detectives started immediately for Boston. They have probably told their story to him by this time."

"What did the young woman look like?" asked Hatch.

"Really, I couldn't say," said the doctor. "She wore an automobile mask which covered all her face except the chin, and there was a veil tied over her cap, concealing her hair. I didn't remove these; I left the body just as it was for the medical examiner."

"How was she dressed?" Hatch went on.

"She wore a long tan automobile dust coat of what seemed to be rich material, and beneath this a handsome—not a fancy—gown. I believe it was tailor-made. She was a woman of superb figure."

That was all that could be learned from Dr. Leonard, and Hatch and the other men raced back to Boston. The next day the newspapers flamed with the mystery of the murder of Miss Melrose, a beautiful Western actress who was visiting Boston. Each newspaper watched the other greedily to see if there was a picture of Miss Melrose; neither had one.

The newspapers also carried the stories of Jack Curtis and Charles Reid in connection with the murder. The stories were in substance just what Dr. Leonard had said, but were given in more detail. It was the general presumption, almost a foregone conclusion, that some one had killed Miss Melrose while the two men were away from the auto.

Who was this some one? Man or woman? No one could answer. Reid's story of being inside the Monarch Inn, where he spoke to a lady he knew—but whose name he refused to give—was verified by Hatch's paper. Three waiters had seen him.

The medical examiner had made only a brief statement, in which he had said, in answer to a question, that the person who killed Miss Melrose might have been either at her right, in the position Curtis would have occupied while driving the car, or might have leaned forward from behind and stabbed her. Thus it was not impossible that one of the men in the car with her had killed her, yet against this possibility was the fact that each of the men was one whom one could not readily associate with such a crime.

The fact that the fatal blow was delivered from the right was proven, said the astute medical examiner, by the fact that the knife slanted as a knife could not have been slanted conveniently by a person on her other side—her left. There were many dark, underlying intimations behind what the medical man said; but he refused to say any more. Meanwhile the body remained in the village where it had been taken. Efforts to get a photograph were unavailing; pleas of newspaper artists for permission to sketch her fell upon deaf ears.

Curtis and Reid, after their first statements, remained in seclusion at the Teutonic. They were not arrested because this did not seem necessary. Both had offered to do anything in their power to solve the riddle, had even employed Pinkerton men who were now on the case; but they would say nothing nor see anyone except the police. The police encouraged them in this attitude, and hinted darkly and mysteriously at clews which "would lead to an arrest within twenty-four hours."

Hatch read these intimations and smiled grimly. Then he went out to try what a little patience and perseverance and human intelligence would do. He learned something of Reid's little romance in Boston. Yet not all of it. It was a fact, however, that Reid had called at the home of Miss Elizabeth Dow on Beacon Hill just after noon and inquired for her.

"She is not in," the maid had replied.

"I'll leave my card for her," said Reid.

"I don't think she'll be back," the girl answered.

"Not be back?" Reid repeated. "Why?"

"Haven't you seen the afternoon papers?" asked the girl. "They will explain. Mrs. Dow, her mother, told me not to talk to anyone."

Reid left the house with a wrinkle in his brow and walked on toward the Common. There he halted a newsboy and bought an afternoon paper—many afternoon papers. The first pages were loaded with details of the murder of Miss Melrose, theories, conjectures, a thousand little things, with long dispatches of her history and her stage career from San Francisco.

Reid passed these over impatiently with a slight shiver and looked inside the paper. There he found the thing to which the maid had referred.

"By George!" he exclaimed.

It was a story of the elopement of Elizabeth Dow with Morgan Mason, Reid's rival. It seemed that Miss Dow and Mason met by appointment at the Monarch Inn and went from there in an automobile. The bride had written to her parents before she started, saying she preferred Mason despite his poverty. The family refused to talk of the matter. But there in fac-simile was the marriage license.

Reid's face was a study as he walked back to the hotel. In a private room off the café he found Curtis, who had been drink-ing heavily, yet who, with the strange mood of some men, was not visibly intoxicated. Reid threw the paper down, open at the elopement announcement.

"See that," he said shortly.

Curtis read it—or glanced at it—but did not make a remark until he came to the name, the Monarch Inn. Then he looked up.

"That's where the other thing happened, isn't it?" he asked, rather thickly.

"Yes."

Curtis rambled off into something else; studiously he avoided any reference to the tragedy, yet that was the one thing which was in his mind. It was in a futile effort to forget it that he was drinking now. He talked on as a drunken man will for a time, then turned suddenly to Reid.

"I loved her," he declared suddenly, passionately. "My God"

"Try not to think of it," Reid advised.

"You'll never say anything about that other thing—the knife—will you?" pleaded Curtis.

"Of course not," said Reid, impatiently. "They couldn't drag it out of me. But you're drinking too much—you want to quit it. First thing you know you'll be saying more than—get up and go out and take a walk."

Curtis stared at Reid vacantly for a moment, as if not understanding, then arose. He had regained possession of himself to a certain extent, but his face was pale.

"I think I will go out," he said.

After a time he passed through the café door into a side street and, refreshed a little by the cool air, started to walk along Tremont Street toward the shopping district. It was two o'clock in the afternoon and the streets were thronged.

Half a dozen reporters were idling in the lobby of the hotel, waiting vainly for either Reid or Curtis. The newspapers were shouting for another story from the only two men who could know a great deal of the circumstances attending the tragedy. Reid, on his return, had marched boldly through the crowd of reporters, paying no attention to their questions. They had not seen Curtis.

As Curtis, now free of the reporters, crossed a side street off Tremont on his way toward the shopping district he met Hutchinson Hatch, who was bound for the hotel to see his man there. Hatch instantly recognized him and fell in behind, curious to see where he would go. At a favorable opportunity, safe beyond reach of the other men, he intended to ask a few questions.

Curtis turned into Winter Street and strolled along through the crowd of women. Half way down Winter Street Hatch followed, and then for a moment he lost sight of him. He had gone into a store, he imagined. As he stood at a door waiting, Curtis came out, rushed through the crowd of women, slinging his arms like a madman, with frenzy in his face. He ran twenty steps, then stumbled and fell.

Hatch immediately ran to his assistance, lifted him up and gazed into the staring, terror-stricken eyes and an ashen face.

"What is it?" asked Hatch, quickly.

"I—I'm very ill. I—I think I need a doctor," gasped Curtis. "Take me somewhere, please."

He fell back limply, half fainting, into Hatch's arms. A cab came worming through the crowd; Hatch climbed into it, assisting Curtis, and gave some directions to the cabby.

"And hurry," he added. "This gentleman is ill."

The cabby applied the whip and drove out into Tremont, then over toward Park Street. Curtis aroused a little.

"Where're we going?" he demanded.

"To a doctor," replied Hatch.

Curtis sank back with eyes closed and his face white—so white that Hatch felt of the pulse to assure himself that the heart was still beating. After a few minutes the cab stopped and, still assisting Curtis, Hatch went to the door. An aged woman answered the bell.

"Professor Van Dusen here?" asked the reporter.

"Yes."

"Please tell him that Mr. Hatch is here with a gentleman who needs immediate attention," Hatch directed, hurriedly.

He knew his way here and, still supporting Curtis, walked in. The woman disappeared. Curtis sank down on a couch in the little reception-room, looked at Hatch glassily for a moment, then without a sound dropped back on the couch unconscious.

After a moment the door opened and there came in Professor Augustus S. F. X. Van Dusen, The Thinking Machine. He squinted inquiringly at Hatch, and Hatch waved his head toward Curtis.

"Dear me, dear me," exclaimed The Thinking Machine.

He leaned over the prostrate figure a moment, then disappeared into another room, returning with a hypodermic. After a few anxious minutes Curtis sat up straight. He stared at the two men with unseeing eyes, and in them was unutterable terror.

"I saw her! I saw her!" he screamed. *"There was a dagger in her heart. Marguerite!"*

Again he fell back unconscious. The Thinking Machine squinted at Hatch.

"The man's got delirium tremens," he snapped impatiently.

III

For fifteen minutes Hatch silently looked on as The Thinking Machine worked over the unconscious man. Once or twice Curtis moved uneasily and moaned slightly. Hatch had started to explain the situation to The Thinking Machine, but the irascible scientist glared at him and the reporter became silent. After ten or fifteen minutes The Thinking Machine turned to Hatch more genially.

"He'll be all right in a little while now," he said. "What is it?"

"Well, it's a murder," Hatch began. "Marguerite Melrose, an actress, was stabbed through the heart last night, and————"

"Murder?" interrupted The Thinking Machine. "Might it not have been suicide?"

"Might have been; yes," said the reporter, after a moment's pause. "But it appears to be murder."

"When you say it *is* murder," said The Thinking Machine, "you immediately give the impression that you were there and saw it. Go on."

From the beginning, then, Hatch told the story as he knew it; of the stopping of The Green Dragon at the Monarch Inn, of the events there, of the whereabouts of Curtis and Reid at the time the girl received the knife thrust and of the confirmation of Reid's story. Then he detailed those incidents of the arrival of the men with the girl at Dr. Leonard's house, of what had transpired there, of the effort Curtis had made to get possession of the knife.

With finger tips pressed together and squinting steadily upward, The Thinking Machine listened. At its end, which bore on the actions of Curtis just preceding his appearance in the room with them, The Thinking Machine arose and walked over to the couch where Curtis lay. He ran his slender fingers idly through the unconscious man's thick hair several times.

"Doesn't it strike you as perfectly possible, Mr. Hatch," he asked finally, "that Miss Melrose *did* kill herself?"

"It may be perfectly possible, but it doesn't appear so," said Hatch. "There was no motive."

"And certainly you've shown no motive for anything else," said the other, crustily. "Still," he mused, "I really can't say anything until I talk to him."

He again turned to his patient, and as he looked saw the red blood surge back into the face.

"Ah, now we're all right," he announced.

Thus it happened, for after another ten minutes the patient

sat up suddenly on the couch and looked at the two men before him, bewildered.

"What's the matter?" he asked. The thickness was gone from his speech; he was himself again, although a little shaky.

Briefly, Hatch explained to him what had happened, and he listened silently. Finally he turned to The Thinking Machine.

"And this gentleman?" he asked. He noted the queer appearance of the scientist, and stared into the squint eyes frankly.

"Professor Van Dusen, a distinguished scientist and physician," Hatch introduced. "I brought you here. He has been working with you for an hour."

"And now, Mr. Curtis," said The Thinking Machine, "if you will tell us *all* you know about the murder of Miss Melrose———"

Curtis paled suddenly.

"Why do you ask me?" he demanded.

"You said a great deal while you were unconscious," remarked The Thinking Machine, as he dreamily stared at the ceiling. "I know that worry over that and too much alcohol have put you in a condition bordering on nervous collapse. I think it would be better if you told it *all*."

Hatch instantly saw the trend of the scientist's remarks, and remained discreetly silent. Curtis stared at both for a moment, then paced nervously across the room. He did not know what he might have said, what chance word might have been dropped. Then, apparently, he made up his mind, for he stopped suddenly in front of The Thinking Machine.

"Do I look like a man who would commit murder?" he asked.

"No, you do not," was the prompt response.

His recital of the story was similar to that of Hatch, but the scientist listened carefully.

"Details! Details!" he interrupted once.

The story was complete from the moment Curtis jumped

out of the car until the return to the hotel of Curtis and Reid. There the narrator stopped.

"Mr. Curtis, why did you try to induce Dr. Leonard to give up the knife to you?" asked The Thinking Machine, finally.

"Because—well, because————" He faltered, flushed and stopped.

"Because you were afraid it would bring the crime home to you?" asked the scientist.

"I didn't know *what* might happen," was the response.

"Is it your knife?"

Again the tell-tale flush overspread Curtis's face.

"No," he said, flatly.

"Is it Reid's knife?"

"Oh, no," he said, quickly.

"You were in love with Miss Melrose?"

"Yes," was the steady reply.

"Had she ever refused to marry you?"

"I had never asked her."

"Why?"

"Is this a third degree?" demanded Curtis, angrily, and he arose. "Am I a prisoner?"

"Not at all," said The Thinking Machine, quietly. "You may be made a prisoner, though, on what you said while unconscious. I am merely trying to help you."

Curtis sank down in a chair with his head in his hands and remained motionless for several minutes. At last he looked up.

"I'll answer your questions," he said.

"Why did you never ask Miss Melrose to marry you?"

"Because—well, because I understood another man, Donald MacLean, was in love with her, and she might have loved him. I understood she would have married him had it not been that by doing so she would have caused his disinheritance. MacLean is now in Boston."

"Ah!" exclaimed The Thinking Machine. "Your friend Reid didn't happen to be in love with her, too, did he?"

"Oh, no," was the reply. "Reid came here hoping to win the love of Miss Dow, a society girl. I came with him."

"Miss Dow?" asked Hatch, quickly. "The girl who eloped last night with Morgan Mason?"

"Yes," replied Curtis. "That elopement and this—crime have put Reid almost in as bad a condition as I am."

"What elopement?" asked The Thinking Machine.

Hatch explained how Mason had procured a marriage license, how Miss Dow and Mason had met at the Monarch Inn—where Miss Melrose must have been killed according to all stories—how Miss Dow had written to her parents from there of the elopement and then of their disappearance. The Thinking Machine listened, but without apparent interest.

"Have you such a knife as was used to kill Miss Melrose?" he asked at the end.

"No."

"Did you ever have such a knife?"

"Well, once."

"Where did you carry it when it was not in your auto kit?"

"In my lower coat pocket."

"By the way, what kind of looking woman was Miss Melrose?"

"One of the most beautiful women I ever met," said Curtis, with a certain enthusiasm. "Of ordinary height, superb fig- ure—a woman who would attract attention anywhere."

"I believe she wore a veil and an automobile mask at the time she was killed?"

"Yes. They covered all her face except her chin."

"Could she, wearing an automobile mask, see either side of

herself without turning?" asked The Thinking Machine, pointedly. "Had you intended to stab her, say while the car was in motion and had the knife in your hand, even in daylight, could she have seen it without turning her head? Or, if she had had the knife, could you have seen it?"

Curtis shuddered a little.

"No, I don't believe so."

"Was she blonde or brunette?"

"Blonde, with great clouds of golden hair," said Curtis, and again there was admiration in his tone.

"Golden hair?" Hatch repeated. "I understood Medical Examiner Francis to say she had dark hair?"

"No, golden hair," was the positive reply.

"Did you see the body, Mr. Hatch?" asked the scientist.

"No. None of us saw it. Dr. Francis makes that a rule."

The Thinking Machine arose, excused himself and passed into another room. They heard the telephone bell ring and then some one closed the door connecting the two rooms. When the scientist returned he went straight to a point which Hatch had impatiently awaited.

"What happened to you this afternoon in Winter Street?"

Curtis had retained his composure well up to this point; now he became uneasy again. Quick pallor on his face was succeeded by a flush which crept up to the roots of his hair.

"I've been drinking too much," he said at last. "That and this thing have completely unnerved me. I am afraid I was not myself."

"What did you *think* you saw?" insisted The Thinking Machine.

"I went into a store for something. I've forgotten what now. I know there was a great crowd of women—they were all about me. There I saw—" He stopped and was silent for a moment. "There

I saw," he went on with an effort, "a woman—just a glimpse of her, over the heads of the others in the store—and————"

"And what?" insisted The Thinking Machine.

"At the moment I would have sworn it was Marguerite Melrose," was the reply.

"Of course you know you were mistaken?"

"I know it now," said Curtis. "It was a chance resemblance, but the effect on me was awful. I ran out of there shrieking—it seemed to me. Then I found myself here."

"And you don't know what you said or did from that time until the present?" asked the scientist, curiously.

"No, except in a hazy sort of way."

After awhile Martha, the scientist's aged servant, appeared in the doorway.

"Mr. Mallory and a gentleman, sir."

"Let them come in," said The Thinking Machine. "Mr. Curtis," and he turned to him gravely, "Mr. Reid is here. I sent for him as if at your request to ask him two questions. If he answers those questions, as I believe he will, I can demonstrate that you are not guilty of and have no connection with the murder of Miss Melrose. Let me ask these questions, without any hint or remark from you as to what the answer must be. Are you willing?"

"I am," replied Curtis. His face was white, but his voice was firm.

Detective Mallory, whom Curtis didn't know, and Charles Reid entered the room. Both looked about curiously. Mallory nodded brusquely at Hatch. Reid looked at Curtis and Curtis looked away.

"Mr. Reid," said The Thinking Machine, without any pre-liminary, "Mr. Curtis tells me that the knife used to kill Miss Melrose was your property. Is that so?" he demanded quickly, as Curtis faced about wonderingly.

"No," thundered Reid, fiercely.

"Is it Mr. Curtis's knife?" asked The Thinking Machine.

"Yes," flashed Reid. "It's a part of his auto kit."

Curtis started to speak; The Thinking Machine waved his hand toward him. Detective Mallory caught the gesture and understood that Jack Curtis was his prisoner for murder.

IV

Curtis was led away and locked up. He raved and bitterly denounced Reid for the information he had given, but he did not deny it. Indeed, after the first burst of fury he said nothing.

Once he was under lock and key the police, led by Detective Mallory, searched his rooms at the Hotel Teutonic and there they found a handkerchief stained with blood. It was slight, still it was a stain. This was immediately placed in the hands of an expert, who pronounced it human blood. Then the case against Curtis seemed complete; it was his knife, he had been in love with Miss Melrose, therefore probably jealous of her, and here was the tell-tale bloodstain.

Meanwhile Reid was permitted to go his way. He seemed crushed by the rapid sequence of events, and read eagerly every line he could find in the public prints concerning both the murder and the elopement of Miss Dow. This latter affair, indeed, seemed to have greater sway over his mind than the murder, or that a lifetime friend was now held as the murderer.

Meanwhile The Thinking Machine had signified to Hatch his desire to visit the scene of the crime and see what might be done there. Late in the afternoon, therefore, they started, taking a train for a village nearest the Monarch Inn.

"It's a most extraordinary case," The Thinking Machine said, "much more extraordinary than you can imagine."

"In what respect?" asked the reporter.

"In motive, in the actual manner of the girl meeting her death and in a dozen other details which I can't state now because I haven't all the facts."

"You don't doubt but what it was murder?"

"It doesn't necessarily follow," said The Thinking Machine, evasively. "Suppose we were seeking a motive for Miss Melrose's suicide, what would we have? We would have her love affair with this man MacLean whom she refused to marry because she knew he would be disinherited. Suppose she had not seen him for a couple of years—suppose she had made up her mind to give him up—that he had suddenly appeared when she sat alone in the automobile in front of the Monarch Inn—suppose, then, finding all her love reawakened, she had decided to end it all?"

"But Curtis's knife and the blood on his handkerchief?"

"Suppose, having made up her mind to kill herself, she had sought a weapon?" went on The Thinking Machine, as if there had been no interruption. "What is more natural than she should have sought something—the knife, say—in the tool bag or kit, which must have been near her? Suppose she stabbed herself while the men were away from the automobile, or even after they had started on again in the darkness?"

Hatch looked a little crestfallen.

"You believe, then, that she did kill herself?" he asked.

"Certainly not," was the prompt response. "I *don't* believe Miss Melrose killed herself—but as yet I know nothing to the contrary. As for the blood on Curtis's handkerchief, remember he helped carry the body to Dr. Leonard; it might have come from that—it might have come from a slight spattering of blood."

"But circumstances certainly implicate Curtis."

"I wouldn't convict any man of any crime on any circumstantial evidence," was the response. "It's worthless unless a man is forced to confess."

The reporter was puzzled, bewildered, and his face showed it. There were many things he did not understand, but the principal question in his mind took form:

"Why did you turn Curtis over to the police, then?"

"Because he is the man who owned the knife," was the reply. "I knew he was lying to me from the first about the knife. Men have been executed on less evidence than that."

The train stopped and they proceeded to the office of the medical examiner, where the body of the woman lay. Professor Van Dusen was readily permitted to see the body, even to offer his expert assistance in an autopsy which was then being performed; but the reporter was stopped at the door. After an hour The Thinking Machine came out.

"She was stabbed from the right," he said in answer to Hatch's inquiring look, "either by some one sitting at her right, by some one leaning over her right shoulder, or she might have done it herself."

Then they went on to Monarch Inn, five miles away. Here, after a comprehensive squint at the landscape, The Thinking Machine entered and for half an hour questioned three waiters there.

Did these waiters see Mr. Reid? Yes. They identified his published picture as a gentleman who had come in and taken a hot Scotch at the bar. Any one with him? No. Speak to anyone in the inn? Yes, a lady.

"What did she look like?" asked The Thinking Machine.

"Couldn't say, sir," the waiter replied. "She came in an automobile and wore a mask, with a veil tied about her head and a long tan automobile coat."

"With the mask on you couldn't see her face?"

"Only her chin, sir."

"No glimpse of her hair?"

"No, sir. It was covered by the veil."

Then The Thinking Machine turned loose a flood of questions. He learned that the woman had been waiting at the inn for nearly an hour when Reid entered; that she had come there alone and at her request had been shown into a private parlor—" to wait for a gentleman," she had told the waiter.

She had opened the door when she heard Reid enter and had glanced out, but he had disappeared into the bar before she saw him. When he started away she looked out again. Then she saw him and he saw her. She seemed surprised and started to close the door, when he spoke to her. No one heard what was said, but he went in and the door was closed.

No one knew just when either Reid or the woman left the inn. Some half an hour or so after Reid entered the room a waiter rapped on the door. There was no answer. He opened the door and went in, but there was no one there. It was presumed then that the gentleman she had been waiting for had appeared and they had gone out together. It was a fact that an automobile had come up meanwhile—in addition to that in which Curtis, Miss Melrose and Reid had come—and had gone away again.

When all this questioning had come to an end and these facts were in possession of The Thinking Machine, the reporter advanced a theory.

"That woman was unquestionably Miss Dow, who knew Reid and who eloped that night with Morgan Mason."

The Thinking Machine looked at him a moment without speaking, then led the way into the private room where the lady had been waiting. Hatch followed. They remained there five or ten minutes, then The Thinking Machine came out and started toward the front door, only eight or ten feet from this room. The road was twenty feet away.

"Let's go," he said, finally.

"Where?" asked Hatch.

"Don't you see?" asked The Thinking Machine, irrelevantly, "that it would have been perfectly possible for Miss Melrose herself to have left the automobile and gone inside the inn for a few minutes?"

Following previously received directions The Thinking Machine now set out to find the man who had charge of the gasoline tank. They went away together and remained half an hour.

On the scientist's return to where Hatch had been waiting impatiently they climbed into the car which had brought them to the inn.

"Two miles down this road, then the first road to your right until I tell you to stop," was the order to the chauffeur.

"Where are you going?" asked Hatch, curiously.

"Don't know yet," was the enigmatic reply.

The car ran on through the night, with great, unblinking lights staring straight out ahead on a road as smooth as asphalt. The turn was made, then more slowly the car proceeded along the cross road. At the second house, dimly discernible through the night, The Thinking Machine gave the signal to stop.

Hatch leaped out, and The Thinking Machine followed. Together they approached the house, a small cottage some distance back from the road. As they went up the path they came upon another automobile, but it had no lights and the engine was still.

Even in the darkness they could see that one of the forward wheels was gone, and the front of the car was demolished.

"That fellow had a bad accident," Hatch remarked.

An old woman and a boy appeared at the door in answer to their rap.

"I am looking for a gentleman who was injured last night in an automobile accident," said The Thinking Machine. "Is he still here?"

"Yes. Come in."

They stepped inside as a man's voice called from another room:

"Who is it?"

"Two gentlemen to see the man who was hurt," the woman called.

"Do you know his name?" asked The Thinking Machine.

"No, sir," the woman replied. Then the man who had spoken appeared.

"Would it be possible for us to see the gentleman who was hurt?" asked The Thinking Machine.

"Well, the doctor said we would have to keep folks away from him," was the reply. "Is there anything I could tell you?"

"We would like to know who he is," said The Thinking Machine. "It may be that we can take him off your hands."

"I don't know his name," the man explained; "but here are the things we took off him. He was hurt on the head, and hasn't been able to speak since he was brought here."

The Thinking Machine took a gold watch, a small notebook, two or three cards of various business concerns, two railroad tickets to New York and one thousand dollars in large bills. He merely glanced at the papers. No name appeared anywhere on them; the same with the railroad tickets. The business cards meant nothing at the moment. It was the gold watch on which the scientist concentrated his attention. He looked on both sides, then inside, carefully. Finally he handed it back.

"What time did this gentleman come here?" he asked.

"We brought him in from the road about nine o'clock," was the reply. "We heard his automobile smash into something and found him there beside it a moment later. He was unconscious. His car had struck a stone on the curve and he was thrown out head first."

"And where is his wife?"

"His wife?" The man looked from The Thinking Machine to the woman. "His wife? We didn't see anybody else."

"Nobody ran away from the machine as you went out?" insisted the scientist.

"No, sir," was the positive reply.

"And no woman has been here to inquire for him?"

"No, sir."

"Has anybody?"

"No, sir."

"What direction was the car going when it struck?"

"I couldn't tell you, sir. It had turned entirely over and was in the middle of the road when we found it."

"What's the number of the car?"

"It didn't have any."

"This gentleman has good medical attention, I suppose?"

"Yes, sir. Dr. Leonard is attending him. He says his condition isn't dangerous, and meanwhile we're letting him stay here, because we suppose he'll make it all right with us when he gets well."

"Thank you—that's all," said The Thinking Machine. "Good-night."

With Hatch he turned and left the house.

"What is all this?" asked Hatch, bewildered.

"That man is Morgan Mason," said The Thinking Machine.

"The man who eloped with Miss Dow?" asked Hatch, breathlessly.

"Now, where is Miss Dow?" asked The Thinking Machine, in turn.

"You mean————"

The Thinking Machine waved his hand off into the vague night; it was a gesture which Hatch understood perfectly.

V

Hutchinson Hatch was deeply thoughtful on the swift run back to the village. There he and The Thinking Machine took train to Boston. Hatch was turning over possibilities. Had Miss Dow eloped with some one besides Mason? There had been no other name mentioned. Was it possible that she killed Miss Melrose? Vaguely his mind clutched for a motive for this, yet none appeared, and he dismissed the idea with a laugh at its absurdity. Then, What? Where? How? Why?

"I suppose the story of an actress having been murdered in an automobile under mysterious circumstances would have been telegraphed all over the country, Mr. Hatch?" asked The Thinking Machine.

"Yes," said Hatch. "If you mean this story, there's not a city in the country that doesn't know of it by this time."

"It's perfectly wonderful, the resources of the press," the scientist mused.

Hatch nodded his acquiescence. He had hoped for a moment that The Thinking Machine had asked the question as a preliminary to something else, but that was apparently all. After awhile the train jerked a little and The Thinking Machine spoke again.

"I think, Mr. Hatch, I wouldn't yet print anything about the disappearance of Miss Dow," he said. "It might be unwise at present. No one else will find it out, so————"

"I understand," said Hatch. It was a command.

"By the way," the other went on, "do you happen to remember the name of that Winter Street store that Curtis went in?"

"Yes," and he named it.

It was nearly midnight when The Thinking Machine and Hatch reached Boston. The reporter was dismissed with a curt:

"Come up at noon to-morrow."

Hatch went his way. Next day at noon promptly he was waiting in the reception-room of The Thinking Machine's home. The scientist was out—down in Winter Street, Martha explained—and Hatch waited impatiently for his return. He came in finally.

"Well?" inquired the reporter.

"Impossible to say anything until day after to-morrow," said The Thinking Machine.

"And then?" asked Hatch.

"The solution," replied the scientist positively. "Now I'm waiting for some one."

"Miss Dow?"

"Meanwhile you might see Reid and find out in some way if he ever happened to make a gift of any little thing, a thing that a woman would wear on the outside of her coat, for instance, to Miss Dow."

"Lord, I don't think *he'll* say anything."

"Find out, too, when he intends to go back West."

It took Hatch three hours, and required a vast deal of patience and skill, to find out that on a recent birthday Miss Dow had received a present of a monogram belt buckle from Reid. That was all; and that was not what The Thinking Machine meant. Hatch had the word of Miss Dow's maid for it that while Miss Dow wore this belt at the time of her elopement, it was underneath the automobile coat.

"Have you heard anything more from Miss Dow?" asked Hatch.

"Yes," responded the maid. "Her father received a letter from her this morning. It was from Chicago, and said that she and her husband were on their way to San Francisco and that the family might not hear from them again until after the honeymoon."

"How? What?" gasped Hatch. His brain was in a muddle. "She in Chicago, *with—her husband*?"

"Yes, sir."

"Is there any question about the letter being in her handwriting?"

"Not at all," replied the maid, positively. "It's perfectly natural," she concluded.

"But————" Hatch began, then he stopped.

For one fleeting instant he was tempted to tell the maid that the man whom the family had supposed was Miss Dow's husband was lying unconscious at a farmhouse not a great way from the Monarch Inn, and that there was no trace of Miss Dow. Now this letter! His head whirled when he thought of it.

"Is there any question but that Miss Dow did elope with Mr. Mason and not some other man?" he asked.

"It was Mr. Mason, all right," the girl responded. "I knew there was to be an elopement and helped arrange for Miss Dow to go," she added, confidentially. "It was Mr. Mason, I know."

Then Hatch rushed away and telephoned to The Thinking Machine. He simply couldn't hold this latest development until he saw him again.

"We've made a mistake," he bellowed through the 'phone.

"What's that?" demanded The Thinking Machine, aggressively.

"Miss Dow is in Chicago with her husband—family has received a letter from her—that man out there with the smashed head can't be Mason," the reporter explained hurriedly.

"Dear me, dear me!" said The Thinking Machine over the wire. And again: "Dear me!"

"Her maid told me all about it," Hatch rushed on, "that is, all about her aiding Miss Dow to elope, and all that. Must be some mistake."

"Dear me!" again came in the voice of The Thinking Machine. Then: "Is Miss Dow a blonde or brunette?"

The irrelevancy of the question caused Hatch to smile in spite of himself.

"A brunette," he answered. "A pronounced brunette."

"Then," said The Thinking Machine, as if this were merely dependent upon or a part of the blonde or brunette proposition, "get immediately a picture of Mason somewhere—I suppose you can—go out and see that man with the smashed head and see if it is Mason. Let me know by 'phone."

"All right," said Hatch, rather hopelessly. "But it is impossible———"

"Don't say that," snapped The Thinking Machine. "Don't say that," he repeated, angrily. "It annoys me exceedingly."

It was nearly ten o'clock that night when Hatch again 'phoned to The Thinking Machine. He had found a photograph, he had seen the man with the smashed head. They were the same. He so informed The Thinking Machine.

"Ah," said that individual, quietly. "Did you find out about any gift that Reid might have made to Miss Dow?" he asked.

"Yes, a monogram belt buckle of gold," was the reply.

Hatch was over his head and knew it. He was finding out things and answering questions which, by the wildest stretch of his imagination, he could not bring to bear on the matter in hand—the mystery surrounding the murder of Marguerite Melrose, an actress.

"Meet me at my place here at one o'clock day after to-morrow," instructed The Thinking Machine. "Publish as little as you can of this matter until you see me. It's extraordinary—perfectly extraordinary. Good-by."

That was all. Hatch groped hopelessly through the tangle, seeking one fact that he could grasp. Then it occurred to him that he had never ascertained when Reid intended to return West, and he went to the Hotel Teutonic for this purpose. The clerk informed him that Reid was to start in a couple of days. Reid had hardly left his room since Curtis was locked up.

Precisely at one o'clock on the second day following, as directed by The Thinking Machine, Hatch appeared and was ushered in. The Thinking Machine was bowed over a retort* in his laboratory, and he looked up at the reporter with a question in his eyes.

"Oh, yes," he said, as if recollecting for the first time the purpose of the visit. "Oh, yes."

He led the way to the reception-room and gave instructions to Martha to admit whoever inquired for him; then he sat down and leaned back in his chair. After awhile the bell rang and two men were shown in. One was Charles Reid; the other a detective whom Hatch knew.

"Ah, Mr. Reid," said The Thinking Machine. "I'm sorry to have troubled you, but there were some questions I wanted to ask before you went away. If you'll wait just a moment."

Reid bowed and took a seat.

"Is he under arrest?" Hatch inquired of the detective, aside.

"Oh, no," was the reply. "Oh, no. Detective Mallory told me to ask him to come up. I don't know what for."

After awhile the bell rang again. Then Hatch heard Detective Mallory's voice in the hall and the rustle of skirts; then the voice of another man. Mallory appeared at the door after a moment;

---

* A retort is a long-necked glass bottle.

behind him came two veiled women and a man who was a stranger to Hatch.

"I'm going to make a request, Mr. Mallory," said The Thinking Machine. "I know it will be a cause of pleasure to Mr. Reid. It is that you release Mr. Curtis, who is charged with the murder of Miss Melrose."

"Why?" demanded Mallory, quickly. Hatch and Reid stared at the scientist curiously.

"This," said The Thinking Machine.

The two women simultaneously removed their veils.

One was Miss Marguerite Melrose.

VI

"Miss Melrose that was," explained The Thinking Machine, "now Mrs. Donald MacLean. This, gentlemen, is her husband. This other young woman is Miss Dow's maid. Together I believe we will be able to throw some light on the death of the young woman who was found in Mr. Curtis's automobile."

Stupefied with amazement, Hatch stared at the woman whose reported murder had startled and puzzled the entire country. Reid had shown only slight emotion—an emotion of a kind hard to read. Finally he advanced to Miss Melrose, or Mrs. MacLean, with outstretched hand.

"Marguerite," he said.

The girl looked deeply into his eyes, then took the proffered hand.

"And Jack Curtis?" she asked.

"If Detective Mallory will have him brought here we can immediately end his connection with this case so far as your murder is concerned," said The Thinking Machine.

"Who—who was murdered, then?" asked Hatch.

"A little circumstantial development is necessary to show," replied The Thinking Machine.

Detective Mallory retired into another room and 'phoned to have Curtis brought up. On his assurance that there had been a mistake which he would explain later, Curtis set out from his cell with a detective and within a few minutes appeared in the room, wonderingly.

One look at Marguerite and he was beside her, gripping her hand. For a time he didn't speak; it was not necessary. Then the actress, with flushed face, indicated MacLean, who had stood quietly by, an interested but silent spectator.

"My husband, Jack," she said.

Quick comprehension swept over Curtis and he looked from one to another. Then he approached MacLean with outstretched hand.

"I congratulate you," he said, with deep feeling. "Make her happy."

Reid had stood unobserved meanwhile. Hatch's glance traveled from one to another of the persons in the room. He was seeking to explain that expression on Reid's face, vainly thus far. There was a little pause as Reid and Curtis came face to face, but neither spoke.

"Now, please, what does it all mean?" asked MacLean, who up to this time had been silent.

"It's a strange study of the human brain," said The Thinking Machine, "and incidentally a little proof that circumstantial evidence is absolutely worthless. For instance, here it was proven that Miss Melrose was dead, that Mr. Curtis was jealous of her, that while drinking he had threatened her—this I learned at the Hotel Yarmouth, but now it is unimportant—that his knife killed her, and finally that there was blood on one of his handkerchiefs. This is the complete circumstantial chain; and Miss Melrose appears, alive.

"Suppose we take the case from the point where I entered it. It will be interesting as showing the methods of a brain which reduces all things to tangible strands which may be woven into a whole, then fitting them together. My knowledge of the affair began when Mr. Curtis was brought to these apartments by Mr. Hatch. Mr. Curtis was ill. I gave him a stimulant; he aroused suddenly and shrieked: 'I saw her. There was a dagger in her heart. Marguerite!'

"My first impression was that he was insane; my next that he had delirium tremens, because I saw he had been drinking heavily. Later I saw it was temporary mental collapse due to excessive drinking and a tremendous strain. Instantly I associated Marguerite with this—'a dagger in her heart.' Therefore, Marguerite dead or wounded. 'I saw her.' Dead or alive? These, then, were my first impressions.

"I asked Mr. Hatch what had happened. He told me Miss Melrose, an actress, had been murdered the night before. I suggested suicide, because suicide is always the first possibility in considering a case of violent death which is not obviously accidental. He insisted that he believed it was murder, and told me why. It was all he knew of the story.

"There was the stopping of The Green Dragon at the Monarch Inn for gasoline; the disappearance of Mr. Curtis, as he told the police, to hunt for gasoline—partly proven by the fact that he brought it back; the statement of Mr. Reid to the police that he had gone into the inn for a hot Scotch, and confirmation of this. Above all, here was the opportunity for the crime—if it were committed by any person other than Curtis or Reid.

"Then Mr. Hatch repeated to me the statement made to him by Dr. Leonard. The first thing that impressed me here was the fact that Curtis had, in taking the girl into the house, carried her by the shoulders. Instantly I saw, knowing that the girl had been stabbed through the heart, how it would be possible for blood to get on Mr. Curtis's hands, thence on his handkerchief or clothing. This was before I knew or considered his connection with the death at all.

"Curtis told Dr. Leonard that the girl was Miss Melrose. The body wasn't yet cold, therefore death must have come just before it reached the doctor. Then the knife was discovered. Here was the first tangible working clew—a rough knife, with a blade six or seven inches long. Obviously not the sort of knife a woman would carry about with her. Therefore, where did it come from?

"Curtis tried to induce the doctor to let him have the knife; probably Curtis's knife, possibly Reid's. Why Curtis's? The nature of the knife, a blade six or seven inches long, indicated a knife used for heavy work, not for a penknife. Under ordinary circumstances such a knife would not have been carried by Reid; therefore it may have belonged to Curtis's auto kit. He might have carried it in his pocket.

"Thus, considering *that it was Miss Melrose who was dead*, we had these facts: Dead only a few minutes, possibly stabbed while the two men were away from the car; Curtis's knife used—not a knife from any other auto kit, mind you, *because Curtis recognized this knife.* Two and two make four, not sometimes, but all the time."

Every person in the room was leaning forward, eagerly listening; Reid's face was perfectly white. The Thinking Machine finally arose, walked over and ran his fingers through Reid's hair, then sat again squinting at the ceiling. He spoke as if to himself.

"Then Mr. Hatch told me another important thing," he went on. "At the moment it appeared a coincidence, later it assumed its complete importance. This was that Dr. Leonard did not actually *see* the face of the girl—only the chin; that the hair was covered by a veil and the mask covered the remainder of the face. Here for the first time I saw that it was wholly possible that the woman *was not Miss Melrose at all*. I saw it as a possibility; not that I believed it. I had no reason to, then.

"The dress of the young woman meant nothing; it was that of thousands of other young women who go automobiling—handsome tailor-made gown, tan dust coat. Then I tricked Mr. Curtis—I suppose it is only fair to use the proper word—into telling me his story by making him believe he made compromising admissions while unconscious. I had, I may say, too, examined his head minutely. I have always maintained that the head of a murderer will show a certain indentation.* Mr. Curtis's head did not show this indentation, neither does Mr. Reid's.

"Mr. Curtis told me the first thing to show that the knife which killed the girl—I still believed her Miss Melrose then—could have passed out of his hands. He said when he leaped from the automobile he thought he dropped something, searched for it a moment, failed to find it, then, being in a hurry, went on. He called back to Mr. Reid to search for what he had lost. That is when Mr. Curtis lost the knife; that is when it passed into the possession of Mr. Reid. He found it."

Every eye was turned on Reid. He sat as if fascinated, staring into the upward turned face of the scientist.

"There we had a girl—presumably Miss Melrose—dead, by a knife owned by Mr. Curtis, last in the possession of Mr. Reid. Mr. Hatch had previously told me that the medical examiner said the wound which killed the girl came from her right, in a general direction. Therefore here was a possibility that Mr. Reid did it in the automobile—a possibility, I say.

"I asked Mr. Curtis why he tried to recover the knife from Dr.

---

* This is the pseudoscience of phrenology at work. See note on page 2.

Leonard. He stammered and faltered, but really it was because, having recognized the knife, he was afraid the crime would come home to him. Mr. Curtis denied flatly that the knife was his, and in denying told me that it was. It was not Mr. Reid's I was assured. Mr. Curtis also told me of his love for Miss Melrose, but there was nothing there, as it appeared, strong enough to suggest a motive for murder. He mentioned you, Mr. MacLean, then.

"Then Mr. Curtis named Miss Dow as one whose hand had been sought by Mr. Reid. Mr. Hatch told me this girl—Miss Dow—had eloped the night before with Morgan Mason from Monarch Inn—or, to be exact, that her family had received a letter from her stating that she was eloping; that Mason had taken out a marriage license. Remember this was the girl that Reid was in love with; it was singular that there should have been a Monarch Inn end to that elopement as well as to this tragedy.

"This meant nothing as bearing on the abstract problem before me until Mr. Curtis described Miss Melrose as having golden hair. With another minor scrap of information Mr. Hatch again opened up vast possibilities by stating that the medical examiner, a careful man, had said Miss Melrose had *dark* hair. I asked him if he had seen the body; he had not. But the medical examiner told him that. Instantly in my mind the question was aroused: Was it *Miss Melrose* who was killed? This was merely a possibility; it still had no great weight with me.

"I asked Mr. Curtis as to the circumstances which caused his collapse in Winter Street. He explained it was because he had seen a woman whom he would have sworn was Miss Melrose if he had not known that she was dead. This, following the dark hair and blonde hair puzzle, instantly caused this point to stand forth sharply in my mind. Was Miss Melrose dead at all? I had good reason then to believe that she was *not*.

"Previously, with the idea of fixing for all time the owner-ship of the knife—yet knowing in my own mind it was Mr. Curtis's—I had sent for Mr. Reid. I told him Mr. Curtis had said it was his knife. Mr. Reid fell into the trap and did the very thing I expected. He declared angrily the knife was Mr. Curtis's, think-ing Curtis had tried to saddle the crime on him. Then I turned Mr. Curtis over to the police. When he was locked up I was rea-sonably certain that he did not commit any crime, because I had traced the knife from him to Mr. Reid."

There was a glitter in Reid's eyes now. It was not fear, only a nervous battle to restrain himself. The Thinking Machine went on:

"I saw the body of the dead woman—indeed, assisted at her autopsy. She was a pronounced brunette—Miss Melrose was a blonde. The mistake in identity was not an impossible one in view of the fact that each wore a mask and had her hair tied up under a veil. That woman was stabbed from the right—still a possibility of suicide."

"Who was the woman?" demanded Curtis. He seemed utterly unable to control himself longer.

"Miss Elizabeth Dow, who was supposed to have eloped with Morgan Mason," was the quiet reply.

Instant amazement was reflected on every face save Reid's, and again every eye was turned to him. Miss Dow's maid burst into tears.

"Mr. Reid knew who the woman was all the time," said The Thinking Machine. "Knowing then that Miss Dow was the dead woman—this belief being confirmed by a monogram gold belt buckle, 'E. D.,' on the body—I proceeded to find out all I could in this direction. The waiters had seen Mr. Reid in the inn; had seen him talking to a masked and veiled lady who had been wait-ing for nearly an hour; had seen him go into a room with her, but had not seen them leave the inn. Mr. Reid had recognized the lady—not she him. How? By a glimpse of the monogram belt buckle which he knew because he probably gave it to her."

"He did," interposed Hatch.

"I did," said Reid, calmly. It was the first time he had spoken.

"Now, Mr. Reid went into the room and closed the door, carrying with him Mr. Curtis's knife," went on The Thinking Machine. "I can't tell you from *personal observation* what happened in that room, but I know. Mr. Reid learned in some way that Miss Dow was going to elope; he learned that she had been waiting long past the time when Mason was due there; that she believed he had humiliated her by giving up the idea at the last minute. Being in a highly nervous condition, she lost faith in Mason and in herself, and perhaps mentioned suicide?"

"She did," said Reid, calmly.

"Go on, Mr. Reid," suggested The Thinking Machine.

"I believed, too, that Mason had changed his mind," the young man continued, with steady voice. "I pleaded with Miss Dow to give up the idea of eloping, because, remember, I loved her, too. She finally consented to go on with our party, as her automobile had gone. We came out of the inn together. When we reached the automobile—The Green Dragon, I mean—I saw Miss Melrose getting into Mr. MacLean's automobile, which had come up meanwhile. Instantly I saw, or imagined, the circumstances, and said nothing to Miss Dow about it, particularly as Mr. MacLean's car dashed away at full speed.

"Now, in taking Miss Dow to The Green Dragon it had been my purpose to introduce her to Miss Melrose. She knew Mr. Curtis. When I saw Miss Melrose was gone I knew Curtis would wonder why. I couldn't explain, because every moment I was afraid Mason would appear to claim Miss Dow and I was anxious to get her as far away as possible. Therefore I requested her not to speak until we reached the next inn, and there I would explain to Curtis.

"Somewhere between the Monarch Inn and the inn we had started for Miss Dow changed her mind; probably was overcome by the humiliation of her position, and she used the knife. She had seen me take the knife from my pocket and throw it into the tool kit on the floor beside her. It was comparatively a trifling matter for her to stoop and pick it up, almost from under her feet, and————"

"Under all these circumstances, as stated by Mr. Reid," interrupted The Thinking Machine, "we understand why, after he found the girl dead, he didn't tell all the truth, even to Curtis. Any jury on earth would have convicted him of murder on circumstantial evidence. Then, when he saw Miss Dow dead, mistaken for Miss Melrose, he *could* not correct the impression without giving himself away. He was forced to silence.

"I realized these things—not in exact detail as Mr. Reid has told them, but in a general way—after my talk with the waiters. Then I set out to find out *why* Mason had not appeared. It was possibly due to accident. On a chance entirely I asked the man in charge of the gasoline tank at the Monarch if he had heard of an accident nearby on the night of the tragedy. He had.

"With Mr. Hatch I found the injured man. A monogram, 'M.M.,' on his watch, told me it was Morgan Mason. Mr. Mason had a serious accident and still lies unconscious. He was going to meet Miss Dow when this happened. He had two railroad tickets to New York—for himself and bride—in his pocket."

Reid still sat staring at The Thinking Machine, waiting. The others were awed into silence by the story of the tragedy.

"Having located both Mason and Miss Dow to my satisfaction, I then sought to find what had become of Miss Melrose. Mr. Reid could have told me this, but he wouldn't have, because it would have turned the light on the very thing which he was trying to keep hidden. With Miss Melrose alive, it was perfectly possible that Curtis *had* seen her in the Winter Street store.

"I asked Mr. Hatch if he remembered what store it was. He did. I also asked Mr. Hatch if such a story as the murder of Miss Melrose would be telegraphed all over the country. He said it would. It did not stand to reason that if Miss Melrose were in any city, or even on a train, she could have failed to hear of her own murder, which would instantly have called forth a denial.

"Therefore, where was she? On the water, out of reach of newspapers? I went to the store in Winter Street and asked if any purchases had been sent from there to any steamer about to sail on the day following the tragedy. There had been several purchases made by a woman who answered Miss Melrose's description as I had it, and these had been sent to a steamer which sailed for Halifax.

"Miss Melrose and Mr. MacLean, married then, were on that steamer. I wired to Halifax to ascertain if they were coming back immediately. They were. I waited for them. Otherwise, Mr. Hatch, I should have given you the solution of the mystery two days ago. As it was, I waited until Miss Melrose, or Mrs. MacLean, returned. I think that's all."

"The letter from Miss Dow in Chicago?" Hatch reminded him.

"Oh, yes," said The Thinking Machine. "That was sent to a friend in her confidence, and mailed on a specified date. As a matter of fact, she and Mason were going to New York and thence to Europe. Of course, as matters happened, the two letters—the other being the one mailed from the Monarch Inn—were sent and could not be recalled."

* * *

This strange story was one of the most astonishing news features the American newspapers ever handled. Charles Reid was arrested, established his story beyond question, and was released. His principal witnesses were Professor Augustus S. F. X. Van Dusen, Jack Curtis and Mrs. Donald MacLean.

THE FLAMING PHANTOM*

I

Hutchinson Hatch, reporter, stood beside the city editor's desk, smoking and waiting patiently for that energetic gentleman to dispose of several matters in hand. City editors always have several matters in hand, for the profession of keeping count of the pulse-beat of the world is a busy one. Finally this city editor emerged from a mass of other things and picked up a sheet of paper on which he had scribbled some strange hieroglyphics, these representing his interpretation of the art of writing.

"Afraid of ghosts?" he asked.

"Don't know," Hatch replied, smiling a little. "I never happened to meet one."

"Well, this looks like a good story," the city editor explained. "It's a haunted house. Nobody can live in it; all sorts of strange happenings, demoniacal laughter, groans and things. House is owned by Ernest Weston, a broker. Better jump down and take a look at it. If it is promising, you might spend a night in it for a Sunday story. Not afraid, are you?"

---

* First published in *Boston American*, November 14, 1905.

"I never heard of a ghost hurting anyone," Hatch replied, still smiling a little. "If this one hurts me it will make the story better."

Thus attention was attracted to the latest creepy mystery of a small town by the sea which in the past had not been wholly lacking in creepy mysteries.

Within two hours Hatch was there. He readily found the old Weston house, as it was known, a two-story, solidly built frame structure, which had stood for sixty or seventy years high upon a cliff overlooking the sea, in the center of a land plot of ten or twelve acres. From a distance it was imposing, but close inspection showed that, outwardly, at least, it was a ramshackle affair.

Without having questioned anyone in the village, Hatch climbed the steep cliff road to the old house, expecting to find some one who might grant him permission to inspect it. But no one appeared; a settled melancholy and gloom seemed to overspread it; all the shutters were closed forbiddingly.

There was no answer to his vigorous knock on the front door, and he shook the shutters on a window without result. Then he passed around the house to the back. Here he found a door and dutifully hammered on it. Still no answer. He tried it, and passed in. He stood in the kitchen, damp, chilly and darkened by the closed shutters.

One glance about this room and he went on through a back hall to the dining-room, now deserted, but at one time a comfortable and handsomely furnished place. Its hardwood floor was covered with dust; the chill of disuse was all-pervading. There was no furniture, only the litter which accumulates of its own accord.

From this point, just inside the dining-room door, Hatch began a sort of study of the inside architecture of the place. To his left was a door, the butler's pantry. There was a passage through, down three steps into the kitchen he had just left.

Straight before him, set in the wall, between two windows, was a large mirror, seven, possibly eight, feet tall and proportionately wide. A mirror of the same size was set in the wall at the end of the room to his left. From the dining-room he passed through a wide archway into the next room. This archway made the two rooms almost as one. This second, he presumed, had been a sort of living-room, but here, too, was nothing save accumulated litter, an old-fashioned fireplace and two long mirrors. As he entered, the fireplace was to his immediate left, one of the large mirrors was straight ahead of him and the other was to his right.

Next to the mirror in the end was a passageway of a little more than usual size which had once been closed with a sliding door. Hatch went through this into the reception-hall of the old house. Here, to his right, was the main hall, connected with the reception-hall by an archway, and through this archway he could see a wide, old-fashioned stairway leading up. To his left was a door, of ordinary size, closed. He tried it and it opened. He peered into a big room beyond. This room had been the library. It smelled of books and damp wood. There was nothing here—not even mirrors.

Beyond the main hall lay only two rooms, one a drawing-room of the generous proportions our old folks loved, with its gilt all tarnished and its fancy decorations covered with dust. Behind this, toward the back of the house, was a small parlor. There was nothing here to attract his attention, and he went upstairs. As he went he could see through the archway into the reception-hall as far as the library door, which he had left closed.

Upstairs were four or five roomy suites. Here, too, in small rooms designed for dressing, he saw the owner's passion for mirrors again. As he passed through room after room he fixed the general arrangement of it all in his mind, and later on paper, to study it, so that, if necessary, he could leave any part of the house in the dark. He didn't know but what this might be necessary, hence his care—the same care he had evidenced downstairs.

After another casual examination of the lower floor, Hatch went out the back way to the barn. This stood a couple of hundred feet back of the house and was of more recent construction. Above, reached by outside stairs, were apartments intended for the servants. Hatch looked over these rooms, but they, too, had the appearance of not having been occupied for several years. The lower part of the barn, he found, was arranged to house half a dozen horses and three or four traps.

"Nothing here to frighten anybody," was his mental comment as he left the old place and started back toward the village. It was three o'clock in the afternoon. His purpose was to learn then all he could of the "ghost," and return that night for developments.

He sought out the usual village bureau of information, the town constable, a grizzled old chap of sixty years, who realized his importance as the whole police department, and who had the gossip and information, more or less distorted, of several generations at his tongue's end.

The old man talked for two hours—he was glad to talk— seemed to have been longing for just such a glorious opportunity as the reporter offered. Hatch sifted out what he wanted, those things which might be valuable in his story.

It seemed, according to the constable, that the Weston house had not been occupied for five years, since the death of the father of Ernest Weston, present owner. Two weeks before the reporter's appearance there Ernest Weston had come down with a contractor and looked over the old place.

"We understand here," said the constable, judicially, "that Mr. Weston is going to be married soon, and we kind of thought he was having the house made ready for his Summer home again."

"Whom do you understand he is to marry?" asked Hatch, for this was news.

"Miss Katherine Everard, daughter of Curtis Everard, a banker up in Boston," was the reply. "I know he used to go around with her before the old man died, and they say since she came out in Newport he has spent a lot of time with her."

"Oh, I see," said Hatch. "They were to marry and come here?"

"That's right," said the constable. "But I don't know when, since this ghost story has come up."

"Oh, yes, the ghost," remarked Hatch. "Well, hasn't the work of repairing begun?"

"No, not inside," was the reply. "There's been some work done on the grounds—in the daytime—but not much of that, and I kind of think it will be a long time before it's all done."

"What is the spook story, anyway?"

"Well," and the old constable rubbed his chin thoughtfully. "It seems sort of funny. A few days after Mr. Weston was down here a gang of laborers, mostly Italians, came down to work and decided to sleep in the house—sort of camp out—until they could repair a leak in the barn and move in there. They got here late in the afternoon and didn't do much that day but move into the house, all upstairs, and sort of settle down for the night. About one o'clock they heard some sort of noise downstairs, and finally all sorts of a racket and groans and yells, and they just naturally came down to see what it was.

"Then they saw the ghost. It was in the reception-hall, some of 'em said, others said it was in the library, but anyhow it was there, and the whole gang left just as fast as they knew how. They slept on the ground that night. Next day they took out their things and went back to Boston. Since then nobody here has heard from 'em."

"What sort of a ghost was it?"

"Oh, it was a man ghost, about nine feet high, and he was blazing from head to foot as if he was burning up," said the constable. "He had a long knife in his hand and waved it at 'em. They didn't stop to argue. They ran, and as they ran they heard the ghost a-laughing at them."

"I should think he would have been amused," was Hatch's somewhat sarcastic comment. "Has anybody who lives in the village seen the ghost?"

"No; we're willing to take their word for it, I suppose," was the grinning reply, "because there never was a ghost there before. I go up and look over the place every afternoon, but everything seems to be all right, and I haven't gone there at night. It's quite a way off my beat," he hastened to explain.

"A man ghost with a long knife," mused Hatch. "Blazing, seems to be burning up, eh? That sounds exciting. Now, a ghost who knows his business never appears except where there has been a murder. Was there ever a murder in that house?"

"When I was a little chap I heard there was a murder or something there, but I suppose if I don't remember it nobody else here does," was the old man's reply. "It happened one Winter when the Westons weren't there. There was something, too, about jewelry and diamonds, but I don't remember just what it was."

"Indeed?" asked the reporter.

"Yes, something about somebody trying to steal a lot of jewelry—a hundred thousand dollars' worth. I know nobody ever paid much attention to it. I just heard about it when I was a boy, and that was at least fifty years ago."

"I see," said the reporter.

* * *

That night at nine o'clock, under cover of perfect blackness, Hatch climbed the cliff toward the Weston house. At one o'clock he came racing down the hill, with frequent glances over his shoulder. His face was pallid with a fear which he had never known before and his lips were ashen. Once in his room in the village hotel Hutchinson Hatch, the nerveless young man, lighted a lamp with trembling hands and sat with wide, staring eyes until the dawn broke through the east.

He had seen the flaming phantom.

II

It was ten o'clock that morning when Hutchinson Hatch called on Professor Augustus S. F. X. Van Dusen—The Thinking Machine. The reporter's face was still white, showing that he had slept little, if at all. The Thinking Machine squinted at him a moment through his thick glasses, then dropped into a chair.

"Well?" he queried.

"I'm almost ashamed to come to you, Professor," Hatch confessed, after a minute, and there was a little embarrassed hesitation in his speech. "It's another mystery."

"Sit down and tell me about it."

Hatch took a seat opposite the scientist.

"I've been frightened," he said at last, with a sheepish grin; "horribly, awfully frightened. I came to you to know what frightened me."

"Dear me! Dear me!" exclaimed The Thinking Machine. "What is it?"

Then Hatch told him from the beginning the story of the haunted house as he knew it; how he had examined the house by daylight, just what he had found, the story of the old murder and the jewels, the fact that Ernest Weston was to be married. The scientist listened attentively.

"It was nine o'clock that night when I went to the house the second time," said Hatch. "I went prepared for something; but not for what I saw."

"Well, go on," said the other, irritably.

"I went in while it was perfectly dark. I took a position on the stairs because I had been told the—the THING—had been seen from the stairs, and I thought that where it had been seen once it would be seen again. I had presumed it was some trick of a shadow, or moonlight, or something of the kind. So I sat waiting calmly. I am not a nervous man—that is, I never have been until now.

"I took no light of any kind with me. It seemed an interminable time that I waited, staring into the reception-room in the general direction of the library. At last, as I gazed into the darkness, I heard a noise. It startled me a bit, but it didn't frighten me, for I put it down to a rat running across the floor.

"But after awhile I heard the most awful cry a human being ever listened to. It was neither a moan nor a shriek—merely a—a cry. Then, as I steadied my nerves a little, a figure—a blazing, burning white figure—grew out of nothingness before my very eyes, in the reception-room. It actually grew and assembled as I looked at it."

He paused, and The Thinking Machine changed his position slightly.

"The figure was that of a man, apparently, I should say, eight feet high. Don't think I'm a fool—I'm not exaggerating. It was all in white and seemed to radiate a light, a ghostly, unearthly light, which, as I looked, grew brighter. I saw no face to the THING, but it had a head. Then I saw an arm raised and in the hand was a dagger, blazing as was the figure.

"By this time I was a coward, a cringing, frightened coward—frightened not at what I saw, but at the weirdness of it. And then, still as I looked, the—the THING—raised the other hand, and there, in the air before my eyes, wrote with his own finger—*on the very face of the air*, mind you—one word: 'Beware!'"

"Was it a man's or woman's writing?" asked The Thinking Machine.

The matter-of-fact tone recalled Hatch, who was again being carried away by fear, and he laughed vacantly.

"I don't know," he said. "I don't know."

"Go on."

"I have never considered myself a coward, and certainly I am not a child to be frightened at a thing which my reason tells me is not possible, and, despite my fright, I compelled myself to action. If the THING were a man I was not afraid of it, dagger and all; if it were not, it could do me no injury.

"I leaped down the three steps to the bottom of the stairs, and while the THING stood there with upraised dagger, with one hand pointing at me, I rushed for it. I think I must have shouted, because I have a dim idea that I heard my own voice. But whether or not I did I———"

Again he paused. It was a distinct effort to pull himself together. He felt like a child; the cold, squint eyes of The Thinking Machine were turned on him disapprovingly.

"Then—the THING disappeared just as it seemed I had my hands on it. I was expecting a dagger thrust. Before my eyes, while I was staring at it, I suddenly saw *only half of it*. Again I heard the cry, and the other half disappeared—my hands grasped empty air.

"Where the THING had been there was nothing. The impetus of my rush was such that I went right on past the spot where the THING had been, and found myself groping in the dark in a room which I didn't place for an instant. Now I know it was the library.

"By this time I was mad with terror. I smashed one of the windows and went through it. Then from there, until I reached my room, I didn't stop running. I couldn't. I wouldn't have gone back to the reception-room for all the millions in the world."

The Thinking Machine twiddled his fingers idly; Hatch sat gazing at him with anxious, eager inquiry in his eyes.

"So when you ran and the—the THING moved away or disappeared you found yourself in the library?" The Thinking Machine asked at last.

"Yes."

"Therefore you must have run from the reception-room through the door into the library?"

"Yes."

"You left that door closed that day?"

"Yes."

Again there was a pause.

"Smell anything?" asked The Thinking Machine.

"No."

"You figure that the THING, as you call it, must have been just about in the door?"

"Yes."

"Too bad you didn't notice the handwriting—that is, whether it seemed to be a man's or a woman's."

"I think, under the circumstances, I would be excused for omitting that," was the reply.

"You said you heard something that you thought must be a rat," went on The Thinking Machine. "What was this?"

"I don't know."

"Any squeak about it?"

"No, not that I noticed."

"Five years since the house was occupied," mused the scientist. "How far away is the water?"

"The place overlooks the water, but it's a steep climb of three hundred yards from the water to the house."

That seemed to satisfy The Thinking Machine as to what actually happened.

"When you went over the house in daylight, did you notice if any of the mirrors were dusty?" he asked.

"I should presume that all were," was the reply. "There's no reason why they should have been otherwise."

"But you didn't notice particularly that some were not dusty?" the scientist insisted.

"No. I merely noticed that they were there."

The Thinking Machine sat for a long time squinting at the ceiling, then asked, abruptly:

"Have you seen Mr. Weston, the owner?"

"No."

"See him and find out what he has to say about the place, the murder, the jewels, and all that. It would be rather a queer state of affairs if, say, a fortune in jewels should be concealed somewhere about the place, wouldn't it?"

"It would," said Hatch. "It would."

"Who is Miss Katherine Everard?"

"Daughter of a banker here, Curtis Everard. Was a reigning belle at Newport for two seasons. She is now in Europe, I think, buying a trousseau, possibly."

"Find out all about her, and what Weston has to say, then come back here," said The Thinking Machine, as if in conclusion. "Oh, by the way," he added, "look up something of the family history of the Westons. How many heirs were there? Who are they? How much did each one get? All those things. That's all."

Hatch went out, far more composed and quiet than when he entered, and began the work of finding out those things The Thinking Machine had asked for, confident now that there would be a solution of the mystery.

That night the flaming phantom played new pranks. The town constable, backed by half a dozen villagers, descended upon the place at midnight, to be met in the yard by the apparition in person. Again the dagger was seen; again the ghostly laughter and the awful cry were heard.

"Surrender or I'll shoot," shouted the constable, nervously.

A laugh was the answer, and the constable felt something warm spatter in his face. Others in the party felt it, too, and wiped their faces and hands. By the light of the feeble lanterns they carried they examined their handkerchiefs and hands. Then the party fled in awful disorder.

The warmth they had felt was the warmth of blood—red blood, freshly drawn.

III

Hatch found Ernest Weston at luncheon with another gentleman at one o'clock that day. This other gentleman was introduced to Hatch as George Weston, a cousin. Hatch instantly remembered George Weston for certain eccentric exploits at Newport a season or so before; and also as one of the heirs of the original Weston estate.

Hatch thought he remembered, too, that at the time Miss Everard had been so prominent socially at Newport George Weston had been her most ardent suitor. It was rumored that there would have been an engagement between them, but her father objected. Hatch looked at him curiously; his face was clearly a dissipated one, yet there was about him the unmistakable polish and gentility of the well-bred man of society.

Hatch knew Ernest Weston as Weston knew Hatch; they had met frequently in the ten years Hatch had been a newspaper reporter, and Weston had been courteous to him always. The reporter was in doubt as to whether to bring up the subject on which he had sought out Ernest Weston, but the broker brought it up himself, smilingly.

"Well, what is it this time?" he asked, genially. "The ghost down on the South Shore, or my forthcoming marriage?"

"Both," replied Hatch.

Weston talked freely of his engagement to Miss Everard, which he said was to have been announced in another week, at which time she was due to return to America from Europe. The marriage was to be three or four months later, the exact date had not been set.

"And I suppose the country place was being put in order as a Summer residence?" the reporter asked.

"Yes. I had intended to make some repairs and changes there, and furnish it, but now I understand that a ghost has taken a hand in the matter and has delayed it. Have you heard much about this ghost story?" he asked, and there was a slight smile on his face.

"I have seen the ghost," Hatch answered.

"You have?" demanded the broker.

George Weston echoed the words and leaned forward, with a new interest in his eyes, to listen. Hatch told them what had happened in the haunted house—all of it. They listened with the keenest interest, one as eager as the other.

"By George!" exclaimed the broker, when Hatch had finished. "How do you account for it?"

"I don't," said Hatch, flatly. "I can offer no possible solution.

I am not a child to be tricked by the ordinary illusion, nor am I of the temperament which imagines things, but I can offer no explanation of this."

"It must be a trick of some sort," said George Weston.

"I was positive of that," said Hatch, "but if it is a trick, it is the cleverest I ever saw."

The conversation drifted on to the old story of missing jewels and a tragedy in the house fifty years before. Now Hatch was asking questions by direction of The Thinking Machine; he himself hardly saw their purport, but he asked them.

"Well, the full story of that affair, the tragedy there, would open up an old chapter in our family which is nothing to be ashamed of, of course," said the broker, frankly; "still it is something we have not paid much attention to for many years. Perhaps George here knows it better than I do. His mother, then a bride, heard the recital of the story from my grandmother."

Ernest Weston and Hatch looked inquiringly at George Weston, who lighted a fresh cigarette and leaned over the table toward them. He was an excellent talker.

"I've heard my mother tell of it, but it was a long time ago," he began. "It seems, though, as I remember it, that my great-grandfather, who built the house, was a wealthy man, as fortunes went in those days, worth probably a million dollars.*

"A part of this fortune, say about one hundred thousand

---

* The jewelry-stasher is confusingly referred to as both Weston's grandfather and his great-grandfather. For our purposes, let us assume that he did mean great-grandfather, a man three generations older than himself. We may therefore assume an age difference of between seventy and ninety years. Weston himself is a youngish man, probably in his mid-thirties. If the events of the story took place in the year 1907 or so, we may assume that the great-grandfather amassed his fortune more than one hundred years earlier. According to Measuring Worth, $1 million in 1807 would be the equivalent of a modern fortune of nearly $25 million—worth a search. Samuel H. Williamson, "Seven Ways to Compute the Relative Value of a US Dollar Amount, 1790 to Present," Measuring Worth, 2022, https://www.measuringworth.com/.

dollars, was in jewels, which had come with the family from England. Many of those pieces would be of far greater value now than they were then, because of their antiquity. It was only on state occasions, I might say, when these were worn, say, once a year.

"Between times the problem of keeping them safely was a difficult one, it appeared. This was before the time of safety deposit vaults. My grandfather conceived the idea of hiding the jewels in the old place down on the South Shore, instead of keeping them in the house he had in Boston. He took them there accordingly.

"At this time one was compelled to travel down the South Shore, below Cohasset anyway, by stagecoach. My grandfather's family was then in the city, as it was Winter, so he made the trip alone. He planned to reach there at night, so as not to attract attention to himself, to hide the jewels about the house, and leave that same night for Boston again by a relay of horses he had arranged for. Just what happened after he left the stagecoach, below Cohasset, no one ever knew except by surmise."

The speaker paused a moment and relighted his cigarette.

"Next morning my great-grandfather was found unconscious and badly injured on the veranda of the house. His skull had been fractured. In the house a man was found dead. No one knew who he was; no one within a radius of many miles of the place had ever seen him.

"This led to all sorts of surmises, the most reasonable of which, and the one which the family has always accepted, being that my grandfather had gone to the house in the dark, had there met some one who was stopping there that night as a shelter from the intense cold, that this man learned of the jewels, that he had tried robbery and there was a fight.

"In this fight the stranger was killed inside the house, and my great-grandfather, injured, had tried to leave the house for aid. He collapsed on the veranda where he was found and died without having regained consciousness. That's all we know or can surmise reasonably about the matter."

"Were the jewels ever found?" asked the reporter.

"No. They were not on the dead man, nor were they in the possession of my grandfather."

"It is reasonable to suppose, then, that there was a third man and that he got away with the jewels?" asked Ernest Weston.

"It seemed so, and for a long time this theory was accepted. I suppose it is now, but some doubt was cast on it by the fact that only two trails of footsteps led to the house and none out. There was a heavy snow on the ground. If none led out it was obviously impossible that anyone came out."

Again there was silence. Ernest Weston sipped his coffee slowly.

"It would seem from that," said Ernest Weston, at last, "that the jewels were hidden before the tragedy, and have never been found."

George Weston smiled.

"Off and on for twenty years the place was searched, according to my mother's story," he said. "Every inch of the cellar was dug up; every possible nook and corner was searched. Finally the entire matter passed out of the minds of those who knew of it, and I doubt if it has ever been referred to again until now."

"A search even now would be almost worth while, wouldn't it?" asked the broker.

George Weston laughed aloud.

"It might be," he said, "but I have some doubt. A thing that was searched for for twenty years would not be easily found."

So it seemed to strike the others after awhile and the matter was dropped.

"But this ghost thing," said the broker, at last. "I'm interested in that. Suppose we make up a ghost party and go down to-night. My contractor declares he can't get men to work there."

"I would be glad to go," said George Weston, "but I'm running over to the Vandergrift ball in Providence to-night."

"How about you, Hatch?" asked the broker.

"I'll go, yes," said Hatch, "as one of several," he added with a smile.

"Well, then, suppose we say the constable and you and I?" asked the broker; "to-night?"

"All right."

After making arrangements to meet the broker later that afternoon he rushed away—away to The Thinking Machine. The scientist listened, then resumed some chemical test he was making.

"Can't you go down with us to-night?" Hatch asked.

"No," said the other. "I'm going to read a paper before a scientific society and prove that a chemist in Chicago is a fool. That will take me all evening."

"To-morrow night?" Hatch insisted.

"No—the next night."

This would be on Friday night—just in time for the feature which had been planned for Sunday. Hatch was compelled to rest content with this, but he foresaw that he would have it all, with a solution. It never occurred to him that this problem, or, indeed, that any problem, was beyond the mental capacity of Professor Van Dusen.

Hatch and Ernest Weston took a night train that evening, and on their arrival in the village stirred up the town constable.

"Will you go with us?" was the question.

"Both of you going?" was the counter-question.

"Yes."

"I'll go," said the constable promptly. "Ghost!" and he laughed scornfully. "I'll have him in the lockup by morning."

"No shooting, now," warned Weston. "There must be somebody back of this somewhere; we understand that, but there is no crime that we know of. The worst is possibly trespassing."

"I'll get him all right," responded the constable, who still remembered the experience where blood—warm blood—had been thrown in his face. "And I'm not so sure there isn't a crime."

That night about ten the three men went into the dark, forbidding house and took a station on the stairs where Hatch had sat when he saw the THING—whatever it was. There they waited. The constable moved nervously from time to time, but neither of the others paid any attention to him.

At last the—the THING appeared. There had been a preliminary sound as of something running across the floor, then suddenly a flaming figure of white seemed to grow into being in the reception-room. It was exactly as Hatch had described it to The Thinking Machine.

Dazed, stupefied, the three men looked, looked as the figure raised a hand, pointing toward them, and wrote a word in the air—positively in the air. The finger merely waved, and there, floating before them, were letters, flaming letters, in the utter darkness. This time the word was: "Death."

Faintly, Hatch, fighting with a fear which again seized him, remembered that The Thinking Machine had asked him if the handwriting was that of a man or woman; now he tried to see. It was as if drawn on a blackboard, and there was a queer twist to the loop at the bottom. He sniffed to see if there was an odor of any sort. There was not.

Suddenly he felt some quick, vigorous action from the constable behind him. There was a roar and a flash in his ear; he knew the constable had fired at the THING. Then came the cry and laugh—almost a laugh of derision—he had heard them before. For one instant the figure lingered and then, before their eyes, faded again into utter blackness. Where it had been was nothing—nothing.

The constable's shot had had no effect.

IV

Three deeply mystified men passed down the hill to the village from the old house. Ernest Weston, the owner, had not spoken since before the—the THING appeared there in the reception-room, or was it in the library? He was not certain—he couldn't have told. Suddenly he turned to the constable.

"I told you not to shoot."

"That's all right," said the constable. "I was there in my official capacity, and I shoot when I want to."

"But the shot did no harm," Hatch put in.

"I would swear it went right through it, too," said the constable, boastfully. "I can shoot."

Weston was arguing with himself. He was a cold-blooded man of business; his mind was not one to play him tricks. Yet now he felt benumbed; he could conceive no explanation of what he had seen. Again in his room in the little hotel, where they spent the remainder of the night, he stared blankly at the reporter.

"Can you imagine any way it could be done?"

Hatch shook his head.

"It isn't a spook, of course," the broker went on, with a nervous smile; "but—but I'm sorry I went. I don't think probably I shall have the work done there as I thought."

They slept only fitfully and took an early train back to Boston. As they were about to separate at the South Station, the broker had a last word.

"I'm going to solve that thing," he declared, determinedly. "I know one man at least who isn't afraid of it—or of anything else. I'm going to send him down to keep a lookout and take care of the place. His name is O'Heagan, and he's a fighting Irishman. If he and that—that—THING ever get mixed up together————"

Like a schoolboy with a hopeless problem, Hatch went straight to The Thinking Machine with the latest developments. The scientist paused just long enough in his work to hear it.

"Did you notice the handwriting?" he demanded.

"Yes," was the reply; "so far as I *could* notice the style of a handwriting that floated in air."

"Man's or woman's?"

Hatch was puzzled.

"I couldn't judge," he said. "It seemed to be a bold style, whatever it was. I remember the capital D clearly."

"Was it anything like the handwriting of the broker—what's-his-name?—Ernest Weston?"

"I never saw his handwriting."

"Look at some of it, then, particularly the capital D's," instructed The Thinking Machine. Then, after a pause: "You say the figure is white and seems to be flaming?"

"Yes."

"Does it give out any light? That is, does it light up a room, for instance?"

"I don't quite know what you mean."

"When you go into a room with a lamp," explained The Thinking Machine, "it lights the room. Does this thing do it? Can you see the floor or walls or anything by the light of the figure itself?"

"No," replied Hatch, positively.

"I'll go down with you to-morrow night," said the scientist, as if that were all.

"Thanks," replied Hatch, and he went away.

Next day about noon he called at Ernest Weston's office. The broker was in.

"Did you send down your man O'Heagan?" he asked.

"Yes," said the broker, and he was almost smiling.

"What happened?"

"He's outside. I'll let him tell you."

The broker went to the door and spoke to some one and O'Heagan entered. He was a big, blue-eyed Irishman, frankly freckled and red-headed—one of those men who look trouble in the face and are glad of it if the trouble can be reduced to a fighting basis. An everlasting smile was about his lips, only now it was a bit faded.

"Tell Mr. Hatch what happened last night," requested the broker.

O'Heagan told it. He, too, had sought to get hold of the flaming figure. As he ran for it, it disappeared, was obliterated, wiped out, gone, and he found himself groping in the darkness of the room beyond, the library. Like Hatch, he took the nearest way out, which happened to be through a window already smashed.

"Outside," he went on, "I began to think about it, and I saw there was nothing to be afraid of, but you couldn't have convinced me of that when I was inside. I took a lantern in one hand and a revolver in the other and went all over that house. There was nothing; if there had been we would have had it out right there. But there was nothing. So I started out to the barn, where I had put a cot in a room.

"I went upstairs to this room—it was then about two o'clock—and went to sleep. It seemed to be an hour or so later when I awoke suddenly—I knew something was happening. And the Lord forgive me if I'm a liar, but there was a cat—a ghost cat in my room, racing around like mad. I just naturally got up to see what was the matter and rushed for the door. The cat beat me to it, and cut a flaming streak through the night.

"The cat looked just like the thing inside the house—that is, it was a sort of shadowy, waving white light like it might be afire. I went back to bed in disgust, to sleep it off. You see, sir," he apologized to Weston, "that there hadn't been anything yet I could put my hands on."

"Was that all?" asked Hatch, smilingly.

"Just the beginning. Next morning when I awoke I was bound to my cot, hard and fast. My hands were tied and my feet were tied, and all I could do was lie there and yell. After awhile, it seemed years, I heard some one outside and shouted louder than ever. Then the constable come up and let me loose. I told him all about it—and then I came to Boston. And with your permission, Mr. Weston, I resign right now. I'm not afraid of anything I can fight, but when I can't get hold of it—well———"

Later Hatch joined The Thinking Machine. They caught a train for the little village by the sea. On the way The Thinking Machine asked a few questions, but most of the time he was silent, squinting out the window. Hatch respected his silence, and only answered questions.

"Did you see Ernest Weston's handwriting?" was the first of these.

"Yes."

"The capital D's?"

"They are not unlike the one the—the THING wrote, but they are not wholly like it," was the reply.

"Do you know anyone in Providence who can get some information for you?" was the next query.

"Yes."

"Get him by long-distance 'phone when we get to this place and let me talk to him a moment."

Half an hour later The Thinking Machine was talking over the long-distance 'phone to the Providence correspondent of Hatch's paper. What he said or what he learned there was not revealed to the wondering reporter, but he came out after several minutes, only to re-enter the booth and remain for another half an hour.

"Now," he said.

Together they went to the haunted house. At the entrance to the grounds something else occurred to The Thinking Machine.

"Run over to the 'phone and call Weston," he directed. "Ask him if he has a motor-boat or if his cousin has one. We might need one. Also find out what kind of a boat it is—electric or gasoline."

Hatch returned to the village and left the scientist alone, sitting on the veranda gazing out over the sea. When Hatch returned he was still in the same position.

"Well?" he asked.

"Ernest Weston has no motor-boat," the reporter informed him. "George Weston has an electric, but we can't get it because it is away. Maybe I can get one somewhere else if you particularly want it."

"Never mind," said The Thinking Machine. He spoke as if he had entirely lost interest in the matter.

Together they started around the house to the kitchen door.

"What's the next move?" asked Hatch.

"I'm going to find the jewels," was the startling reply.

"Find them?" Hatch repeated.

"Certainly."

They entered the house through the kitchen and the scientist squinted this way and that, through the reception-room, the library, and finally the back hallway. Here a closed door in the flooring led to a cellar.

In the cellar they found heaps of litter. It was damp and chilly and dark. The Thinking Machine stood in the center, or as near the center as he could stand, because the base of the chimney occupied this precise spot, and apparently did some mental calculation.

From that point he started around the walls, solidly built of stone, stooping and running his fingers along the stones as he walked. He made the entire circuit as Hatch looked on. Then he made it again, but this time with his hands raised above his head, feeling the walls carefully as he went. He repeated this at the chimney, going carefully around the masonry, high and low.

"Dear me, dear me!" he exclaimed, petulantly. "You are taller than I am, Mr. Hatch. Please feel carefully around the top of this chimney base and see if the rocks are all solidly set."

Hatch then began a tour. At last one of the great stones which made this base trembled under his hand.

"It's loose," he said.

"Take it out."

It came out after a deal of tugging.

"Put your hand in there and pull out what you find," was the next order. Hatch obeyed. He found a wooden box, about eight inches square, and handed it to The Thinking Machine.

"Ah!" exclaimed that gentleman.

A quick wrench caused the decaying wood to crumble. Tumbling out of the box were the jewels which had been lost for fifty years.

V

Excitement, long restrained, burst from Hatch in a laugh—almost hysterical. He stooped and gathered up the fallen jewelry and handed it to The Thinking Machine, who stared at him in mild surprise.

"What's the matter?" inquired the scientist.

"Nothing," Hatch assured him, but again he laughed.

The heavy stone which had been pulled out of place was lifted up and forced back into position, and together they returned to the village, with the long-lost jewelry loose in their pockets.

"How did you do it?" asked Hatch.

"Two and two always make four," was the enigmatic reply. "It was merely a sum in addition." There was a pause as they walked on, then: "Don't say anything about finding this, or even hint at it in any way, until you have my permission to do so."

Hatch had no intention of doing so. In his mind's eye he saw a story, a great, vivid, startling story spread all over his newspaper about flaming phantoms and treasure trove—$100,000 in jewels. It staggered him. Of course he would say nothing about it—even hint at it, yet. But when he did say something about it———!

In the village The Thinking Machine found the constable.

"I understand some blood was thrown on you at the Weston place the other night?"

"Yes. Blood—warm blood."

"You wiped it off with your handkerchief?"

"Yes."

"Have you the handkerchief?"

"I suppose I might get it," was the doubtful reply. "It might have gone into the wash."

"Astute person," remarked The Thinking Machine. "There might have been a crime and you throw away the one thing which would indicate it—the bloodstains."

The constable suddenly took notice.

"By ginger!" he said. "Wait here and I'll go see if I can find it."

He disappeared and returned shortly with the handkerchief. There were half a dozen bloodstains on it, now dark brown.

The Thinking Machine dropped into the village drug store and had a short conversation with the owner, after which he disappeared into the compounding room at the back and remained for an hour or more—until darkness set in. Then he came out and joined Hatch, who, with the constable, had been waiting.

The reporter did not ask any questions, and The Thinking Machine volunteered no information.

"Is it too late for anyone to get down from Boston to-night?" he asked the constable.

"No. He could take the eight o'clock train and be here about half-past nine."

"Mr. Hatch, will you wire to Mr. Weston—Ernest Weston— and ask him to come to-night, sure. Impress on him the fact that it is a matter of the greatest importance."

Instead of telegraphing, Hatch went to the telephone and spoke to Weston at his club. The trip would interfere with some other plans, the broker explained, but he would come. The Thinking Machine had meanwhile been conversing with the constable and had given some sort of instructions which evidently amazed that official exceedingly, for he kept repeating "By ginger!" with considerable fervor.

"And not one word or hint of it to anyone," said The Thinking Machine. "Least of all to the members of your family."

"By ginger!" was the response, and the constable went to supper.

The Thinking Machine and Hatch had their supper thoughtfully that evening in the little village "hotel." Only once did Hatch break this silence.

"You told me to see Weston's handwriting," he said. "Of course you knew he was with the constable and myself when we saw the THING, therefore it would have been impossible————"

"Nothing is impossible," broke in The Thinking Machine. "Don't say that, please."

"I mean that, as he was with us————"

"We'll end the ghost story to-night," interrupted the scientist.

Ernest Weston arrived on the nine-thirty train and had a long, earnest conversation with The Thinking Machine, while Hatch was permitted to cool his toes in solitude. At last they joined the reporter.

"Take a revolver by all means," instructed The Thinking Machine.

"Do you think that necessary?" asked Weston.

"It is—absolutely," was the emphatic response.

Weston left them after awhile. Hatch wondered where he had gone, but no information was forthcoming. In a general sort of way he knew that The Thinking Machine was to go to the haunted house, but he didn't know when; he didn't even know if he was to accompany him.

At last they started, The Thinking Machine swinging a hammer he had borrowed from his landlord. The night was perfectly black, even the road at their feet was invisible. They stumbled frequently as they walked on up the cliff toward the house, dimly standing out against the sky. They entered by way of the kitchen, passed through to the stairs in the main hall, and there Hatch indicated in the darkness the spot from which he had twice seen the flaming phantom.

"You go in the drawing-room behind here," The Thinking Machine instructed. "Don't make any noise whatever."

For hours they waited, neither seeing the other. Hatch heard his heart thumping heavily; if only he could see the other man; with an effort he recovered from a rapidly growing nervousness and waited, waited. The Thinking Machine sat perfectly rigid on the stair, the hammer in his right hand, squinting steadily through the darkness.

At last he heard a noise, a slight nothing; it might almost have been his imagination. It was as if something had glided across the floor, and he was more alert than ever. Then came the dread misty light in the reception-hall, or was it in the library? He could not say. But he looked, looked, with every sense alert.

Gradually the light grew and spread, a misty whiteness which was unmistakably light, but which did not illuminate anything around it. The Thinking Machine saw it without the tremor of a nerve; saw the mistiness grow more marked in certain places, saw these lines gradually grow into the figure of a person, a person who was the center of a white light.

Then the mistiness fell away and The Thinking Machine saw the outline in bold relief. It was that of a tall figure, clothed in a robe, with head covered by a sort of hood, also luminous. As The Thinking Machine looked he saw an arm raised, and in the hand he saw a dagger. The attitude of the figure was distinctly a threat. And yet The Thinking Machine had not begun to grow nervous; he was only interested.

As he looked, the other hand of the apparition was raised and seemed to point directly at him. It moved through the air in bold sweeps, and The Thinking Machine saw the word "Death," written in air luminously, swimming before his eyes. Then he blinked incredulously. There came a wild, demoniacal shriek of laughter from somewhere. Slowly, slowly the scientist crept down the steps in his stocking feet, silent as the apparition itself, with the hammer still in his hand. He crept on, on toward the figure.

Hatch, not knowing the movements of The Thinking Machine, stood waiting for something, he didn't know what. Then the thing he had been waiting for happened. There was a sudden loud clatter as of broken glass, the phantom and writing faded, crumbled up, disappeared, and somewhere in the old house there was the hurried sound of steps. At last the reporter heard his name called quietly. It was The Thinking Machine.

"Mr. Hatch, come here."

The reporter started, blundering through the darkness toward the point whence the voice had come. Some irresistible thing swept down upon him; a crashing blow descended on his head, vivid lights flashed before his eyes; he fell. After awhile, from a great distance, it seemed, he heard faintly a pistol shot.

VI

When Hatch fully recovered consciousness it was with the flickering light of a match in his eyes—a match in the hand of The Thinking Machine, who squinted anxiously at him as he grasped his left wrist. Hatch, instantly himself again, sat up suddenly.

"What's the matter?" he demanded.

"How's your head?" came the answering question.

"Oh," and Hatch suddenly recalled those incidents which had immediately preceded the crash on his head. "Oh, it's all right, my head, I mean. What happened?"

"Get up and come along," requested The Thinking Machine, tartly. "There's a man shot down here."

Hatch arose and followed the slight figure of the scientist through the front door, and toward the water. A light glimmered down near the water and was dimly reflected; above, the clouds had cleared somewhat and the moon was struggling through.

"What hit me, anyhow?" Hatch demanded, as they went. He rubbed his head ruefully.

"The ghost," said the scientist. "I think probably he has a bullet in him now—the ghost."

Then the figure of the town constable separated itself from the night and approached.

"Who's that?"

"Professor Van Dusen and Mr. Hatch."

"Mr. Weston got him all right," said the constable, and there was satisfaction in his tone. "He tried to come out the back way, but I had that fastened, as you told me, and he came through the front way. Mr. Weston tried to stop him, and he raised the knife to stick him; then Mr. Weston shot. It broke his arm, I think. Mr. Weston is down there with him now."

The Thinking Machine turned to the reporter.

"Wait here for me, with the constable," he directed. "If the man is hurt he needs attention. I happen to be a doctor; I can aid him. Don't come unless I call."

For a long while the constable and the reporter waited. The constable talked, talked with all the bottled-up vigor of days. Hatch listened impatiently; he was eager to go down there where The Thinking Machine and Weston and the phantom were.

After half an hour the light disappeared, then he heard the swift, quick churning of waters, a sound as of a powerful motorboat maneuvering, and a long body shot out on the waters.

"All right down there?" Hatch called.

"All right," came the response.

There was again silence, then Ernest Weston and The Thinking Machine came up.

"Where is the other man?" asked Hatch.

"The ghost—where is he?" echoed the constable.

"He escaped in the motor-boat," replied Mr. Weston, easily.

"Escaped?" exclaimed Hatch and the constable together.

"Yes, escaped," repeated The Thinking Machine, irritably. "Mr. Hatch, let's go to the hotel."

Struggling with a sense of keen disappointment, Hatch followed the other two men silently. The constable walked beside him, also silent. At last they reached the hotel and bade the constable, a sadly puzzled, bewildered and crestfallen man, good-night.

"By ginger!" he remarked, as he walked away into the dark.

Upstairs the three men sat, Hatch impatiently waiting to hear the story. Weston lighted a cigarette and lounged back; The Thinking Machine sat with finger tips pressed together, studying the ceiling.

"Mr. Weston, you understand, of course, that I came into this thing to aid Mr. Hatch?" he asked.

"Certainly," was the response. "I will only ask a favor of him when you conclude."

The Thinking Machine changed his position slightly, re-adjusted his thick glasses for a long, comfortable squint, and told the story, from the beginning, as he always told a story. Here it is:

"Mr. Hatch came to me in a state of abject, cringing fear and told me of the mystery. It would be needless to go over his examination of the house, and all that. It is enough to say that he noted and told me of four large mirrors in the dining-room and living-room of the house; that he heard and brought to me the stories in detail of a tragedy in the old house and missing jewels, valued at a hundred thousand dollars, or more.

"He told me of his trip to the house that night, and of actually seeing the phantom. I have found in the past that Mr. Hatch is a cool, level-headed young man, not given to imagining things which are not there, and controls himself well. Therefore I knew that anything of charlatanism must be clever, exceedingly clever, to bring about such a condition of mind in him.

"Mr. Hatch saw, as others had seen, the figure of a phantom in the reception-room near the door of the library, or in the library near the door of the reception-room, he couldn't tell exactly. He knew it was near the door. Preceding the appearance of the figure he heard a slight noise which he attributed to a rat running across the floor. Yet the house had not been occupied for five years. Rodents rarely remain in a house—I may say never—for that long if it is uninhabited. Therefore what was this noise? A noise made by the apparition itself? How?

"Now, there is only one white light of the kind Mr. Hatch described known to science. It seems almost superfluous to name it. It is phosphorus, compounded with Fuller's earth and glycerine and one or two other chemicals, so it will not instantly flame as it does in the pure state when exposed to air.* Phosphorus has a very pronounced odor if one is within, say, twenty feet of it. Did Mr. Hatch smell anything? No.

"Now, here we have several facts, these being that the apparition in appearing made a slight noise; that phosphorus was the luminous quality; that Mr. Hatch did not smell phosphorus even when he ran through the spot where the phantom had appeared. Two and two make four; Mr. Hatch saw phosphorus, passed through the spot where he had seen it, but did not smell it, therefore it was not there. It was a reflection he saw—a reflection of phosphorus. So far, so good.

"Mr. Hatch saw a finger lifted and write a luminous word in the air. Again he did not actually see this; he saw a reflection of it. This first impression of mine was substantiated by the fact that when he rushed for the phantom *a part of it* disappeared,

---

* Phosphorus produces a white, glowing light through chemiluminescence, not burning, when exposed to oxygen, but the reaction can cause severe burns. Sherlock Holmes, in *The Hound of the Baskervilles* (London: George Newnes, 1902), remarked on the villain's use of a "cunning preparation" of phosphorus on the glowing canine that haunted the moors, noting that it had no scent and of course did not burn the dog (323). Fuller's earth is a generic name for any absorbent clay or mineral, used in various processes to decolorize oil or other liquids. Glycerin or glycerol is a simple compound in the form of a colorless, odorless, viscous liquid.

first half of it, he said—then the other half. So his extended hands grasped only air.

"Obviously those reflections had been made on something, probably a mirror as the most perfect ordinary reflecting surface. Yet he actually passed through the spot where he had seen the apparition and had not struck a mirror. He found himself in another room, the library, having gone through a door which, that afternoon, he had himself closed. He did not open it then.

"Instantly a sliding mirror suggested itself to me to fit all these conditions. He saw the apparition in the door, then saw only half of it, then all of it disappeared. He passed through the spot where it had been. All of this would have happened easily if a large mirror, working as a sliding door, and hidden in the wall, were there. Is it clear?"

"Perfectly," said Mr. Weston.

"Yes," said Hatch, eagerly. "Go on."

"This sliding mirror, too, might have made the noise which Mr. Hatch imagined was a rat. Mr. Hatch had previously told me of four large mirrors in the living- and dining-rooms. With these, from the position in which he said they were, I readily saw how the reflection could have been made.

"In a general sort of way, in my own mind, I had accounted for the phantom. Why was it there? This seemed a more difficult problem. It was possible that it had been put there for amusement, but I did not wholly accept this. Why? Partly because no one had ever heard of it until the Italian workmen went there. Why did it appear just at the moment they went to begin the work Mr. Weston had ordered? Was it the purpose to keep the workmen away?

"These questions arose in my mind in order. Then, as Mr. Hatch had told me of a tragedy in the house and hidden jewels, I asked him to learn more of these. I called his attention to the fact that it would be a queer circumstance if these jewels were still somewhere in the old house. Suppose some one who knew of their existence were searching for them, believed he could find them, and wanted something which would effectually drive away any inquiring persons, tramps or villagers, who might appear there at night. A ghost? Perhaps.

"Suppose some one wanted to give the old house such a reputation that Mr. Weston would not care to undertake the work of repair and refurnishing. A ghost? Again perhaps. In a shallow mind this ghost might have been interpreted even as an effort to prevent the marriage of Miss Everard and Mr. Weston. Therefore Mr. Hatch was instructed to get all the facts possible about you, Mr. Weston, and members of your family. I reasoned that members of your own family would be more likely to know of the lost jewels than anyone else after a lapse of fifty years.

"Well, what Mr. Hatch learned from you and your cousin, George Weston, instantly, in my mind, established a motive for the ghost. It was, as I had supposed possible, an effort to drive workmen away, perhaps only for a time, while a search was made for the jewels. The old tragedy in the house was a good pretext to hang a ghost on. A clever mind conceived it and a clever mind put it into operation.

"Now, what one person knew most about the jewels? Your cousin George, Mr. Weston. Had he recently acquired any new information as to these jewels? I didn't know. I thought it possible. Why? On his own statement that his mother, then a bride, got the story of the entire affair direct from his grandmother, who remembered more of it than anybody else—who might even have heard his grandfather say where he intended hiding the jewels."

The Thinking Machine paused for a little while, shifted his position, then went on:

"George Weston refused to go with you, Mr. Weston, and Mr. Hatch, to the ghost party, as you called it, because he said he was going to a ball in Providence that night. He did not go to Providence; I learned that from your correspondent there, Mr. Hatch; so George Weston might, possibly, have gone to the ghost party after all.

"After I looked over the situation down there it occurred to me that the most feasible way for a person, who wished to avoid being seen in the village, as the perpetrator of the ghost did, was to go to and from the place at night in a motor-boat. He could easily run in the dark and land at the foot of the cliff, and no soul in the village would be any the wiser. Did George Weston have a motor-boat? Yes, an electric, which runs almost silently.

"From this point the entire matter was comparatively simple. I *knew*—the pure logic of it told me—how the ghost was made to appear and disappear; one look at the house inside convinced me beyond all doubt. I knew the motive for the ghost—a search for the jewels. I knew, or thought I knew, the name of the man who was seeking the jewels; the man who had fullest knowledge and fullest opportunity, the man whose brain was clever enough to devise the scheme. Then, the next step to prove what I knew. The first thing to do was to find the jewels."

"Find the jewels?" Weston repeated, with a slight smile.

"Here they are," said The Thinking Machine, quietly.

And there, before the astonished eyes of the broker, he drew out the gems which had been lost for fifty years. Mr. Weston was not amazed; he was petrified with astonishment and sat staring at the glittering heap in silence. Finally he recovered his voice.

"How did you do it?" he demanded. "Where?"

"I used my brain, that's all," was the reply. "I went into the old house seeking them where the owner, under all conditions, would have been most likely to hide them, and there I found them."

"But—but————" stammered the broker.

"The man who hid these jewels hid them only temporarily, or at least that was his purpose," said The Thinking Machine, irritably. "Naturally he would not hide them in the woodwork of the house, because that might burn; he did not bury them in the cellar, because that has been carefully searched. Now, in that house there is nothing except woodwork and chimneys above the cellar. Yet he hid them in the house, proven by the fact that the man he killed was killed in the house, and that the outside ground, covered with snow, showed two sets of tracks into the house and none out. Therefore he did hide them in the cellar. Where? In the stonework. There was no other place.

"Naturally he would not hide them on a level with the eye, because the spot where he took out and replaced a stone would be apparent if a close search were made. He would, therefore, place them either above or below the eye level. He placed them above. A large loose stone in the chimney was taken out and there was the box with these things."

Mr. Weston stared at The Thinking Machine with a new wonder and admiration in his eyes.

"With the jewels found and disposed of, there remained only to prove the ghost theory by an actual test. I sent for you, Mr. Weston, because I thought possibly, as no actual crime had been committed, it would be better to leave the guilty man to you. When you came I went into the haunted house with a hammer—an ordinary hammer—and waited on the steps.

"At last the ghost laughed and appeared. I crept down the steps where I was sitting in my stocking feet. I knew what it was. Just when I reached the luminous phantom I disposed of it for all time by smashing it with a hammer. It shattered a large sliding mirror which ran in the door inside the frame, as I had thought. The crash startled the man who operated the ghost from the top of a box, giving it the appearance of extreme height, and he started out through the kitchen, as he had entered. The constable had barred that door after the man entered; therefore the ghost turned and came toward the front door of the house. There he ran into and struck down Mr. Hatch, and ran out through the front door, which I afterwards found was not securely fastened. You know the rest of it; how you found the motor-boat and waited there for him; how he came there, and————"

"Tried to stab me," Weston supplied. "I had to shoot to save myself."

"Well, the wound is trivial," said The Thinking Machine. "His arm will heal up in a little while. I think then, perhaps, a little trip of four or five years in Europe, at your expense, in return for the jewels, might restore him to health."

"I was thinking of that myself," said the broker, quietly. "Of course, I couldn't prosecute."

"The ghost, then, was——?" Hatch began.

"George Weston, my cousin," said the broker. "There are some things in this story which I hope you may see fit to leave unsaid, if you can do so with justice to yourself."

Hatch considered it.

"I think there are," he said, finally, and he turned to The Thinking Machine. "Just where was the man who operated the phantom?"

"In the dining-room, beside the butler's pantry," was the reply. "With that pantry door closed he put on the robe already covered with phosphorus, and merely stepped out. The figure was reflected in the tall mirror directly in front, as you enter the dining-room from the back, from there reflected to the mirror on the opposite wall in the living-room, and thence reflected to the sliding mirror in the door which led from the reception-hall to the library. This is the one I smashed."

"And how was the writing done?"

"Oh, that? Of course that was done by reversed writing on a piece of clear glass held before the apparition as he posed. This made it read straight to anyone who might see the last reflection in the reception-hall."

"And the blood thrown on the constable and the others when the ghost was in the yard?" Hatch went on.

"Was from a dog. A test I made in the drug store showed that.* It was a desperate effort to drive the villagers away and keep them away. The ghost cat and the tying of the watchman to his bed were easily done."

All sat silent for a time. At length Mr. Weston arose, thanked the scientist for the recovery of the jewels, bade them all good-night and was about to go out. Mechanically Hatch was following. At the door he turned back for the last question.

"How was it that the shot the constable fired didn't break the mirror?"

"Because he was nervous and the bullet struck the door beside the mirror," was the reply. "I dug it out with a knife. Good-night."

---

* It wasn't until 1901 that Paul Uhlenhuth, a German immunologist, developed the so-called "Uhlenhuth test," which could distinguish between animal and human blood. The basis of the test was Uhlenhuth's discovery that the blood of different species involved unique proteins. The test involved adding soluble antigens to the blood (in this case, likely scrapings mixed with fluid) and identifying the antibodies that precipitated. The test assumed great importance to forensics; it is a little surprising that the Thinking Machine, who was certainly no detective, was familiar with it, and identification of the blood as dog blood would have required very specific testing. It is more likely that the Thinking Machine merely confirmed that the blood was not human. In light of the presence of the "ghost cat," cat blood is a more likely candidate than an unseen dog.

THE RALSTON BANK BURGLARY[*]

I

With expert fingers Phillip Dunston, receiving teller, verified the last package of one-hundred-dollar bills he had made up—ten thousand dollars in all—and tossed it over on the pile beside him, while he checked off a memorandum. It was correct; there were eighteen packages of bills, containing $107,231. Then he took the bundles, one by one, and on each placed his initials, "P. D." This was a system of checking in the Ralston National Bank.

It was care in such trivial details, perhaps, that had a great deal to do with the fact that the Ralston National had advanced from a small beginning to the first rank of those banks which were financial powers. President Quinton Fraser had inaugurated the system under which the Ralston National had so prospered, and now, despite his seventy-four years, he was still its active head. For fifty years he had been in its employ; for thirty-five years of that time he had been its president.

Publicly the aged banker was credited with the possession of a vast fortune, this public estimate being based on large sums he

[*] First published in *Boston American*, November 7, 1905.

had given to charity. But as a matter of fact the private fortune of the old man, who had no one to share it save his wife, was not large; it was merely a comfortable living sum for an aged couple of simple tastes.

Dunston gathered up the packages of money and took them into the cashier's private office, where he dumped them on the great flat-top desk at which that official, Randolph West, sat figuring. The cashier thrust the sheet of paper on which he had been working into his pocket and took the memorandum which Dunston offered.

"All right?" he asked.

"It tallies perfectly," Dunston replied.

"Thanks. You may go now."

It was an hour after closing time. Dunston was just pulling on his coat when he saw West come out of his private office with the money to put it away in the big steel safe which stood between depositors and thieves. The cashier paused a moment to allow the janitor, Harris, to sweep the space in front of the safe. It was the late afternoon scrubbing and sweeping.

"Hurry up," the cashier complained, impatiently.

Harris hurried, and West placed the money in the safe. There were eighteen packages.

"All right, sir?" Dunston inquired.

"Yes."

West was disposing of the last bundle when Miss Clarke— Louise Clarke—private secretary to President Fraser, came out of his office with a long envelope in her hand. Dunston glanced at her and she smiled at him.

"Please, Mr. West," she said to the cashier, "Mr. Fraser told me before he went to put these papers in the safe. I had almost forgotten."

She glanced into the open safe and her pretty blue eyes

opened wide. Mr. West took the envelope, stowed it away with the money without a word, the girl looking on interestedly, and then swung the heavy door closed. She turned away with a quick, reassuring smile at Dunston, and disappeared inside the private office.

West had shot the bolts of the safe into place and had taken hold of the combination dial to throw it on, when the street door opened and President Fraser entered hurriedly.

"Just a moment, West," he called. "Did Miss Clarke give you an envelope to go in there?"

"Yes. I just put it in."

"One moment," and the aged president came through a gate which Dunston held open and went to the safe. The cashier pulled the steel door open, unlocked the money compartment where the envelope had been placed, and the president took it out.

West turned and spoke to Dunston, leaving the president looking over the contents of the envelope. When the cashier turned back to the safe the president was just taking his hand away from his inside coat pocket.

"It's all right, West," he instructed. "Lock it up."

Again the heavy door closed, the bolts were shot and the combination dial turned. President Fraser stood looking on curiously; it just happened that he had never witnessed this operation before.

"How much have you got in there to-night?" he asked.

"One hundred and twenty-nine thousand,"* replied the cashier. "And all the securities, of course."

"Hum," mused the president. "That would be a good haul for some one—if they could get it, eh, West?" and he chuckled dryly.

---

* A "real price" of over $4 million in 2022's money. Williamson, Measuring Worth.

"Excellent," returned West, smilingly. "But they can't."

Miss Clarke, dressed for the street, her handsome face almost concealed by a veil which was intended to protect her pink cheeks from boisterous winds, was standing in the door of the president's office.

"Oh, Miss Clarke, before you go, would you write just a short note for me?" asked the president.

"Certainly," she responded, and she returned to the private office. Mr. Fraser followed her.

West and Dunston stood outside the bank railing, Dunston waiting for Miss Clarke. Every evening he walked over to the subway with her. His opinion of her was an open secret. West was waiting for the janitor to finish sweeping.

"Hurry up, Harris," he said again.

"Yes, sir," came the reply, and the janitor applied the broom more vigorously. "Just a little bit more. I've finished inside."

Dunston glanced through the railing. The floor was spick and span and the hardwood glistened cleanly. Various bits of paper came down the corridor before Harris's broom. The janitor swept it all up into a dustpan just as Miss Clarke came out of the president's room. With Dunston she walked up the street. As they were going they saw Cashier West come out the front door, with his handkerchief in his hand, and then walk away rapidly.

"Mr. Fraser is doing some figuring," Miss Clarke explained to Dunston. "He said he might be there for another hour."

"You are beautiful," replied Dunston, irrelevantly.

* * *

These, then, were the happenings in detail in the Ralston National Bank from 4:15 o'clock on the afternoon of November 11. That night the bank was robbed. The great steel safe which was considered impregnable was blown and $129,000 was missing.

The night watchman of the bank, William Haney, was found senseless, bound and gagged, inside the bank. His revolver lay beside him with all the cartridges out. He had been beaten into insensibility; at the hospital it was stated that there was only a bare chance of his recovery.

The locks, hinges and bolts of the steel safe had been smashed by some powerful explosive, possibly nitro-glycerine. The tiny dial of the time-lock showed that the explosion came at 2:39; the remainder of the lock was blown to pieces.

Thus was fixed definitely the moment at which the robbery occurred. It was shown that the policeman on the beat had been four blocks away. It was perfectly possible that no one heard the explosion, because the bank was situated in a part of the city wholly given over to business and deserted at night.

The burglars had entered the building through a window of the cashier's private office, in the full glare of an electric light. The window sash here had been found unfastened and the pro-tecting steel bars, outside from top to bottom, seemed to have been dragged from their sockets in the solid granite. The granite crumbled away, as if it had been chalk.

Only one possible clew was found. This was a white linen handkerchief, picked up in front of the blown safe. It must have been dropped there at the time of the burglary, because Dunston distinctly recalled it was not there before he left the bank. He would have noticed it while the janitor was sweeping.

This handkerchief was the property of Cashier West. The cashier did not deny it, but could offer no explanation of how it came there. Miss Clarke and Dunston both said that they had seen him leave the bank with a handkerchief in his hand.

II

President Fraser reached the bank at ten o'clock and was informed of the robbery. He retired to his office, and there he sat, apparently stunned into inactivity by the blow, his head bowed on his arms. Miss Clarke, at her typewriter, frequently glanced at the aged figure with an expression of pity on her face. Her eyes seemed weary, too. Outside, through the closed door, they could hear the detectives.

From time to time employees of the bank and detectives entered the office to ask questions. The banker answered as if dazed; then the board of directors met and voted to personally make good the loss sustained. There was no uneasiness among depositors, because they knew the resources of the bank were practically unlimited.

Cashier West was not arrested. The directors wouldn't listen to such a thing; he had been cashier for eighteen years, and they trusted him implicitly. Yet he could offer no possible explanation of how his handkerchief had come there. He asserted stoutly that he had not been in the bank from the moment Miss Clarke and Dunston saw him leave it.

After investigation the police placed the burglary to the credit of certain expert cracksmen, identity unknown. A general alarm, which meant a rounding up of all suspicious persons, was sent out, and this drag-net was expected to bring important facts to light. Detective Mallory said so, and the bank officials placed great reliance on his word.

Thus the situation at the luncheon hour. Then Miss Clarke, who, wholly unnoticed, had been waiting all morning at her typewriter, arose and went over to Fraser.

"If you don't need me now," she said, "I'll run out to luncheon."

"Certainly, certainly," he responded, with a slight start. He had apparently forgotten her existence.

She stood silently looking at him for a moment.

"I'm awfully sorry," she said, at last, and her lips trembled slightly.

"Thanks," said the banker, and he smiled faintly. "It's a shock, the worst I ever had."

Miss Clarke passed out with quiet tread, pausing for a moment in the outer office to stare curiously at the shattered steel safe. The banker arose with sudden determination and called to West, who entered immediately.

"I know a man who can throw some light on this thing," said Fraser, positively. "I think I'll ask him to come over and take a look. It might aid the police, anyway. You may know him? Professor Van Dusen."

"Never heard of him," said West, tersely, "but I'll welcome anybody who can solve it. My position is uncomfortable."

President Fraser called Professor Van Dusen—The Thinking Machine—and talked for a moment through the 'phone. Then he turned back to West.

"He'll come," he said, with an air of relief. "I was able to do him a favor once by putting an invention on the market."

Within an hour The Thinking Machine, accompanied by Hutchinson Hatch, reporter, appeared. President Fraser knew the scientist well, but on West the strange figure made a startling, almost uncanny, impression. Every known fact was placed before The Thinking Machine. He listened without comment, then arose and wandered aimlessly about the offices. The employees were amused by his manner; Hatch was a silent looker-on.

"Where was the handkerchief found?" demanded The Thinking Machine, at last.

"Here," replied West, and he indicated the exact spot.

"Any draught through the office—ever?"

"None. We have a patent ventilating system which prevents that."

The Thinking Machine squinted for several minutes at the window which had been unfastened—the window in the cashier's private room—with the steel bars guarding it, now torn out of their sockets, and at the chalklike softness of the granite about the sockets. After awhile he turned to the president and cashier.

"Where is the handkerchief?"

"In my desk," Fraser replied. "The police thought it of no consequence, save, perhaps—perhaps———," and he looked at West.

"Except that it might implicate me," said West, hotly.

"Tut, tut, tut," said Fraser, reprovingly. "No one thinks for a———"

"Well, well, the handkerchief?" interrupted The Thinking Machine, in annoyance.

"Come into my office," suggested the president.

The Thinking Machine started in, saw a woman—Miss Clarke, who had returned from luncheon—and stopped. There was one thing on earth he was afraid of—a woman.

"Bring it out here," he requested.

President Fraser brought it and placed it in the slender hands of the scientist, who examined it closely by a window, turning it over and over. At last he sniffed at it. There was the faint, clinging odor of violet perfume. Then abruptly, irrelevantly, he turned to Fraser.

"How many women employed in the bank?" he asked.

"Three," was the reply; "Miss Clarke, who is my secretary, and two general stenographers in the outer office."

"How many men?"

"Fourteen, including myself."

If the president and Cashier West had been surprised at the actions of The Thinking Machine up to this point, now they were amazed. He thrust the handkerchief at Hatch, took his own handkerchief, briskly scrubbed his hands with it, and also passed that to Hatch.

"Keep those," he commanded.

He sniffed at his hands, then walked into the outer office, straight toward the desk of one of the young women stenographers. He leaned over her, and asked one question:

"What system of shorthand do you write?"

"Pitman," was the astonished reply.

The scientist sniffed. Yes, it was unmistakably a sniff. He left her suddenly and went to the other stenographer. Precisely the same thing happened; standing close to her he asked one question, and at her answer sniffed. Miss Clarke passed through the outer office to mail a letter. She, too, had to answer the question as the scientist squinted into her eyes, and sniffed.

"Ah," he said, at her answer.

Then from one to another of the employees of the bank he went, asking each a few questions. By this time a murmur of amusement was running through the office. Finally The Thinking Machine approached the cage in which sat Dunston, the receiving teller. The young man was bent over his work, absorbed.

"How long have you been employed here?" asked the scientist, suddenly.

Dunston started and glanced around quickly.

"Five years," he responded.

"It must be hot work," said The Thinking Machine. "You're perspiring."

"Am I?" inquired the young man, smilingly.

He drew a crumpled handkerchief from his hip pocket, shook it out, and wiped his forehead.

"Ah!" exclaimed The Thinking Machine, suddenly.

He had caught the faint, subtle perfume of violets—an odor identical with that on the handkerchief found in front of the safe.

III

The Thinking Machine led the way back to the private office of the cashier, with President Fraser, Cashier West and Hatch following.

"Is it possible for anyone to overhear us here?" he asked.

"No," replied the president. "The directors meet here."

"Could anyone outside hear that, for instance?" and with a sudden sweep of his hand he upset a heavy chair.

"I don't know," was the astonished reply. "Why?"

The Thinking Machine went quickly to the door, opened it softly and peered out. Then he closed the door again.

"I suppose I may speak with absolute frankness?" he inquired.

"Certainly," responded the old banker, almost startled. "Certainly."

"You have presented an abstract problem," The Thinking Machine went on, "and I presume you want a solution of it, no matter where it hits?"

"Certainly," the president again assured him, but his tone expressed a grave, haunting fear.

"In that case," and The Thinking Machine turned to the reporter, "Mr. Hatch, I want you to ascertain several things for me. First, I want to know if Miss Clarke uses or has ever used violet perfume—if so, when she ceased using it."

"Yes," said the reporter. The bank officials exchanged wondering looks.

"Also, Mr. Hatch," and the scientist squinted with his strange eyes straight into the face of the cashier, "go to the home of Mr. West, here, see for yourself his laundry mark, and ascertain beyond any question if he has ever, or any member of his family has ever, used violet perfume."

The cashier flushed suddenly.

"I can answer that," he said, hotly. "No."

"I knew you would say that," said The Thinking Machine, curtly. "Please don't interrupt. Do as I say, Mr. Hatch."

Accustomed as he was to the peculiar methods of this man, Hatch saw faintly the purpose of the inquiries.

"And the receiving teller?" he asked.

"I know about him," was the reply.

Hatch left the room, closing the door behind him. He heard the bolt shot in the lock as he started away.

"I think it only fair to say here, Professor Van Dusen," explained the president, "that we understand thoroughly that it would have been impossible for Mr. West to have had anything to do with or know————"

"Nothing is impossible," interrupted The Thinking Machine.

"But I won't————" began West, angrily.

"Just a moment, please," said The Thinking Machine. "No one has accused you of anything. What I am doing may explain to your satisfaction just how your handkerchief came here and bring about the very thing I suppose you want—exoneration."

The cashier sank back into a chair; President Fraser looked from one to the other. Where there had been worry on his face there was now only wonderment.

"Your handkerchief was found in this office, apparently having been dropped by the persons who blew the safe," and the long, slender fingers of The Thinking Machine were placed tip to tip as he talked. "It was not there the night before. The janitor who swept says so; Dunston, who happened to look, says so; Miss Clarke and Dunston both say they saw you with a handkerchief as you left the bank. Therefore, that handkerchief reached that spot after you left and before the robbery was discovered."

The cashier nodded.

"You say you don't use perfume; that no one in your family uses it. If Mr. Hatch verifies this, it will help to exonerate you. But some person who handled that handkerchief after it left your possession and before it appeared here did use perfume. Now who was that person? Who would have had an opportunity?

"We may safely dismiss the possibility that you lost the handkerchief, that it fell into the hands of burglars, that those burglars used perfume, that they brought it to your bank—your own bank, mind you!—and left it. The series of coincidences necessary to bring that about would not have occurred once in a million times."

The Thinking Machine sat silent for several minutes, squinting steadily at the ceiling.

"If it had been lost anywhere, in the laundry, say, the same rule of coincidence I have just applied would almost eliminate it. Therefore, because of an opportunity to get that handkerchief, we will assume—there is—there must be—some one employed in this bank who had some connection with or actually participated in the burglary."

The Thinking Machine spoke with perfect quiet, but the effect was electrical. The aged president staggered to his feet and stood staring at him dully; again the flush of crimson came into the face of the cashier.

"Some one," The Thinking Machine went on, evenly, "who

either found the handkerchief and unwittingly lost it at the time of the burglary, or else stole it and deliberately left it. As I said, Mr. West seems eliminated. Had he been one of the robbers, he would not wittingly have left his handkerchief; we will still assume that he does not use perfume, therefore personally did not drop the handkerchief where it was found."

"Impossible! I can't believe it, and of my employees———" began Mr. Fraser.

"Please don't keep saying things are impossible," snapped The Thinking Machine. "It irritates me exceedingly. It all comes to the one vital question: Who in the bank uses perfume?"

"I don't know," said the two officials.

"I do," said The Thinking Machine. "There are two—only two, Dunston, your receiving teller, and Miss Clarke."

"But they———"

"Dunston uses a violet perfume not *like* that on the handkerchief, but *identical* with it," The Thinking Machine went on. "Miss Clarke uses a strong rose perfume."

"But those two persons, above all others in the bank, I trust implicitly," said Mr. Fraser, earnestly. "And, besides, they wouldn't know how to blow a safe. The police tell me this was the work of experts."

"Have you, Mr. Fraser, attempted to raise, or have you raised lately, any large sum of money?" asked the scientist, suddenly.

"Well, yes," said the banker, "I have. For a week past I have tried to raise ninety thousand dollars on my personal account."

"And you, Mr. West?"

The face of the cashier flushed slightly—it might have been at the tone of the question—and there was the least pause.

"No," he answered finally.

"Very well," and the scientist arose, rubbing his hands; "now we'll search your employees."

"What?" exclaimed both men. Then Mr. Fraser added: "That would be the height of absurdity; it would never do. Besides, any person who robbed the bank would not carry proofs of the robbery, or even any of the money about with them—to the bank, above all places."

"The bank would be the safest place for it," retorted The Thinking Machine. "It is perfectly possible that a thief in your employ would carry some of the money; indeed, it is doubtful if he would dare do anything else with it. He could see you would have no possible reason for suspecting anyone here—unless it is Mr. West."

There was a pause. "I'll do the searching, except the three ladies, of course," he added, blushingly. "With them each combination of two can search the other one."

Mr. Fraser and Mr. West conversed in low tones for several minutes.

"If the employees will consent I am willing," Mr. Fraser explained, at last; "although I see no use of it."

"They will agree," said The Thinking Machine. "Please call them all into this office."

Among some confusion and wonderment the three women and fourteen men of the bank were gathered in the cashier's office, the outer doors being locked. The Thinking Machine addressed them with characteristic terseness.

"In the investigation of the burglary of last night," he explained, "it has been deemed necessary to search all employees of this bank." A murmur of surprise ran around the room. "Those who are innocent will agree readily, of course; will all agree?"

There were whispered consultations on all sides. Dunston flushed angrily; Miss Clarke, standing near Mr. Fraser, paled slightly. Dunston looked at her and then spoke.

"And the ladies?" he asked.

"They, too," explained the scientist. "They may search one another—in the other room, of course."

"I for one will not submit to such a proceeding," Dunston declared, bluntly, "not because I fear it, but because it is an insult."

Simultaneously it impressed itself on the bank officials and The Thinking Machine that the one person in the bank who used a perfume identical with that on the handkerchief was the first to object to a search. The cashier and president exchanged startled glances.

"Nor will I," came in the voice of a woman.

The Thinking Machine turned and glanced at her. It was Miss Willis, one of the outside stenographers; Miss Clarke and the other woman were pale, but neither had spoken.

"And the others?" asked The Thinking Machine.

Generally there was acquiescence, and as the men came forward the scientist searched them, perfunctorily, it seemed. Nothing! At last there remained three men, Dunston, West and Fraser. Dunston came forward, compelled to do so by the attitude of his fellows. The three women stood together. The Thinking Machine spoke to them as he searched Dunston.

"If the ladies will retire to the next room they may proceed with their search," he suggested. "If any money is found, bring it to me—nothing else."

"I will not, I will not, I will not," screamed Miss Willis, suddenly. "It's an outrage."

Miss Clarke, deathly white and half fainting, threw up her hands and sank without a sound into the arms of President Fraser. There she burst into tears.

"It is an outrage," she sobbed. She clung to President Fraser, her arms flung upward and her face buried on his bosom. He was soothing her with fatherly words, and stroked her hair awkwardly. The Thinking Machine finished the search of Dunston. Nothing! Then Miss Clarke roused herself and dried her eyes.

"It is an outrage," she sobbed.

"Of course I will have to agree," she said, with a flash of anger in her eyes.

Miss Willis was weeping, but, like Dunston, she was

compelled to yield, and the three women went into an adjoining room. There was a tense silence until they reappeared. Each shook her head. The Thinking Machine nearly looked disappointed.

"Dear me!" he exclaimed. "Now, Mr. Fraser." He started toward the president, then paused to pick up a scarf pin.

"This is yours," he said. "I saw it fall," and he made as if to search the aged man.

"Well, do you really think it necessary in my case?" asked the president, in consternation, as he drew back, nervously. "I—I am the president, you know."

"The others were searched in your presence, I will search you in their presence," said The Thinking Machine, tartly.

"But—but————" the president stammered.

"Are you afraid?" the scientist demanded.

"Why, of course not," was the hurried answer; "but it seems so—so unusual."

"I think it best," said The Thinking Machine, and before the banker could draw away his slender fingers were in the inside breast pocket, whence they instantly drew out a bundle of money—one hundred $100 bills—ten thousand dollars—with the initials of the receiving teller, "P. D."—"o. k.—R. W."

"Great God!" exclaimed Mr. Fraser, ashen white.

"Dear me, dear me!" said The Thinking Machine again. He sniffed curiously at the bundle of bank notes, as a hound might sniff at a trail.

IV

President Fraser was removed to his home in a dangerous condition. His advanced age did not withstand the shock. Now alternately he raved and muttered incoherently, and the old eyes were wide, staring fearfully always. There was a consultation between The Thinking Machine and West after the removal of President Fraser, and the result was another hurried meeting of the board of directors. At that meeting West was placed, temporarily, in command. The police, of course, had been informed of the matter, but no arrest was probable.

Immediately after The Thinking Machine left the bank Hatch appeared and inquired for him. From the bank he went to the home of the scientist. There Professor Van Dusen was bending over a retort, busy with some problem.

"Well?" he demanded, as he glanced up.

"West told the truth," began Hatch. "Neither he nor any member of his family uses perfume; he has few outside acquaintances, is regular in his habits, but is a man of considerable wealth, it appears."

"What is his salary at the bank?" asked The Thinking Machine.

"Fifteen thousand a year," said the reporter. "But he must have a large fortune. He lives like a millionaire."

"He couldn't do that on fifteen thousand dollars a year," mused the scientist. "Did he inherit any money?"

"No," was the reply. "He started as a clerk in the bank and has made himself what he is."

"That means speculation," said The Thinking Machine. "You can't save a fortune from a salary, even fifteen thousand dollars a year. Now, Mr. Hatch, find out for me all about his business connections. His source of income particularly I would like to know. Also whether or not he has recently sought to borrow or has received a large sum of money; if he got it and what he did with it. He says he has not sought such a sum. Perhaps he told the truth."

"Yes, and about Miss Clarke————"

"Yes; what about her?" asked The Thinking Machine.

"She occupies a little room in a boarding-house for women in an excellent district," the reporter explained. "She has no friends who call there, at any rate. Occasionally, however, she goes out at night and remains late."

"The perfume?" asked the scientist.

"She uses a perfume, the housekeeper tells me, but she doesn't recall just what kind it is—so many of the young women in the house use it. So I went to her room and looked. There was no perfume there. Her room was considerably disarranged, which seemed to astonish the housekeeper, who declared that she had carefully arranged it about nine o'clock. It was two when I was there."

"How was it disarranged?" asked the scientist.

"The couch cover was jerked awry and the pillows tumbled down, for one thing," said the reporter. "I didn't notice any further."

The Thinking Machine relapsed into silence.

"What happened at the bank?" inquired Hatch.

Briefly the scientist related the facts leading up to the search, the search itself and its startling result. The reporter whistled.

"Do you think Fraser had anything to do with it?"

"Run out and find out those other things about West," said The Thinking Machine, evasively. "Come back here to-night. It doesn't matter what time."

"But who do you think committed the crime?" insisted the newspaper man.

"I may be able to tell you when you return."

For the time being The Thinking Machine seemed to forget the bank robbery, being busy in his tiny laboratory. He was aroused from his labors by the ringing of the telephone bell.

"Hello," he called. "Yes, Van Dusen. No, I can't come down

to the bank now. What is it? Oh, it has disappeared? When? Too bad! How's Mr. Fraser? Still unconscious? Too bad! I'll see you to-morrow."

The scientist was still engrossed in some delicate chemical work just after eight o'clock that evening when Martha, his housekeeper and maid of all work, entered.

"Professor," she said, "there's a lady to see you."

"Name?" he asked, without turning.

"She didn't give it, sir."

"There in a moment."

He finished the test he had under way, then left the little laboratory and went into the hall leading to the sitting-room, where unprivileged callers awaited his pleasure. He sniffed a little as he stepped into the hall. At the door of the sitting-room he paused and peered inside. A woman arose and came toward him. It was Miss Clarke.

"Good-evening," he said. "I knew you'd come."

Miss Clarke looked a little surprised, but made no comment.

"I came to give you some information," she said, and her voice was subdued. "I am heartbroken at the awful things which have come out concerning—concerning Mr. Fraser. I have been closely associated with him for several months, and I won't believe that he could have had anything to do with this affair, although I know positively that he was in need of a large sum of money—ninety thousand dollars—because his personal fortune was in danger. Some error in titles to an estate, he told me."

"Yes, yes," said The Thinking Machine.

"Whether he was able to raise this money I don't know," she went on. "I only hope he did without having to—to do that—to have any———"

"To rob his bank," said the scientist, tartly. "Miss Clarke, is young Dunston in love with you?"

The girl's face changed color at the sudden question.

"I don't see————" she began.

"You may not see," said The Thinking Machine, "but I can have him arrested for robbery and convict him."

The girl gazed at him with wide, terror-stricken eyes, and gasped.

"No, no, no," she said, hurriedly. "He could have had nothing to do with that at all."

"Is he in love with you?" again came the question.

There was a pause.

"I've had reason to believe so," she said, finally, "though————"

"And you?"

The girl's face was flaming now, and, squinting into her eyes, the scientist read the answer.

"I understand," he commented, tersely. "Are you going to be married?"

"I could—could never marry him," she gasped suddenly. "No, no," emphatically. "We are not, ever."

She slowly recovered from her confusion, while the scientist continued to squint at her curiously.

"I believe you said you had some information for me?" he asked.

"Y—yes," she faltered. Then more calmly: "Yes. I came to tell you that the package of ten thousand dollars which you took from Mr. Fraser's pocket has again disappeared."

"Yes," said the other, without astonishment.

"It was presumed at the bank that he had taken it home with him, having regained possession of it in some way, but a careful search has failed to reveal it."

"Yes, and what else?"

The girl took a long breath and gazed steadily into the eyes of the scientist, with determination in her own.

"I have come, too, to tell you," she said, "the name of the man who robbed the bank."

V

If Miss Clarke had expected that The Thinking Machine would show either astonishment or enthusiasm, she must have been disappointed, for he neither altered his position nor looked at her. Instead, he was gazing thoughtfully away with lackluster eyes. "Well?" he asked. "I suppose it's a story. Begin at the beginning."

With a certain well-bred air of timidity, the girl began the story; and occasionally as she talked there was a little tremor of the lips.

"I have been a stenographer and typewriter for seven years," she said, "and in that time I have held only four positions. The first was in a law office in New York, where I was left an orphan to earn my own living; the second was with a manufacturing concern, also in New York. I left there three years ago to accept the position of private secretary to William T. Rankin, president of the——National Bank, at Hartford, Connecticut. I came from there to Boston and later went to work at the Ralston Bank, as private secretary to Mr. Fraser. I left the bank in Hartford because of the failure of that concern, following a bank robbery."

The Thinking Machine glanced at her suddenly.

"You may remember from the newspapers——" she began again.

"I never read the newspapers," he said.

"Well, anyway," and there was a shade of impatience at the interruption, "there was a bank burglary there similar to this. Only seventy thousand dollars was stolen, but it was a small institution and the theft precipitated a run which caused a collapse after I had been in that position for only six months."

"How long have you been with the Ralston National?"

"Nine months," was the reply.

"Had you saved any money while working in your other positions?"

"Well, the salary was small—I couldn't have saved much."

"How did you live those two years from the time you left the Hartford bank until you accepted this position?"

The girl stammered a little.

"I received assistance from friends," she said, finally.

"Go on."

"That bank in Hartford," she continued, with a little gleam of resentment in her eyes, "had a safe similar to the one at the Ralston National, though not so large. It was blown in identically the same way as this one was blown."

"Oh, I see," said the scientist. "Some one was arrested for this, and you want to give me the name of that man?"

"Yes," said the girl. "A professional burglar, William Dineen, was arrested for that robbery and confessed. Later he escaped. After his arrest he boasted of his ability to blow any style of safe. He used an invention of his own for the borings to place the charges. I noticed that safe and I noticed this one. There is a striking similarity in the two."

The Thinking Machine stared at her.

"Why do you tell me?" he asked.

"Because I understood you were making the investigation for the bank," she responded, unhesitatingly, "and I dreaded the notoriety of telling the police."

"If this William Dineen is at large you believe he did this?"

"I am almost positive."

"Thank you," said The Thinking Machine.

Miss Clarke went away, and late that night Hatch appeared. He looked weary and sank into a chair gratefully, but there was satisfaction in his eye. For an hour or more he talked. At last The Thinking Machine was satisfied, nearly.

"One thing more," he said, in conclusion. "Notify the police to look out for William Dineen, professional bank burglar, and his pals, whose names you can get from the newspapers in connection with a bank robbery in Hartford. They are wanted in connection with this case."

The reporter nodded.

"When Mr. Fraser recovers I intend to hold a little party here," the scientist continued. "It will be a surprise party."

It was two days later, and the police were apparently seeking some tangible point from which they could proceed, when The Thinking Machine received word that there had been a change for the better in Mr. Fraser's condition. Immediately he sent for Detective Mallory, with whom he held a long conversation. The detective went away tugging at his heavy mustache and smiling. With three other men he disappeared from police haunts that afternoon on a special mission.

That night the little "party" was held in the apartments of The Thinking Machine. President Fraser was first to arrive. He was pale and weak, but there was a fever of impatience in his manner. Then came West, Dunston, Miss Clarke, Miss Willis and Charles Burton, a clerk whose engagement to the pretty Miss Willis had been recently announced.

The party gathered, each staring at the other curiously, with questions in their eyes, until The Thinking Machine entered, rubbing his fingers together briskly. Behind him came Hatch, bearing a shabby gripsack. The reporter's face showed excitement despite his rigid efforts to repress it. There were some preliminaries, and then the scientist began.

"To come to the matter quickly," he said, in preface, "we will take it for granted that no employee of the Ralston Bank is a professional burglar. But the person who was responsible for that burglary, who shared the money stolen, who planned it and actually assisted in its execution is in this room—now."

Instantly there was consternation, but it found no expression in words, only in the faces of those present.

"Further, I may inform you," went on the scientist, "that no one will be permitted to leave this room until I finish."

"Permitted?" demanded Dunston. "We are not prisoners."

"You will be if I give the word," was the response, and Dunston sat back, dazed. He glanced uneasily at the faces of the others; they glanced uneasily at him.

"The actual facts in the robbery you know," went on The Thinking Machine. "You know that the safe was blown, that a large sum of money was stolen, that Mr. West's handkerchief was found near the safe. Now, I'll tell you what I have learned. We will begin with President Fraser.

"Against Mr. Fraser is more direct evidence than against anyone else, because in his pocket was found one of the stolen bundles of money, containing ten thousand dollars. Mr. Fraser needed ninety thousand dollars previous to the robbery."

"But———" began the old man, with deathlike face.

"Never mind," said the scientist. "Next, Miss Willis." Curious eyes were turned on her, and she, too, grew suddenly white. "Against her is less direct evidence than against anyone else. Miss Willis positively declined to permit a search of her person until she was compelled to do so by the fact that the other two permitted it. The fact that nothing was found has no bearing on the subject. She did refuse.

"Then Charles Burton," the inexorable voice went on, calmly, as if in mere discussion of a problem of mathematics.

"Burton is engaged to Miss Willis. He is ambitious. He recently lost twenty thousand dollars in stock speculation—all he had. He needed more money in order to give this girl, who refused to be searched, a comfortable home.

"Next Miss Clarke, secretary to Mr. Fraser. Originally she came under consideration through the fact that she used perfume, and that Mr. West's handkerchief carried a faint odor of perfume. Now it is a fact that for years Miss Clarke used violet perfume, then on the day following the robbery suddenly began to use strong rose perfume, which smothers a violet odor. Miss Clarke, you will remember, fainted at the time of the search. I may add that a short while ago she was employed in a bank which was robbed in the identical manner of this one."

Miss Clarke sat apparently calm, and even faintly smiling, but her face was white. The Thinking Machine squinted at her a moment, then turned suddenly to Cashier West.

"Here is the man," he said, "whose handkerchief was found, but he does not use perfume, has never used it. He is the man who would have had best opportunity to leave unfastened the window in his private office by which the thieves entered the bank; he is the man who would have had the best opportunity to apply a certain chemical solution to the granite sockets of the steel bars, weakening the granite so they could be pulled out; he is the man who misrepresented facts to me. He told me he did not have and had not tried to raise any especially large sum of money. Yet on the day following the robbery he deposited one hundred and twenty-five thousand dollars in cash in a bank in Chicago. The stolen sum was one hundred and twenty-nine thousand dollars. That man, there."

All eyes were now turned on the cashier. He seemed choking, started to speak, then dropped back into his chair.

"And last, Dunston," resumed The Thinking Machine, and

he pointed dramatically at the receiving teller. "He had equal opportunity with Mr. West to know of the amount of money in the bank; he refused first to be searched, and you witnessed his act a moment ago. To this man now there clings the identical odor of violet perfume which was on the handkerchief—not a perfume like it, but the identical odor."

There was silence, dumfounded silence, for a long time. No one dared to look at his neighbor now; the reporter felt the tension. At last The Thinking Machine spoke again.

"As I have said, the person who planned and participated in the burglary is now in this room. If that person will stand forth and confess it will mean a vast difference in the length of the term in prison."

Again silence. At last there came a knock at the door, and Martha thrust her head in.

"Two gentlemen and four cops are here," she announced.

"There are the accomplices of the guilty person, the men who actually blew that safe," declared the scientist, dramatically. "Again, will the guilty person confess?"

No one stirred.

VI

There was tense silence for a moment. Dunston was the first to speak.

"This is all a bluff," he said. "I think, Mr. Fraser, there are some explanations and apologies due to all of us, particularly to Miss Clarke and Miss Willis," he added, as an afterthought. "It is humiliating, and no good has been done. I had intended asking Miss Clarke to be my wife, and now I assert my right to speak for her. I demand an apology."

Carried away by his own anger and by the pleading face of

Miss Clarke and the pain there, the young man turned fiercely on The Thinking Machine. Bewilderment was on the faces of the two banking officials.

"You feel that an explanation is due?" asked The Thinking Machine, meekly.

"Yes," thundered the young man.

"You shall have it," was the quiet answer, and the stooped figure of the scientist moved across the room to the door. He said something to some one outside and returned.

"Again I'll give you a chance for a confession," he said. "It will shorten your prison term." He was speaking to no one in particular; yet to them all. "The two men who blew the safe are now about to enter this room. After they appear it will be too late."

Startled glances were exchanged, but no one stirred. Then came a knock at the door. Silently The Thinking Machine looked about with a question in his eyes. Still silence, and he threw open the door. Three policemen in uniform and Detective Mallory entered, bringing two prisoners.

"These are the men who blew the safe," The Thinking Machine explained, indicating the prisoners. "Does anyone here recognize them?"

Apparently no one did, for none spoke.

"Do you recognize any person in this room?" he asked of the prisoners.

One of them laughed shortly and said something aside to the other, who smiled. The Thinking Machine was nettled and when he spoke again there was a touch of sarcasm in his voice.

"It may enlighten at least one of you in this room," he said, "to tell you that these two men are Frank Seranno and Gustave Meyer, Mr. Meyer being a pupil and former associate of the notorious bank burglar, William Dineen. You may lock them up now," he said to Detective Mallory. "They will confess later."

"Confess!" exclaimed one of them. Both laughed.

The prisoners were led out and Detective Mallory returned to lave in the font of analytical wisdom, although he would not have expressed it in those words. Then The Thinking Machine began at the beginning and told his story.

"I undertook to throw some light on this affair a few hours after its occurrence, at the request of President Fraser, who had once been able to do me a very great favor," he explained. "I went to the bank—you all saw me there—looked over the premises, saw how the thieves had entered the building, looked at the safe and at the spot where the handkerchief was found. To my mind it was demonstrated clearly that the handkerchief appeared there at the time of the burglary. I inquired if there was any draught through the office, seeking in that way to find if the handkerchief might have been lost at some other place in the bank, overlooked by the sweeper and blown to the spot where it was found. There was no draught.

"Next I asked for the handkerchief. Mr. Fraser asked me into his office to look at it. I saw a woman—Miss Clarke it was—in there and declined to go. Instead, I examined the handkerchief outside. I don't know that my purpose there can be made clear to you. It was a possibility that there would be perfume on the handkerchief, and the woman in the office might use perfume. I didn't want to confuse the odors. Miss Clarke was not in the bank when I arrived; she had gone to luncheon.

"Instantly I got the handkerchief I noticed the odor of perfume—violet perfume. Perfume is used by a great many women, by very few men. I asked how many women were employed in the bank. There were three. I handed the scented handkerchief to Mr. Hatch, removed all odor of the clinging perfume from my hands with my own handkerchief and also handed that to Mr. Hatch, so as to completely rid myself of the odor.

"Then I started through the bank and spoke to every person in it, standing close to them so that I might catch the odor if they used it. Miss Clarke was the first person who I found used it—but the perfume she used was a strong rose odor. Then I went on until I came to Mr. Dunston. The identical odor of the handkerchief he revealed to me by drawing out his own handkerchief while I talked to him."

Dunston looked a little startled, but said nothing; instead he glanced at Miss Clarke, who sat listening, interestedly. He could not read the expression on her face.

"This much done," continued The Thinking Machine, "we retired to Cashier West's office. There I knew the burglars had entered; there I saw a powerful chemical solution had been applied to the granite around the sockets of the protecting steel bars to soften the stone. Its direct effect is to make it of chalk-like consistency. I was also curious to know if any noise made in that room would attract attention in the outer office, so I upset a heavy chair, then looked outside. No one moved or looked back; therefore no one heard.

"Here I explained to President Fraser and to Mr. West why I connected some one in the bank with the burglary. It was because of the scent on the handkerchief. It would be tedious to repeat the detailed explanation I had to give them. I sent Mr. Hatch to find out, first, if Miss Clarke here had ever used violet perfume instead of rose; also to find out if any members of Mr. West's family used any perfume, particularly violet. I knew that Mr. Dunston used it.

"Then I asked Mr. Fraser if he had sought to raise any large sum of money. He told me the truth. But Mr. West did not tell me the truth in answer to a question along the same lines. Now I know why. It was because as cashier of the bank he was not supposed to operate in stocks, yet he has made a fortune at it. He didn't want Fraser to know this, and willfully misrepresented the facts.

"Then came the search. I expected to find just what was found, money, but considerably more of it. Miss Willis objected, Mr. Dunston objected and Miss Clarke fainted in the arms of Mr. Fraser. I read the motives of each aright. Dunston objected because he is an egotistical young man and, being young, is foolish. He considered it an insult. Miss Willis objected also through a feeling of pride."

The Thinking Machine paused for a moment, locked his fingers behind his head and leaned far back in his chair.

"Shall I tell what happened next?" he asked, "or will you tell it?"

Everyone in the room knew it was a question to the guilty person. Which? Whom? There came no answer, and after a moment The Thinking Machine resumed, quietly, very quietly.

"Miss Clarke fainted in Mr. Fraser's arms. While leaning against him, and while he stroked her hair and tried to soothe her, she took from the bosom of her loose shirtwaist a bundle of money, ten thousand dollars, and slipped it into the inside pocket of Mr. Fraser's coat."

There was deathlike silence.

"It's a lie!" screamed the girl, and she rose to her feet with anger-distorted face. "It's a lie!"

Dunston arose suddenly and went to her. With his arm about her he turned defiantly to The Thinking Machine, who had not moved or altered his position in the slightest. Dunston said nothing, because there seemed to be nothing to say.

"Into the inside pocket of Mr. Fraser's coat," The Thinking Machine repeated. "When she removed her arms his scarf pin clung to the lace on one of her sleeves. That I saw. That pin could not have caught on her sleeve where it did if her hand had not been to the coat pocket. Having passed this sum of money—her pitiful share of the theft—she agreed to the search."

"It's a lie!" shrieked the girl again. And her every tone and every gesture said it was the truth.

Dunston gazed into her eyes with horror in his own and his arm fell limply. Still he said nothing.

"Of course nothing was found," the quiet voice went on. "When I discovered the bank notes in Mr. Fraser's pocket I smelled of them—seeking the odor, this time not of violet perfume, but of rose perfume. I found it."

Suddenly the girl whose face had shown only anger and defiance leaned over with her head in her hands and wept bitterly. It was a confession. Dunston stood beside her, helplessly; finally his hand was slowly extended and he stroked her hair.

"Go on, please," he said to Professor Van Dusen, meekly. His suffering was no less than hers.

"These facts were important, but not conclusive," said The Thinking Machine, "so next, with Mr. Hatch's aid here, I ascertained other things about Miss Clarke. I found out that when she went out to luncheon that day she purchased some powerful rose perfume; that, contrary to custom, she went home; that she used it liberally in her room; and that she destroyed a large bottle of violet perfume which you, Mr. Dunston, had given her. I ascertained also that her room was disarranged, particularly the couch. I assume from this that when she went to the office in the morning she did not have the money about her; that she left it hidden in the couch; that through fear of its discovery she rushed back home to get it; that she put it inside her shirtwaist, and there she had it when the search was made. Am I right, Miss Clarke?"

The girl nodded her head and looked up with piteous, tear-stained face.

"That night Miss Clarke called on me. She came ostensibly to tell me that the package of money, ten thousand dollars, had disappeared again. I knew that previously by telephone, and I knew, too, that she had that money then about her. She has it now. Will you give it up?"

Without a word the girl drew out the bundle of money, ten thousand dollars. Detective Mallory took it, held it, amazed for an instant, then passed it to The Thinking Machine, who sniffed at it.

"An odor of strong rose perfume," he said. Then: "Miss Clarke also told me that she had worked in a bank which had been robbed under circumstances identical with this by one William Dineen, and expressed the belief that he had something to do with this. Mr. Hatch ascertained that two of Dineen's pals were living in Cambridge. He found their rooms and searched them, later giving the address to the police.

"Now, why did Miss Clarke tell me that? I considered it in all points. She told me either to aid honestly in the effort to catch the thief, or to divert suspicion in another direction. Knowing as much as I did then, I reasoned it was to divert suspicion from you, Mr. Dunston, and from herself possibly. Dineen is in prison, and was there three months before this robbery; I believed she knew that. His pals are the two men in the other room; they are the men who aided Dineen in the robbery of the Hartford bank, with Miss Clarke's assistance; they are the men who robbed the Ralston National with her assistance. She herself indicated her profit from the Hartford robbery to me by a remark she made indicating that she had not found it necessary to work for two years from the time she left the Hartford bank until she became Mr. Fraser's secretary."

There was a pause. Miss Clarke sat sobbing, while Dunston stood near her studying the toe of his shoe. After awhile the girl became more calm.

"Miss Clarke, would you like to explain anything?" asked The Thinking Machine. His voice was gentle, even deferential.

"Nothing," she said, "except admit it all—all. I have nothing to conceal. I went to the bank, as I went to the bank in Hartford, for the purpose of robbery, with the assistance of those men in the next room. We have worked together for years. I planned this robbery; I had the opportunity, and availed myself of it, to put a solution on the sockets of the steel bars of the window in Mr. West's room, which would gradually destroy the granite and make it possible to pull out the bars. This took weeks, but I could reach that room safely from Mr. Fraser's.

"I had the opportunity to leave the window unfastened and did so. I dressed in men's clothing and accompanied those two men to the bank. We crept in the window, after pulling the bars out. The men attacked the night watchman and bound him. The handkerchief of Mr. West's I happened to pick up in the office one afternoon a month ago and took it home. There it got the odor of perfume from being in a bureau with my things. On the night we went to the bank I needed something to put about my neck and used it. In the bank I dropped it. We had arranged all details at night, when I met them."

She stopped and looked at Dunston, a long, lingering look, that sent the blood to his face. It was not an appeal; it was nothing save the woman love in her, mingled with desperation.

"I intended to leave the bank in a little while," she went on. "Not immediately, because I was afraid that would attract attention, but after a few weeks. And then, too, I wanted to get forever out of sight of this man," and she indicated Dunston.

"Why?" he asked.

"Because I loved you as no woman ever loved a man before,"

she said, "and I was not worthy. There was another reason, too—I am married already. This man, Gustave Meyer, is my husband."

She paused and fumbled nervously at the veil fastening at her throat. Silence lay over the room; The Thinking Machine reached behind him and picked up the shabby-looking gripsack which had passed unnoticed.

"Are there any more questions?" the girl asked, at last.

"I think not," said The Thinking Machine.

"And, Mr. Dunston, you will give me credit for some good, won't you—some good in that I loved you?" she pleaded.

"My God!" he exclaimed in a sudden burst of feeling.

"Look out!" shouted The Thinking Machine.

He had seen the girl's hand fly to her hat, saw it drawn suddenly away, saw something slender flash at her breast. But it was too late. She had driven a heavy hat pin straight through her breast, piercing the heart. She died in the arms of the man she loved, with his tears on her face.

Detective Mallory appeared before the two prisoners in an adjoining room.

"Miss Clarke has confessed," he said.

"Well, the little devil!" exclaimed Meyer. "I knew some day she would throw us. I'll kill her!"

"It isn't necessary," remarked Mallory.

* * *

In the room where the girl lay The Thinking Machine pushed with his foot the shabby-looking grip toward President Fraser and West.

"There's the money," he said.

"Where—how did you get it?"

"Ask Mr. Hatch."

"Professor Van Dusen told me to search the rooms of those men in there, find the shabbiest looking bag or receptacle that was securely locked, and bring it to him. I—I did so. I found it under the bed, but I didn't know what was in it until he opened it."

THE MYSTERY OF A STUDIO[*]

I

Where the light slants down softly into one corner of a noted art museum in Boston there hangs a large picture. Its title is "Fulfillment." Discriminating art critics have alternately raved at it and praised it; from the day it appeared there it has been a fruitful source of acrimonious discussion. As for the public, it accepts the picture as a startling, amazing thing of beauty, and there is always a crowd around it.

"Fulfillment" is typified by a woman. She stands boldly forth against a languorous background of deep tones. Flesh tints are daringly laid on the semi-nude figure, diaphanous draperies hide, yet, reveal, the exquisite lines of the body. Her arms are outstretched straight toward the spectator, the black hair ripples down over her shoulders, the red lips are slightly parted. The mysteries of complete achievement and perfect life lie in her eyes.

Into this picture the artist wove the spiritual and the worldly; here he placed on canvas an elusive portrayal of success in its

---

[*] First published in *Boston American*, December 4, 1905.

fullest and widest meaning. One's first impression of the picture is that it is sensual; another glance shows the underlying typification of success, and love and life are there. One by one the qualities stand forth.

The artist was Constans St. George.[*] After the first flurry of excitement which the picture caused there came a whirlwind of criticism. Then the artist, who had labored for months on the work which he had intended and which proved to be his masterpiece, collapsed. Some said it was overwork—they were partly right; others that it was grief at the attacks of critics who did not see beyond the surface of the painting. Perhaps they, too, were partly right.

However that may be, it is a fact that for several months after the picture was exhibited St. George was in a sanitarium. The physicians said it was nervous collapse—a total breaking-down, and there were fears for his sanity. At length there came an improvement in his condition, and he returned to the world. Since then he had lived quietly in his studio, one of many in a large office building. From time to time he had been approached with offers for the picture, but always he refused to sell. A New York millionaire made a flat proposition of fifty thousand dollars,[†] which was as flatly refused.

The artist loved the picture as a child of his own brain; every day he visited the museum where it was exhibited and stood looking at it with something almost like adoration in his eyes. Then he went away quietly, tugging at his straggling beard and with the dim blindness of tears in his eyes. He never spoke to anyone; and always avoided that moment when a crowd was about.

---

[*] A fictional artist. Curiously, there is indeed a work titled "Fulfillment" by the Viennese artist Gustave Klimt (1862–1918), created as part of the Stoclet Frieze he worked on from 1905 to 1911.

[†] Over $1.5 million in 2022, according to Williamson, Measuring Worth.

Whatever the verdict of the critics or of the public on "Fulfillment," it was an admitted fact that the artist had placed on canvas a representation of a wonderfully beautiful woman. Therefore, after awhile the question of who had been the model for "Fulfillment" was aroused. No one knew, apparently. Artists who knew St. George could give no idea—they only knew that the woman who had posed was not a professional model.

This led to speculation, in which the names of some of the most beautiful women in the United States were mentioned. Then a romance was woven. This was that the artist was in love with the original and that his collapse was partly due to her refusal to wed him. This story, as it went, was elaborated until the artist was said to be pining away for love of one whom he had immortalized in oils.

As the story grew it gained credence, and a search was still made occasionally for the model. Half a dozen times Hutchinson Hatch, a newspaper reporter of more than usual astuteness, had been on the story without success; he had seen and studied the picture until every line of it was firmly in his mind. He had seen and talked to St. George twice. The artist would answer no questions as to the identity of the model.

This, then, was the situation on the morning of Friday, November 27, when Hatch entered the reportorial rooms of his newspaper. At sight of him the city editor removed his cigar, placed it carefully on the "official block"* which adorned his flat-topped desk, and called to the reporter.

"Girl reported missing," he said, brusquely. "Name is Grace Field, and she lived at No. 195———Street, Dorchester.

---

* In architecture, the "official block" is the suite of rooms in a larger facility (e.g., a hospital or prison) where offices are located. In this context, Futrelle means the work space on the desk (as contrasted with the portions of the desktop occupied by decorative items or stacks of papers).

Employed in the photographic department of the Star, a big department store.* Report of her disappearance made to the police early to-day by Ellen Stanford, her roommate, also employed at the Star. Jump out on it and get all you can. Here is the official police description."

Hatch took a slip of paper and read:

"Grace Field, twenty-one years, five feet seven inches tall, weight 151 pounds, profuse black hair, dark-brown eyes, superb figure, oval face, said to be beautiful."†

Then the description went into details of her dress and other things which the police note in their minute records for a search. Hatch absorbed all these things and left his office. He went first to the department store, where he was told Miss Stanford had not appeared that day, sending a note that she was ill.

From the store Hatch went at once to the address given in Dorchester. Miss Stanford was in. Would she see a reporter? Yes. So Hatch was ushered into the modest little parlor of a boarding-house, and after awhile Miss Stanford entered. She was a petite blonde, with pink cheeks and blue eyes, now reddened by weeping.

Briefly Hatch explained the purpose of his visit—an effort to find Grace Field, and Miss Stanford eagerly and tearfully expressed herself as willing to tell him all she knew.

"I have known Grace for five months," she explained; "that is, from the time she came to work at the Star. Her counter is next to mine. A friendship grew up between us, and we began rooming together. Each of us is alone in the East. She comes from the West, somewhere in Nevada, and I come from Quebec.

---

* A fictional department store.

† In 1907, the idealized standard for women was the "Gibson Girl" with an hourglass figure, depicted by the illustrator Charles Dana Gibson in countless publications between the 1890s and the 1910s.

"Grace has never said much about herself, but I know that she had been in Boston a year or so before I met her. She lived somewhere in Brookline, I believe, but it seems that she had some funds and did not go to work until she came to the Star. This is as I understand it.

"Three days ago, on Tuesday it was, there was a letter for Grace when we came in from work. It seemed to agitate her, although she said nothing to me about what was in it, and I did not ask. She did not sleep well that night, but next morning, when we started to work, she seemed all right. That is, she was all right until we got to the subway station, and then she told me to go on to the store, saying she would be there after awhile.

"I left her, and at her request explained to the manager of our floor that she would be late. From that time to this no one has seen her or heard of her. I don't know where she could have gone," and the girl burst into tears. "I'm sure something dreadful has happened to her."

"Possibly an elopement?" Hatch suggested.

"No," said the girl, quickly. "No. She was in love, but the man she was in love with has not heard of her either. I saw him the night after she disappeared. He called here and asked for her, and seemed surprised that she had not returned home, or had not been at work."

"What's his name?" asked Hatch.

"He's a clerk in a bank," said Miss Stanford. "His name is Willis—Victor Willis. If she had eloped with him I would not have been surprised, but I am positive she did not, and if she did not, where is she?"

"Were there any other admirers you know of?" Hatch asked.

"No," said the girl, stoutly. "There may have been others who admired her, but none she cared for. She has told me too much—I—I know," she faltered.

"How long have you known Mr. Willis?" asked Hatch.

The girl's face flamed scarlet instantly.

"Only since I've known Grace," she replied. "She introduced us."

"Has Mr. Willis ever shown you any attention?"

"Certainly not," Miss Stanford flashed, angrily. "All his attention was for Grace."

There was the least trace of bitterness in the tone, and Hatch imagined he read it aright. Willis was a man whom both perhaps loved; it might be in that event that Miss Stanford knew more than she had said of the whereabouts of Grace Field. The next step was to see Willis.

"I suppose you'll do everything possible to find Miss Field?" he asked.

"Certainly," said the girl.

"Have you her photograph?"

"I have one, yes, but I don't think—I don't believe Grace———"

"Would like to have it published?" asked Hatch. "Possibly not, under ordinary circumstances—but now that she is missing it is the surest way of getting a trace of her. Will you give it to me?"

Miss Stanford was silent for a time. Then apparently she made up her mind, for she arose.

"It might be well, too," Hatch suggested, "to see if you can find the letter you mentioned."

The girl nodded and went out. When she returned she had a photograph in her hand; a glimpse of it told Hatch it was a bust picture of a woman in evening dress. The girl was studying a scrap of paper.

"What is it?" asked Hatch, quickly.

"I don't know," she responded. "I was searching for the letter when I remembered she frequently tore them up and dropped them into the waste-basket. It had been emptied every day, but I looked and found this clinging to the bottom, caught between the cane."

"May I see it?" asked the reporter. The girl handed it to him. It was evidently a piece of a letter torn from the outer edge just where the paper was folded to put it into the envelope. On it were these words and detached letters, written in a bold hand:

> **sday**
>
> **ill you**
>
> **to the**
>
> **ho**

Hatch's eyes opened wide.

"Do you know the handwriting?" he asked.

The girl faltered an instant.

"No," she answered, finally.

Hatch studied her face a moment with cold eyes, then turned the scrap of paper over. The other side was blank. Staring down at it he veiled a glitter of anxious interest.

"And the picture?" he asked, quietly.

The girl handed him the photograph. Hatch took it and as he looked it was with difficulty he restrained an exclamation of astonishment—triumphant astonishment. Finally, with his brain teeming with possibilities, he left the house, taking the photograph and the scrap of paper. Ten minutes later he was talking to his city editor over the 'phone.

"It's a great story," he explained, briefly. "The missing girl is the mysterious model of St. George's picture, 'Fulfillment.'"

"Great," came the voice of the city editor.

II

Having laid his story before his city editor, Hatch sat down to consider the fragmentary writing. Obviously "sday" represented a day of the week—either Tuesday, Wednesday, or Thursday, these being the only days where the letter "s" preceded the "day." This seemed to be a definite fact, but still it meant nothing. True, Miss Field had last been seen on Wednesday, but then?—nothing.

To the next part of the fragment Hatch attached the greatest importance. It was the possibility of a threat,————"ill you." Did it mean "kill you" or "will you" or "till you" or—or what? There might be dozens of other words ending in "ill" which he did not recall at the moment. His imagination hammered the phrase into his brain as "kill you." The "to the"—the next words—were clear, but meant nothing at all. The last letters were distinctly "ho," possibly "hope."

Then Hatch began real work on the story. First he saw the bank clerk, Victor Willis, who Miss Stanford had said loved Grace Field, and whom Hatch suspected Miss Stanford loved. He found Willis a grim, sullen-faced young man of twenty-eight years, who would say nothing.

From that point Hatch worked vigorously for several hours. At the end of that time he had found out that on Wednesday, the day of Miss Field's disappearance, a veiled woman—probably Grace Field—had called at the bank and inquired for Willis. Later, Willis, urging necessity, had asked to be allowed the day off and left the bank. He did not appear again until next morning. His actions did not impress any of his associates with the idea that he was a bridegroom; in fact, Hatch himself had given up the idea that Miss Field had eloped. There seemed no reason for an elopement.

When Hatch called at the studio, and home, of Constans St.

George, to inform him of the disappearance of the model whose identity had been so long guarded, he was told that Mr. St. George was not in; that is, St. George refused to answer knocks at the door, and had not been seen for a day or so. He frequently disappeared this way, his informant said.

With these facts—and lack of facts—in his possession on Friday evening, Hatch called on Professor S. F. X. Van Dusen. The Thinking Machine received him as cordially as he ever received anybody.

"Well, what is it?" he asked.

"I don't believe this is really worth your while, Professor," Hatch said, finally. "It's just a case of a girl who disappeared. There are some things about it which are puzzling, but I'm afraid it's only an elopement."

The Thinking Machine dragged up a footstool, planted his small feet on it comfortably and leaned back in his chair.

"Go on," he directed.

Then Hatch told the story, beginning at the time when the picture was placed in the art museum, and continuing up to the point where he had seen Willis after finding the photograph and the scrap of paper. He had always found that it saved time to begin at the beginning with The Thinking Machine; he did it now as a matter of course.

"And the scrap of paper?" asked The Thinking Machine.

"I have it here," replied the reporter.

For several minutes the scientist examined the fragment and then handed it back to the reporter.

"If one could establish some clear connection between that and the disappearance of the girl it might be valuable," he said. "As it is now, it means nothing. Any number of letters might be thrown into the waste-basket in the room the two girls occupied, therefore dismiss this for the moment."

"But isn't it possible————" Hatch began.

"Anything is possible, Mr. Hatch," retorted the other, belligerently. "You might take occasion to see the handwriting of St. George, the artist, and see if that is his—also look at Willis's. Even if it were Willis's, however, it may mean nothing in connection with this."

"But what could have happened to Miss Field?"

"Any one of fifty things," responded the other. "She might have fallen dead in the street and been removed to a hospital or undertaking establishment; she might have been arrested for shoplifting and given a wrong name; she might have gone mad and gone away; she might have eloped with another man; she might have committed suicide; she might have been murdered. The question is not what *could* have happened, but what *did* happen."

"Yes, I thoroughly understand that," Hatch replied, with a slight smile. "But still I don't see————"

"Probably you don't," snapped the other. "We'll take it for granted that she did none of these things, with the possible exception of eloping, killing herself, or was murdered. You are convinced that she did not elope. Yet you have only run down one possible end of this—that is, the possibility of her elopement with Willis. You don't believe she did elope with him. Well, why not with St. George?"

"St. George?" gasped Hatch. "A great artist elope with a shop-girl?"

"She was his ideal in a picture which you say is one of the greatest in the world," replied the other, testily. "That being true, it is perfectly possible that she was his ideal for a wife, isn't it?"

The matter had not occurred to Hatch in just that light. He nodded his head, with a feeling of having been weighed and found wanting.

"Now, you say, too, that St. George has not been seen around his studio for a couple of days," said the scientist. "What is more possible than that they are together somewhere?"

"I see," said the reporter.

"It was understood, too, as I understand it, that St. George was in love with her," went on The Thinking Machine. "So, I should imagine a solution of the mystery might be reached by taking St. George as the center of the affair. Suicide may be passed by for the moment, because she had no known motive for suicide—rather, if she loved Willis, she had every reason to live. Murder, too, may be passed for the moment—although there is a possibility that we might come back to that. Question St. George. He will listen if you make him, and then he must answer."

"But his place is all closed up," said Hatch. "It is supposed he is half crazy."

"Possibly he might be," said The Thinking Machine. "Or it is possible that he is keeping to his studio at work—or he might even be married to Miss Field and she might be there with him."

"Well, I see no way to ascertain definitely that he is there," said the reporter, and a puzzled wrinkle came into his face. "Of course I might remain on watch night and day to see if he comes out for food, or if anything to eat is sent in."

"That would take too long, and besides it might not happen at all," said The Thinking Machine. He arose and went into the adjoining room. He returned after a moment, and glanced at the clock on the mantel. "It is just nine o'clock now," he commented. "How long would it take you to get to the studio?"

"Half an hour."

"Well, go there now," directed the scientist. "If Mr. St. George is in his studio he will come out of it to-night at thirty-two minutes past nine. He will be running, and may not wear either a hat or coat."

"What?" and Hatch grinned, a weak, puzzled grin.

"You wait where he can't see you when he comes out," the scientist went on. "When he goes he may leave the door open. If he does go on see if you find any trace of Miss Field, and then, on his return, meet him at the outer door, ask him what you please, and come to see me to-morrow morning. He will be out of his studio about twenty minutes."

Vaguely Hatch felt that the scientist was talking rot, but he had seen this strange mind bring so many odd things to pass that he could not doubt this, even if it were absurd on its face.

"At thirty-two minutes past nine to-night," said the reporter, and he glanced at his watch.

"Come to see me to-morrow after you see the handwriting of Willis and St. George," directed the scientist. "Then you may also tell me just what happens to-night."

* * *

Hatch was feeling like a fool. He was waiting in a darkened corner, just a few feet from St. George's studio. It was precisely half-past nine o'clock. He had been there for seven minutes. What strange power was to bring St. George, who for two days had denied himself to everyone, out of that studio, if, indeed, he were there?

For the twentieth time Hatch glanced at his watch, which he had set with the little clock in The Thinking Machine's home. Slowly the minute hand crept around, to 9:31, 9:31½, and he heard the door of the studio rattle. Then suddenly it was thrown open and St. George appeared.

Without a glance to right or left, hatless and coatless, he rushed out of the building. Hatch got only a glimpse of his face; his lips were pressed tightly together; there was a glint of madness in his eyes. He jerked at the door once, then ran through the hall and disappeared down the stairs leading to the street. The studio door stood open behind him.

III

When the clatter of the running footsteps had died away and Hatch heard the outer door slam, he entered the studio, closing the door behind him. It was close here, and there was a breath of Chinese incense which was almost stifling. One quick glance by the light of an incandescent told Hatch that he stood in the reception-room. Typically, from floor to ceiling, the place was the abode of an artist; there was a rich gradation of color and everywhere were scraps of art and half-finished studies.

The reporter had given up the idea of solving the mystery of why St. George had so suddenly left his apartments; now he devoted himself to a quick, minute search of the place. He found nothing to interest him in the reception-room, and went on into the studio where the artist did his work.

Hatch glanced around quickly, his eyes taking in all the details, then went to a little table which stood, half-covered with newspapers. He turned these over, then bent forward suddenly and picked up—a woman's glove. Beside it lay its mate. He stuffed them into his pocket.

Eagerly he sought now for anything that might come to hand. At last he reached another door, leading into the bedroom. Here on a large table was a chafing dish, many dishes which had not been washed, and all the other evidences of a careless man who did a great deal of his own cooking. There was a dresser here, too, a gorgeous, mahogany affair. Hatch didn't stop to admire this because his eye was attracted by a woman's veil which lay on it. He thrust it into his pocket.

"Quite a haul I'm making," he mused, grimly.

From this room a door, half open, led into a bathroom. Hatch merely glanced in, then looked at his watch. Fifteen minutes had elapsed. He must get out, and he started for the outer door. As he opened it quietly and stepped into the hall he heard the street door open one flight below, and started down the steps. There, half way, he met St. George.

"Mr. St. George?" he asked.

"No," was the reply.

Hatch knew his man perfectly, because he had seen him half a dozen times and had talked to him twice. The denial of identity therefore was futile.

"I came to tell you that Grace Field, the model for your 'Fulfillment,' has disappeared," Hatch went on, as the other glared at him.

"I don't care," snapped the other. He darted up the steps. Hatch listened until he heard the door of the studio close.

It was ten minutes to ten o'clock when Hatch left the building. Now he would see Miss Stanford and have her identify the gloves and the veil. He boarded a car and drew out and closely examined the gloves and veil. The gloves were tan, rather heavy, but small, and the veil was of some light, cobwebby material which he didn't know by name.

"If these are Grace Field's," the reporter argued, to himself, "it means something. If they are not, I'm simply a burglar."

There was a light in the Dorchester house where Miss Stanford lived, and the reporter rang the bell. A servant appeared.

"Would it be possible for me to see Miss Stanford for just a moment?" he asked.

"If she has not gone to bed."

He was ushered into the little parlor again. The servant disappeared, and after a moment Miss Stanford came in.

"I hated to trouble you so late," said the reporter, and she smiled at him frankly, " but I would like to ask if you have ever seen these?"

He laid in her hands the gloves and the veil. Miss Stanford studied them carefully and her hands trembled.

"The gloves, I know, are Grace's—the veil I am not so positive about," she replied.

Hatch felt a great wave of exultation sweep over him, and it stopped his tongue for an instant.

"Did you—did you find them in Mr. Willis's possession?" asked the girl.

"I am not at liberty to tell just where I found them," Hatch replied. "If they are Miss Field's—and you can swear to that, I suppose—it may mean that we have a clew."

"Oh, I was afraid it would be this way," gasped the girl, and she sank down weeping on a couch.

"Knew what would be which way?" asked Hatch, puzzled.

"I knew it! I knew it!" she sobbed. "Is there anything to connect Mr. Willis directly with the—*the murder*?"

The reporter started to say something, then paused. He wasn't quite sure of himself. He had uncovered something, he didn't know what yet.

"It would be better, Miss Stanford," he explained, gently, "if you would tell me all you know about this affair. The things which are now in my possession are fragmentary—if you could give me any new detail it would be only serving the ends of justice."

For a little while the girl was silent, then she arose and faced him.

"Is Mr. Willis yet under arrest?" she asked, calmly now.

"Not yet," said the reporter.

"Then I will say nothing else," she declared, and her lips closed in a straight line.

"What was the motive for murder?" Hatch insisted.

"I will say nothing else," she replied, firmly.

"And what makes you positive there was murder?"

"Good-night. You need not come again, for I will not see you."

Miss Stanford turned and left the room. Hatch, sadly puzzled, bewildered, stood staring after her a moment, then went out, his brain alive with possibilities, with intangible ends which would not be connected. He was eager to lay the new facts before The Thinking Machine.

From Dorchester the reporter took a car for his home. In his room, with the tangible threads of the mystery spread out on a table, he thought and surmised far into the night, and when he finally replaced them all in his pocket and turned down the light it was with a hopeless shake of his head.

On the following morning when Hatch arose he picked up a paper and went to breakfast. He spread the paper before him and there—the first thing he saw—was a huge headline, stating that a burglar had entered the room of Constans St. George and had tried to kill Mr. St. George. A shot had been fired at him and had passed through his left arm.

Mr. St. George had been asleep when the door of his apartments was burst in by the thief. The artist arose at the noise, and as he stepped into the reception-room had been shot. The wound was trivial. The burglar escaped; there was no clew.

IV

It was a long story of seemingly hopeless complications that Hatch told The Thinking Machine that morning. Nothing connected with anything, and yet here was a series of happenings, all apparently growing out of the disappearance of Miss Field, and which must have some relation one to the other. At the conclusion of the story, Hatch passed over the newspaper containing the account of the burglary in the studio. The artist had been removed to a hospital.

The Thinking Machine read the newspaper account and turned to the reporter with a question:

"Did you see Willis's handwriting?"

"Not yet," replied the reporter.

"See it at once," instructed the other. "If possible, bring me a sample of it. Did you see St. George's handwriting?"

"No," the reporter confessed.

"See that and bring me a sample if you can. Find out first if Willis has a revolver now or has ever had. If so, see it and see if it is loaded or empty—its exact condition. Find out also if St. George has a revolver—and if he has one, get possession of it if it is in your power."

The scientist twisted the two gloves and the veil which Hatch had given to him in his fingers idly, then passed them to the reporter again.

Hatch arose and stood waiting, hat in hand.

"Also find out," The Thinking Machine went on, "the exact condition of St. George—his mental condition particularly. Find out if Willis is at his office in the bank to-day, and, if possible, where and how he spent last night. That's all."

"And Miss Stanford?" asked Hatch.

"Never mind her," replied The Thinking Machine. "I may see her myself. These other things are of immediate consequence. The minute you satisfy yourself come back to me. Quickness on your part may prevent a tragedy."

The reporter went away hurriedly. At four o'clock that afternoon he returned. The Thinking Machine greeted him; he held a piece of letter-paper in his hand.

"Well?" he asked.

"The handwriting is Willis's," said Hatch, without hesitation. "I saw a sample—it is identical, and the paper on which he writes is identical."

The scientist grunted.

"I also saw some of St. George's writing," the reporter went on, as if he were reciting a lesson. "It is wholly dissimilar."

The Thinking Machine nodded.

"Willis has no revolver that anyone ever heard of," Hatch continued. "He was at dinner with several of his fellow employees last night, and left the restaurant at eight o'clock."

"Been drinking?"

"Might have had a few drinks," responded the reporter. "He is not a drinking man."

"Has St. George a revolver?"

"I was unable to find that out or do anything except get a sample of his writing from another artist," the reporter explained. "He is in a hospital, raving crazy. It seems to be a return of the trouble he had once before, except it is worse. The wound itself is not bad."

The scientist was studying the sheet of paper.

"Have you that scrap?" he asked.

Hatch produced it, and the scientist placed it on the sheet; Hatch could only conjecture that he was fitting it to something else already there. He was engaged in this work when Martha entered.

"The young lady who was here earlier to-day wants to see you again," she announced.

"Show her in," directed The Thinking Machine, without raising his eyes.

Martha disappeared, and after a moment Miss Stanford entered. Hatch, himself unnoticed, stared at her curiously, and arose, as did the scientist. The girl's face was flushed a little, and there was an eager expression in her eyes.

"I know he didn't do it," she began. "I've just gotten a letter from Springfield stating that he was there on the day Grace went away—and—"

"Know who didn't do what?" asked the scientist.

"That Mr. Willis didn't kill Grace," replied the girl, her enthusiasm suddenly checked. "See here."

The scientist read a letter which she offered, and the girl sank into a chair. Then for the first time she saw Hatch and her eyes expressed her surprise. She stared at him a moment, then nodded a greeting, after which she fell to watching The Thinking Machine.

"Miss Stanford," he said, at length, "you made several mistakes when you were here before in not telling me the truth—all of it. If you will tell me all you know of this case I may be able to see it more clearly."

The girl reddened and stammered a little, then her lips trembled.

"Do you *know*—not conjecture, but *know*—whether or not Miss Field, or Grace, as you call her, was engaged to Willis?" the irritated voice asked.

"I—I know it, yes," she stammered.

"And you were in love with Mr. Willis—you *are* in love with him?"

Again the tell-tale blush swept over her face. She glanced at Hatch; it was the nervousness of a girl who is driven to a confession of love.

"I regard Mr. Willis very highly," she said, finally, her voice low.

"Well," and the scientist arose and crossed to where the girl sat, "don't you see that a very grave charge might be brought

home to you if you don't tell all of this? The girl has disappeared. There might be even a hint of murder in which your
name would be mentioned. Don't you see?"

There was a long pause, and the girl stared steadily into the
squint eyes above her. Finally her eyes fell.

"I think I understand. Just what is it you want me to answer?"

"Did or did you not ever hear Mr. Willis threaten Miss Field?"

"I did once, yes."

"Did or did you not know that Miss Field was the original of
the painting?"

"I did not."

"It is a semi-nude picture, isn't it?"

Again there was a flush in the girl's face.

"I have heard it was," she said. "I have never seen it. I suggested to Grace several times that we go to see it, but she never
would. I understand why now."

"Did Willis know she was the original of that painting? That
is, knowing it yourself now, do you have any reason to suppose
that he previously knew?"

"I don't know," she said, frankly. "I know that there was
something which was always causing friction between them—
something they quarreled about. It might have been that. That
was when I heard Mr. Willis threaten her—it was something
about shooting her if she ever did something—I don't know
what."

"Miss Field knew him before you did, I think you said?"

"She introduced me to him."

The Thinking Machine fingered the sheet of paper he held.

"Did you know what those scraps of paper you brought me
contained?"

"Yes, in a way," said the girl.

"Why did you bring them, then?"

"Because you told me you knew I had them, and I was afraid it might make more trouble for me and for Mr. Willis if I did not."

The Thinking Machine passed the sheet to Hatch.

"This will interest you, Mr. Hatch," he explained. "Those words and letters in parentheses are what I have supplied to complete the full text of the note, of which you had a mere scrap. You will notice how the scrap you had fitted into it."

The reporter read this:

"If you go to th(at stud)io Wednesday to see that artist, (I will k)ill you bec(ause I w)on't have it known to the world tha(t you a)re a model. I hope you will heed this warning.

"V. W."

The reporter stared at the patched-up letter, pasted together with infinite care, and then glanced at The Thinking Machine, who settled himself again comfortably in the chair.

"And now, Miss Stanford," asked the scientist, in a most matter-of-fact tone, "where is the body of Miss Field?"

V

The blunt question aroused the girl, and she arose suddenly, staring at The Thinking Machine. He did not move. She stood as if transfixed, and Hatch saw her bosom rise and fall rapidly with the emotion she was seeking to repress.

"Well?" asked The Thinking Machine.

"I don't know," flamed Miss Stanford, suddenly, almost fiercely. "I don't even know she is dead. I know that Mr. Willis did not kill her, because, as that letter I gave you shows, he was in Springfield. I won't be tricked into saying anything further."

The outburst had no appreciable effect on The Thinking Machine beyond causing him to raise his eyebrows slightly as he looked at the defiant little figure.

"When did you last see Mr. Willis have a revolver?"

"I know nothing of any revolver. I know only that Victor Willis is innocent as you are, and that I love him. Whatever has become of Grace Field I don't know."

Tears leaped suddenly to her eyes, and, turning, she left the room. After a moment they heard the outer door slam as she passed out. Hatch turned to the scientist with a question in his eyes.

"Did you smell anything like chloroform or ether when you were in St. George's apartments?" asked The Thinking Machine as he arose.

"No," said Hatch. "I only noticed that the place seemed close, and there was an odor of Chinese incense—joss sticks—which was almost stifling."

The Thinking Machine looked at the reporter quickly, but said nothing. Instead, he passed out of the room, to return a few minutes later with his hat and coat on.

"Where are we going?" asked Hatch.

"To St. George's studio," was the answer.

Just then the telephone bell in the next room rang. The scientist answered it in person.

"Your city editor," he called to Hatch.

Hatch went to the 'phone and remained there several minutes. When he came back there was a new excitement in his face.

"What is it?" asked the scientist.

"Another queer thing my city editor told me," Hatch responded. "Constans St. George, raving mad, has escaped from the hospital and disappeared."

"Dear me, dear me!" exclaimed the scientist, quickly. It was as near surprise as he ever showed. "Then there is danger."

With quick steps he went to the telephone and called up police headquarters.

"Detective Mallory," Hatch heard him ask for. "Yes. This is Professor Van Dusen. Please meet me immediately here at my house. Be here in ten minutes? Good. I'll wait. It's a matter of great importance. Good-by."

Then impatiently The Thinking Machine moved about, waiting. The reporter, whose acquaintance with the logician was an extended one, had never seen him in just such a state. It started when he heard St. George had escaped.

At last they left the house and stood waiting on the steps until Detective Mallory appeared in a cab. Into that Hatch and The Thinking Machine climbed, after the latter had given some direction, and the cabby drove rapidly away. It was all a mystery to Hatch, and he was rather glad of it when Detective Mallory asked what it meant.

"Means that there is danger of a tragedy," said The Thinking Machine, crustily. "We may be in time to avert it. There is just a chance. If I'd only known this an hour ago—even half an hour ago—it might have been stopped."

The Thinking Machine was the first man out of the cab when it stopped, and Hatch and the detective followed quickly.

"Is Mr. St. George in his apartments?" asked the scientist of the elevator boy.

"No, sir," said the boy. "He's in hospital, shot."

"Is there a key to his place? Quick."

"I think so, sir, but I can't give it to you."

"Here, give it to me, then!" exclaimed the detective. He flashed a badge in the boy's eyes, and the youth immediately lost a deal of his coolness.

"Gee, a detective! Yes, sir."

"How many rooms has Mr. St. George?" asked the scientist.

"Three and a bath," the boy responded.

Two minutes later the three men stood in the reception-room of the apartments. There came to them from somewhere inside a deadly, stifling odor of chloroform. After one glance around The Thinking Machine rushed into the next room, the studio.

"Dear me, dear me!" he exclaimed.

There on the floor lay huddled the figure of a man. Blood had run from several wounds on his head. The Thinking Machine stooped a moment, and his slender fingers fumbled over the heart.

"Unconscious, that's all," he said, and he raised the man up.

"Victor Willis!" exclaimed Hatch.

"Victor Willis!" repeated The Thinking Machine, as if puzzled. "Are you sure?"

"Certain," said Hatch, positively. "It's the bank clerk."

"Then we are too late," declared the scientist.

He arose and looked about the room. A door to his right attracted his attention. He jerked it open and peered in. It was a clothes press. Another small door on the other side of the room was also thrown open. Here was a kitchenette, with a great quantity of canned stuffs.

The Thinking Machine went on into the little bedroom which Hatch had searched. He flung open the bathroom and peered in, only to shut it immediately. Then he tried the handle of another door, a closet. It was fastened.

"Ah!" he exclaimed.

Then on his hands and knees he sniffed at the crack between the door and the flooring. Suddenly, as if satisfied, he arose and stepped away from the door.

"Smash that door in," he directed.

Detective Mallory looked at him stupefied. There was a similar expression on Hatch's face.

"What's—what's in there?" the detective asked.

"Smash it," said the other, tartly. "Smash it, or God knows what you'll find in there."

The detective, a powerful man, and Hatch threw their weight against the door; it stood rigid. They pulled at the handle; it refused to yield.

"Lend me your revolver?" asked The Thinking Machine.

The weapon was in his hand almost before the detective was aware of it, and, placing the barrel to the keyhole, The Thinking Machine pulled the trigger. There was a resonant report, the lock was smashed and the detective put out his hand to open the door.

"Look out for a shot," warned The Thinking Machine, sharply.

VI

The Thinking Machine drew Detective Mallory and Hatch to one side, out of immediate range of any person who might rush out, then pulled the closet door open. A cloud of suffocating fumes—the sweet, sickening odor of chloroform—gushed out, but there was no sound from inside. The detective looked at The Thinking Machine inquiringly.

Carefully, almost gingerly, the scientist peered around the edge of the door. What he saw did not startle him, because it was what he expected. It was Constans St. George lying prone on the floor as if dead, with a blood-spattered revolver clasped loosely in one hand; the other hand grasped the throat of a woman, a woman of superb physical beauty, who also lay with face upturned, staring glassily.

"Open the windows—all of them, then help me," commanded the scientist.

As Detective Mallory and Hatch turned to obey the instructions, The Thinking Machine took the revolver from the inert fingers of the artist. Then Hatch and Mallory returned and together they lifted the unconscious forms toward a window.

"It's Grace Field," said the reporter.

In silence for half an hour the scientist labored over the unconscious forms of his three patients. The detective and reporter stood by, doing only what they were told to do. The wind, cold and stinging, came pouring through the windows, and it was only a few minutes until the chloroform odor was dissipated. The first of the three unconscious ones to show any sign of returning comprehension was Victor Willis, whose presence at all in the apartments furnished one of the mysteries which Hatch could not fathom.

It was evident that his condition was primarily due to the wounds on his head—two of which bled profusely. The chloroform had merely served to further deaden his mentality. The wounds were made with the butt of the revolver, evidently in the hands of the artist. Willis's eyes opened finally and he stared at the faces bending over him with uncomprehending eyes.

"What happened?" he asked.

"You're all right now," was the scientist's assuring answer. "This man is your prisoner, Detective Mallory, for breaking and entering and for the attempted murder of Mr. St. George."

Detective Mallory was delighted. Here was something he could readily understand; a human being given over to his care; a tangible thing to put handcuffs on and hold. He immediately proceeded to put the handcuffs on.

"Any need of an ambulance?" he asked.

"No," replied The Thinking Machine. "He'll be all right in half an hour."

Gradually as reason came back Willis remembered.

He turned his head at last and saw the inert bodies of St. George and Grace Field, the girl whom he had loved.

"She was here, then!" he exclaimed suddenly, violently. "I knew it. Is she dead?"

"Shut up that young fool's mouth, Mr. Mallory," commanded the scientist, sharply. "Take him in the other room or send him away."

Obediently Mallory did as directed; there was that in the voice of this cold, calm being, The Thinking Machine, which compelled obedience. Mallory never questioned motives or orders.

Willis was able to walk to the other room with help. Miss Field and St. George lay side by side in the cold wind from the open window. The Thinking Machine had forced a little whiskey down their throats, and after a time St. George opened his eyes.

The artist was instantly alert and tried to rise. He was weak, however, and even a strength given to him by the madness which blazed in his eyes did not avail. At last he lay raving, cursing, shrieking. The Thinking Machine regarded him closely.

"Hopeless," he said, at last.

Again for many minutes the scientist worked with the girl. Finally he asked that an ambulance be sent for. The detective called up the City Hospital on the telephone in the apartments and made the request. The Thinking Machine stared alternately at the girl and at the artist.

"Hopeless," he said again. "St. George, I mean."

"Will the girl recover?" asked Hatch.

"I don't know," was the frank reply. "She's been partly

stupefied for days—ever since she disappeared, as a matter of fact. If her physical condition was as good as her appearance indicates she may recover. Now the hospital is the best place for her."

It was only a few minutes before two ambulances came and the three persons were taken away; Willis a prisoner, and a sullen, defiant prisoner, who refused to speak or answer questions; St. George raving hideously and cursing frightfully; the woman, beautiful as a marble statue, and colorless as death.

When they had all gone, The Thinking Machine went back into the bedroom and examined more carefully the little closet in which he had found the artist and Grace Field. It was practically a padded cell, relatively six feet each way. Heavy cushions of felt two or three inches thick covered the interior of the little room closely. In the top of it there was a small aperture, which had permitted some of the fumes of the chloroform to escape. The place was saturated with the poison.

"Let's go," he said, finally.

Detective Mallory and Hatch followed him out and a few minutes later sat opposite him in his little laboratory. Hatch had told a story over the telephone that made his city editor rejoice madly; it was news, great, big, vital news.

"Now, Mr. Hatch, I suppose you want some details," said The Thinking Machine, as he relapsed into his accustomed attitude. "And you, too, Mr. Mallory, since you are holding Willis a prisoner on my say-so. Would you like to know why?"

"Sure," said the detective.

"Let's go back a little—begin at the beginning, where Mr. Hatch called on me," said The Thinking Machine. "I can make the matter clearer that way. And I believe the cause of justice, Mr. Mallory, requires absolute accuracy and clarity in all things, does it not?"

"Sure," said the detective again.

"Well, Mr. Hatch told me at some length of the preliminaries of this case," explained The Thinking Machine. "He told me the history of the picture; the mystery as to the identity of the model; her great beauty; how he found her to be Grace Field, a shop-girl. He also told me of the mental condition of the artist, St. George, and repeated the rumor as he knew it about the artist being heartbroken because the girl—his model—would not marry him.

"All this brought the artist into the matter of the girl's disappearance. She represented to him, physically, the highest ideal of which he could conceive—hope, success, life itself. Therefore it was not astonishing that he should fall in love with her; and it is not difficult to imagine that the girl did not fall in love with him. She is a beautiful woman, but not necessarily a woman of mentality; he is a great artist, eccentric, childish even in certain things. They were two natures totally opposed.

"These things I could see instantly. Mr. Hatch showed me the photograph and also the scrap of paper. At the time the scrap of paper meant nothing. As I pointed out, it might have no bearing at all, yet it made it necessary for me to know whose handwriting it was. If Willis's, it still might mean nothing; if St. George's, a great deal, because it showed a direct thread to him. There was reason to believe that any friendship between them had ended when the picture was exhibited.

"It was necessary, therefore, even that early in the work of reducing the mystery to logic to center it about St. George. This I explained to Mr. Hatch and pointed out the fact that the girl and the artist might have eloped—were possibly together somewhere. First it was necessary to get to the artist; Mr. Hatch had not been able to do so.

"A childishly simple trick, which seemed to amaze Mr. Hatch

considerably, brought the artist out of his rooms after he had been there closely for two days. I told Mr. Hatch that the artist would leave his rooms, if he were there, one night at 9:32, and told him to wait in the hall, then if he left the door open to enter the apartments and search for some trace of the girl. Mr. St. George did leave his apartments at the time I mentioned, and————"

"But why, how?" asked Hatch.

"There was one thing in the world that St. George loved with all his heart," explained the scientist. "That was his picture. Every act of his life has demonstrated that. I looked at a telephone book; I found he had a 'phone. If he were in his rooms, locked in, it was a bit of common sense that his telephone was the best means of reaching him. He answered the 'phone; I told him, just at 9:30, that the art museum was on fire and his picture in danger.

"St. George left his apartments to go and see, just as I knew he would, hatless and coatless, and leaving the door open. Mr. Hatch went inside and found two gloves and a veil, all belonging to Miss Field. Miss Stanford identified them and asked if he had gotten them from Willis, and if Willis had been arrested. Why did she ask these questions? Obviously because she knew, or thought she knew, that Willis had some connection with the affair.

"Mr. Hatch detailed all his discoveries and the conversation with Miss Stanford to me on the day after I 'phoned to St. George, who, of course, had found no fire. It showed that Miss Stanford suspected Willis, whom she loved, of the murder of Miss Field. Why? Because she had heard him threaten. He's a hare-brained young fool, anyway. What motive? Jealousy. Jealousy of what? He knew in some way that she had posed for a semi-nude picture, and that the man who painted it loved her. There is your jealousy. It explains Willis's every act."

The Thinking Machine paused a moment, then went on:

"This conversation with Mr. Hatch made me believe Miss Stanford knew more than she was willing to tell. In what way? By a letter? Possibly. She had given Mr. Hatch a scrap of a letter; perhaps she had found another letter, or more of this one. I sent her a note, telling her I knew she had these scraps of letters, and she promptly brought them to me. She had found them after Mr. Hatch saw her first somewhere in the house—in a bureau drawer she said, I think.

"Meanwhile, Mr. Hatch had called my attention to the burglary of St. George's apartments. One reading of that convinced me that it was Willis who did this. Why? Because burglars don't burst in doors when they think anyone is inside; they pick the lock. Knowing, too, Willis's insane jealousy, I figured that he would be the type of man who would go there to kill St. George if he could, particularly if he thought the girl was there.

"Thus it happened that I was not the only one to think that St. George knew where the girl was. Willis, the one most interested, thought she was there. I questioned Miss Stanford mercilessly, trying to get more facts about the young man from her which would bear on this, trying to trick her into some statement, but she was loyal to the last.

"All these things indicated several things. First, that Willis didn't actually know where the girl was, as he would have known had he killed her; second, that if she had disappeared with a man, it was St. George, as there was no other apparent possibility; third, that St. George would be with her or near her, even if he had killed her; fourth, the pistol shot through the arm had brought on again a mental condition which threatened his entire future, and now as it happens has blighted it.

"Thus, Miss Field and St. George were together. She loved Willis devotedly, therefore she was with St. George against her

will, or she was dead. Where? In his rooms? Possibly. I determined to search there. I had just reached this determination
when I heard St. George, violently insane, had escaped from the
hospital. He had only one purpose then—to get to the woman.
Then she was in danger.

"I reasoned along these lines, rushed to the artist's apartments, found Willis there wounded. He had evidently been
there searching when St. George returned, and St. George had
attacked him, as a madman will, and with the greater strength of
a madman. Then I knew the madman's first step. It would be the
end of everything for him; therefore the death of the girl and his
own. How? By poison preferably, because he would not shoot
her—he loved beauty too much. Where? Possibly in the place
where she had been all along, the closet, carefully padded and
prepared to withstand noises. It is really a padded cell. I have an
idea that the artist, sometimes overcome by his insane fits, and
knowing when they would come, prepared this closet and used
it himself occasionally. Here the girl could have been kept and
her shrieks would never have been heard. You know the rest."

The Thinking Machine stopped and arose, as if to end the
matter. The others arose, too.

"I took you, Mr. Mallory, because you were a detective, and I
knew I could force a way into the apartments which I imagined
would be locked. I think that's all."

"But how did the girl get there?" asked Hatch.

"St. George evidently asked her to come, possibly to pose
again. It was a gratification to the girl to do this—a little touch of
vanity caused her to pose in the first place. It was this vanity that
Willis was fighting so hard, and which led to his threats and his
efforts to kill St. George. Of course the artist was insane when
she came; his frantic love for her led him to make her a prisoner
and hold her against her will. You saw how well he did it."

There was an awed pause. Hatch was rubbing the nap of his hat against his sleeve, thoughtfully. Detective Mallory had nothing to say; it was all said. Both turned as if to go, but the reporter had two more questions.

"I suppose St. George's case is hopeless?"

"Absolutely. It will end in a few months with his death."

"And Miss Field?"

"If she is not dead by this time she will recover. Wait a minute." He went into the next room and they heard the telephone bell jingle. After a time he came out. "She will recover," he said. "Good-afternoon."

Wonderingly, Hutchinson Hatch, reporter, and Detective Mallory passed down the street together.

THE END

READING GROUP GUIDE

1. Do you like the Thinking Machine? What do you see as his redeeming personal qualities?

2. How does Professor Van Dusen compare to Sherlock Holmes? Hutchison Hatch to Dr. Watson?

3. Do you find these stories dated? Or do they play well to today's readers?

4. How realistic are the other principal characters—Hutchinson Hatch, Detective Mallory?

5. How do you think Jacques Futrelle's writing might have changed if he had survived the sinking of the *Titanic*? Do you think he would have been a giant in the field?

FURTHER READING

BY JACQUES FUTRELLE

The Thinking Machine Series

Novels

The Chase of the Golden Plate. New York: Dodd, Mead, 1906. First published in three parts, spread over five issues: "The Burglar and the Girl," *Saturday Evening Post*, September 8, 15, 1906; "The Girl and the Plate," *Saturday Evening Post*, September 22, 29, 1906; and "The Thinking Machine," *Saturday Evening Post*, October 6, 1906.

Short Stories*

"Kidnapped Baby Blake, Millionaire." *Boston American,*
November 27, 1905. Also published as "The Disappearance
of Baby Blake."
"Mystery of the Golden Dagger." *Boston American,* December 26,
1905.
"Mystery of the Fatal Cipher." *Boston American,* January 1–7,
1906, also published in *Associated Sunday Magazines,*
February 3, 1907, as "The Thinking Machine Looks into
the Cipher Message."
"The Mystery of the Grip of Death." *Boston American,* January
8–14, 1906.
"Problem of Dressing Room A." *Associated Sunday Magazines,*
September 2, 1906. Collected in *The Thinking Machine on
the Case* (1908) as a two-part story: "Dressing Room A" and
"Fitting the Hypothesis." In the original magazine version, there
is also a short introductory essay titled "The Thinking Machine"
that tells of a legendary chess challenge and how that resulted in
the naming of the Professor. That brief story also appears as the
introduction to *The Thinking Machine on the Case* (1908).

---

* Many of the early stories first appeared in multiple parts, occasionally even in the
same issue of the newspaper. Only the copyright date of the first part of these stories is
given here. In addition, some stories appeared with variant titles as "The Problem of…"
or "Problem of…" or without this phrase at all; some appeared as "The Mystery of…"
or "The Strange Case of…" Futrelle only published two collections of the Thinking
Machine stories during his lifetime, *The Thinking Machine* (New York: Dodd, Mead,
1907) and *The Thinking Machine on the Case* (New York: D. Appleton, 1908; English
title: *The Professor on the Case*). The list here excludes those collected in *The Thinking
Machine*. Futrelle wrote a total of forty-seven short stories; some scholars count forty-
eight, wrongly treating "My Experience with the Great Logician" as two stories. They
were printed together and are essentially two parts of the same piece. In 2003, Stan
Smith edited an exhaustive collection of Futrelle's stories about the Thinking Machine,
titled *The Thinking Machine Omnibus* (Shelburne, Ontario: Battered Silicon Dispatch
Box, 2003), including *The Chase of the Golden Plate*. Many thanks to FictionMags
Chum Phil Stephensen-Payne for his careful checking of original sources!

"Problem of the Motor Boat." *Associated Sunday Magazines,*
September 9, 1906. Collected in *The Thinking Machine on
the Case* (1908) as a two-part story: "The Motor Boat" and
"The Woman in the Case."

"A Piece of String." *Associated Sunday Magazines,* September 16,
1906.

"Problem of the Crystal Gazer." *Associated Sunday Magazines,*
September 23, 1906. Collected in *The Thinking Machine on
the Case* (1908) as a two-part story: "The Crystal Gazer"
and "A Matter of Logic."

"Problem of the Roswell Tiara." *Associated Sunday Magazines,*
September 30, 1906. Collected in *The Thinking Machine on
the Case* (1908) as a two-part story: "The Roswell Tiara"
and "A Fool of Good Intention."

"Problem of the Lost Radium." *Associated Sunday Magazines,*
October 7, 1906. Collected in *The Thinking Machine on the
Case* (1908) as a two-part story: "The Lost Radium" and
"The Suit Case."

"The Problem of the Opera Box." *Associated Sunday Magazines,*
October 14, 1906. Collected in *The Thinking Machine on
the Case* (1908) as a two-part story: "An Opera Box" and
"Before Midnight."

"Problem of the Missing Necklace." *Associated Sunday Magazines,*
October 21, 1906. Collected in *The Thinking Machine on the
Case* (1908) as a two-part story: "The Missing Necklace"
and "Master of His Profession."

"Problem of the Green Eyed Monster." *Associated Sunday
Magazines,* October 28, 1906. Collected in *The Thinking
Machine on the Case* (1908) as a two-part story: "The Green-
Eyed Monster" and "Two and Two Again Make Four."

"Problem of the Perfect Alibi." *Associated Sunday Magazines,*
November 4, 1906. Collected in *The Thinking Machine on*

the Case (1908) as a two-part story: "His Perfect Alibi" and "A Question of Time."

"Problem of the Phantom Auto." *Associated Sunday Magazines*, November 11, 1906. Collected in *The Thinking Machine on the Case* (1908) as a two-part story: "The Phantom Motor" and "The Gap in the Trail."

"The Haunted Bell." *Saturday Evening Post*, November 17, 1906.

"Problem of the Stolen Bank Notes." *Associated Sunday Magazines*, November 18, 1906. Collected in *The Thinking Machine on the Case* (1908) as a two-part story: "The Brown Coat" and "A Human Problem."

"Problem of the Superfluous Finger." *Associated Sunday Magazines*, November 25, 1906. Collected in *The Thinking Machine on the Case* (1908) as a two-part story: "The Superfluous Finger" and "The Case Is Closed."

"The Thinking Machine." *Associated Sunday Magazines*, January 20, 1907. The story includes "The Problem of the Knotted Cord." This issue contained two sections. The first, titled "My First Experience with the Great Logician," tells of a personal adventure of the narrator and begins with, "It was once my good fortune to meet..." The second is the story, "The Problem of the Knotted Cord," which begins with, "With the brilliant glare..." Subsequent reprints have treated these as separate stories.

"Problem of the Souvenir Cards." *Associated Sunday Magazines*, February 3, 1907.

"Problem of the Stolen Rubens." *Associated Sunday Magazines*, February 17, 1907.

"The Three Overcoats." *Associated Sunday Magazines*, March 3, 1907.

"Problem of the Organ Grinder." *Associated Sunday Magazines*, March 17, 1907.

"Problem of the Hidden Million." *Associated Sunday Magazines,* March 31, 1907.

"Problem of the Auto Cab." *Associated Sunday Newspapers,* April 14, 1907.

"Problem of the Private Compartment." *Associated Sunday Newspapers,* April 28, 1907.

"Problem of the Cross Mark." *Associated Sunday Magazines,* May 12, 1907.

"Problem of the Ghost Woman." *Associated Sunday Newspapers,* May 26, 1907.

"The Silver Box." *Associated Sunday Newspapers,* June 9, 1907. Also published as "The Leak."

"Problem of Convict No. 97." *Associated Sunday Newspapers,* June 23, 1907.

"Problem of the Deserted House." *Associated Sunday Magazines,* July 7, 1907.

"Problem of the Red Rose." *Associated Sunday Magazines,* July 21, 1907.

"Problem of the Vanishing Man." *Associated Sunday Magazines,* August 11, 1907.

"Problem of the Broken Bracelet." *Associated Sunday Magazines,* September 8, 1907.

"Problem of the Interrupted Wireless." *Associated Sunday Magazines,* November 3, 1907. Collected in *The Thinking Machine on the Case* (1908) as a two-part story: "The Interrupted Wireless" and "The Midnight Message."

"The Grinning God: Part 2: The House That Was." *Associated Sunday Magazines,* December 1, 1907. Part one, "Wraiths of the Storm," was written by his wife, May Futrelle.

"The Mystery of Prince Otto." *Cassell's Magazine of Fiction,* July 1912. Also published as "Five Millions by Wireless."

"The Tragedy of the Life Raft." *Popular Magazine*, August 1, 1912.

"The Case of the Scientific Murderer." *Popular Magazine*, September 1, 1912. Revised as "The Case of the Mysterious Weapon." *Ellery Queen's Mystery Magazine*, October 1950.

"The Jackdaw." *Popular Magazine*, September 15, 1912. Also published as "The Jackdaw Girl."

Other Works

"The Great Suit Case Mystery." *Boston American*, October 5–8, 1905. Reprinted Sandwich, MA: Seymour-Kyper Productions, 1997.

The Simple Case of Susan. New York: D. Appleton, 1908.

Elusive Isabel. Indianapolis: Bobbs-Merrill, 1909.

The Diamond Master. Indianapolis: Bobbs-Merrill, 1909.

The High Hand. Indianapolis: Bobbs-Merrill, 1911.

My Lady's Garter. Chicago: Rand, McNally, 1912.

Blind Man's Buff. London: Hodder & Stoughton, 1914.*

Critical Studies

Binyon, T. J. *"Murder Will Out": The Detective in Fiction*. Oxford: Oxford University Press, 1989, 50.

Futrelle, Jacques. *Best "Thinking Machine" Detective Stories*. Edited by E. F. Bleiler. New York: Dover, 1973.

The Great Cases of The Thinking Machine. Edited by E. F. Bleiler. New York: Dover, 1976.

---

* "The Knife," *Mystery*, October 1933, is occasionally attributed to Futrelle. However, it is a reworking by Donald Rust of Futrelle's "The Great Auto Mystery" (unfortunately published with no indication that it was such, though Futrelle and Rust are listed as coauthors).

Marks, Jeffrey A. "No Escape: Jacques Futrelle and the Titanic." *Mystery Scene*. https://www.mysteryscenemag.com /article/92-articles/feature/37-blurb-jaques-futrelle-and -the-titanic?showall=1.

Panek, Leroy Lad. *Probable Cause: Crime Fiction in America*. Bowling Green, OH: Bowling Green State University Popular Press, 1990, 73–76.

Seymour, Freddie and Bettina Kyper. *The Thinking Machine: Jacques Futrelle: Discovering the Titanic Talent of a Pioneer American Mystery Author*. Dennisport, MA: Graphic Illusions, 1995.

ABOUT THE AUTHOR

Although he may be best remembered today for his tragic death on the *Titanic* in 1912 after urging his wife into a lifeboat, John "Jacques" Heath Futrelle (1875–1912) had an all-too-short but prolific career as a writer of fiction. Born in Pike County, Georgia, south of Atlanta, he was the son of Wiley Harmon Heath Futrelle, a teacher in an Atlanta preparatory college, and Lillie Bevill Futrelle, a Southern belle. They nurtured him in the classics, including French, in deference to his French Huguenot ancestry. Early on, he later remarked, he had set his sights on journalism. "I'd have done anything—*anything*—to get into the newspaper business."*

At the age of eighteen, after apprenticing for a printer, Futrelle was hired as a stenographer to the business manager of the *Atlanta Journal*. There, he seized any opportunity that came his way to write a story. Futrelle's early work for the *Journal* was

---

* Quoted in *The Thinking Machine: Jacques Futrelle—Discovering the Titanic Talent of a Pioneer American Mystery Author* by Freddie Seymour and Bettina Kyper (Dennisport, MA: Graphic Illusions, 1995), part 3, 3. Seymour and Kyper were friends with Futrelle's daughter, Virginia Futrelle Raymond, and interviewed her extensively. Futrelle's wife, May, also gave several interviews about her husband after his tragic death. However, the book does not rigorously source its material.

well regarded, but in 1894, he accepted a spot on the staff of the *Boston Post*. After a few months in Boston, Futrelle sorely missed his family, and especially his sweetheart, a young woman named Lillie May Peel (known as May). He returned to Atlanta, where he set up the *Journal*'s sports department. In 1895, however, his employer urged him to accept an opportunity to work for the *Journal*'s sister newspaper, the *New York Herald*. He and May married and moved to New York, where they soon became immersed in the active life of the city. The Futrelles had two children, Virginia in 1897 and John Heath (Jacques, Jr.) in 1899.

When the Spanish-American War broke out in 1898, the *Herald* staff was caught up in the jingoism of the day, and Futrelle, working around the clock, broke down with exhaustion. In the spring of 1899, he and May relocated to Futrelle's older sister's summer home in Scituate, Massachusetts, for a respite. During this time, it appears that Futrelle read a great deal of mystery fiction—especially Poe, Doyle, and the memoirs of Eugene Vidocq—and took notes on his ideas for stories.*

In 1902, short of funds, he took a position as a theatrical manager in Virginia, where he tried his hand at acting and directing. In 1904, however, his chance to return to journalism arrived, with an offer to work for William Randolph Hearst's newest paper, the *Boston American*. He plunged into newspaper work, meanwhile trying his hand at mystery fiction. One of his first efforts was a pastiche of Sherlock Holmes titled "The Great Suit Case Mystery," in which Holmes solves an actual Boston crime (before the police).† The success of this piece apparently led to an opportunity to publish wholly original work, his now-classic

---

* Seymour and Kyper, part 3, 17.

† First published in the *Boston American* from October 5 to October 8, 1905, as front-page news, the pastiche never appeared again until Seymour-Kyper Productions published it in book form in 1997.

tale "The Mystery of Cell 13," in the context of a contest for readers. The first installment appeared three weeks after his Holmes tale, and it was highly popular.

After Futrelle's success with the Thinking Machine with "The Mystery of Cell 13" in 1905, ten more stories featuring the sleuth appeared in the *Boston American* in rapid succession, similarly presented as contests. In the spring of 1906, Futrelle came to the momentous decision to give up journalism to become a full-time writer of fiction. His Thinking Machine stories began to appear in the *Associated Sunday Magazines*, a supplement that was included with numerous newspapers around the United States, and he produced another thirty-one tales before the end of 1907. He was also able to publish his first novel, *The Chase of the Golden Plate* (featuring the Thinking Machine) in 1906, and in 1907, a collection of seven Thinking Machine stories—this volume—appeared in both the United States and England. A second collection, *The Thinking Machine on the Case*, came out in 1908.*

In 1908, the Futrelles moved into a permanent residence in Scituate, and they remained there for the rest of Futrelle's life. They became the center of a small artist's colony and entertained frequently. Futrelle published an enormous quantity of short stories—mostly about the Thinking Machine[†]—in a variety of outlets, and he wrote several novels. *The Simple Case of Susan* (1908) is a romance involving a mix-up of identities. *The Diamond Master*, probably the least obscure of his novels, is a science-fiction mystery. *Elusive Isabel* (1909) takes place in an embassy and involves crime and espionage. *The High Hand* (1911) is a cynical look at politics.

---

* The English edition is known as *The Professor on the Case*.

† Bleiler notes that these include other detectives as well: Fred Boyd, Dr. Spence, and Garron and Louis Harding. E. F. Bleiler, "Introduction," in Jacques Futrelle, *The Best "Thinking Machine" Detective Stories* (New York: Dover, 1973), ix.

In 1912, the Futrelles traveled to Europe to promote his books and secure European publishing deals. Reportedly, Jacques also worked on new story ideas while they were there, though whether he wrote any actual stories is unknown. After Jacques's death on his doomed voyage home, May pursued her own career as a writer* but also undertook to promote her husband's legacy. She published two of his novels posthumously, *My Lady's Garter* (1912) and *Blind Man's Buff* (1914). May also wrote two novels of her own, *Secretary of Frivolous Affairs* (1911) and *Lieutenant What's-His-Name* (1915), the latter an expansion of her husband's own work, *The Simple Case of Susan*. She was active in the Authors' League of America and instrumental in the passage of the 1940 copyright reform act. May died in 1967, fifty-five years after her husband.

"[Futrelle] had a fine hand for devising astounding plots; he knew men and women; he wrote with plausibility and aplomb; and above all, he tempered the hot steel of derring-do in the oil of humor," mourned H. L. Mencken in his review of Futrelle's last work.† Little remembered today, if only he had lived to midcentury or longer, he could have been part of the pantheon of the American greats such as Ellery Queen and Erle Stanley Gardner, whose puzzles and indelible characters continue to fascinate readers.

---

* May and Jacques cowrote one story, "The Grinning God." May wrote the first part in its entirety, as a challenge for her husband. It appeared as "Wraiths of the Storm" in *Associated Sunday Magazines*, November 24, 1907; Jacques was given a printer's galley of the story and wrote the wrap-up, featuring the Thinking Machine, titled "The Grinning God: Part 2: The House That Was," which appeared the following week in *Associated Sunday Magazines*, December 1, 1907.

† Review, *My Lady's Garter*, in *The Smart Set* 38, no. 4 (December 1912): 158.